THE BEAST HUNTERS
DARK SOVEREIGN

Published in Norway by C. A. Lende Publishing 2022
Text © Christer Lende 2022
Cover Design © Andrei Bat 2022

ISBN 978-82-692150-2-1

THE BEAST HUNTERS
DARK SOVEREIGN

Christer Lende

C. A. Lende Publishing

DEDICATION

*This book is dedicated to mamma (Norwegian for "mother").
You've taught me more than you can possibly know. I love you, and
I'm proud to be your son.*

ALSO BY

CHRISTER LENDE

THE BEAST HUNTER OF ASHBOURN SERIES:
The Beast Hunters
The Beast Hunters Dark Sovereign
The Beast Hunters Blood Oath

The Dollmaker of Kalastra
Bleeding Ink

SIGN UP FOR MY AUTHOR NEWSLETTER

Be the first to find out all the super-duper exciting news about Christer Lende's new releases and life, and get some free short stories while you're at it: https://www.authorcal-ende.com/newsletter-signup

ACKNOWLEDGEMENT

My mother still won't read my books, but I still have to thank you for raising me, so thank you, Anette Lende, for that.

I must thank both my extremely good editors, Chris D. Tavenor, and Anna Windgätter, for making this book readable.

Nicola Schramm was the first to read this book from beginning to end as well. I remember finding it extremely cool that the first person to read my book was someone I have never met. And being the cousin of the girlfriend of my good friend, you had no obligation to read of friendship, so I know you really liked it.

I was again surprised when a veteran, who only read Warhammer 40k, wanted the second book, and Tom Haugen read this book with haste as well. Thank you so much for your longer talks at the gym about the book, until we were yelled at for slacking too much.

Brage Ariell Lindell Eidsvik will always tell me his current theories while reading, and I truly loved to hear them. Sometimes, they were so sinister and insane. Thank you for reading.

Ole-Marius Skulbru, you're a fantastic guy, and we've been making entertainment together since we were young. Thank you for your love for these books and these characters. You're my most passionate reader, I think.

Sin Jace Blix-Torres might be the fastest reader there is. This book took under a day for you to read. It was the wildest of rides. I was vacationing in Rotterdam at the time, but spent more time on my phone, chatting things up with you.

I am actually a great friend of Are Bråthen's brother, but he is not the one to read my books. It was such a surprise when you, one night talking online, wanted to read my book. I was even more surprised when you asked if I had more. And before long, all three books had been read. Thank you for that, it really meant a lot to me.

My best friend during my studies, Tom Christian Klingsheim, randomly told me he wanted to read my books. As of today, I think he is my biggest fan, asking me every other day for the next chapter of what I am currently working on. I love it, and love sending you the next 'episode' as you call it. Thank you, Tom. You're a great dude.

My girlfriend of eight years, Emma Kristine Skjæveland, actually took to reading the first book in the series, and then the second one. So I guess I have to give you credit. So lastly, thank you, Emma, for giving a crap about what I do when I get lost in front of the computer.

THE ASSISTANT

Adenar sat in his small office below the staircase and filled out some forms for the next gala. Well, an office was an exaggeration. He'd been given a small room behind the receptionist's desk, together with his own smaller desk and crooked chair. The rain drummed on the windows of the massive building, and he dreaded going outside. With Ashbourn being such a gargantuan city, going from one district to the neighbouring one took time, even by carriage.

His mood was sombre, partly from being generally overworked, but mostly from Callan dropping more work on him again just as he left for the evening. Being the assistant to basically everybody in the Meritocrat Headquarters made him an easy target for other 'overworked' employees. But Adenar did it all, working every week as if his life depended on it. He'd been lucky to actually get a job working directly for the political party after his studies, which he still didn't know how had happened. And it didn't seem like *anyone* else knew why or how he got the job either.

In truth, he liked working during the night better than the day. No surprise work would suddenly land in his lap and he could silently work on the papers Callan had ordered him to finish before dawn. Adenar didn't understand why the work needed to be done before tomorrow, but he couldn't object, as Callan would just say 'that information is classified for an assistant,' and walk smugly away. Barely of higher position than Adenar, Callan pulled his rank on every possible occasion. So he'd learned to just accept the work and shut up.

Adenar pushed through the paperwork mindlessly, filling out forms upon forms concerning the next large political celebration, orchestrated by the Meritocrats. And being the lowest assistant in the Meritocrat Headquarters, he had to do all the most tedious work before every gala, having to make *all* the tickets for *all* the guests, place them at the designated tables for the dinner, and order the correct amount of food.

The food had to be individually chosen to fit each attendee, of course, the utmost elite of the giant city expecting the best at all times.

Adenar was finally done making the tickets and preparing the food list for three of the different parties attending: the Passionists, the Royalists, and, of course, the Meritocrats, lacking only information from the Warborn Party. He sighed, having neglected this task for as long as he could. Unfortunately, the rain hadn't stopped during his many hours of work.

This last task was all Callan's fault, not having collected the documents from the Warborn Headquarters himself, before passing the work on to Adenar. Now Adenar had to travel over there and get them, and after that, he'd have to make tickets and food lists for all the individuals once more. *Remember how lucky you are,* he forced himself to think. *Getting a job in the headquarters right after my studies is rare. That's how the king did it.* But the king hadn't become a lowly assistant. Everybody knew that. He'd become a member of the council.

Adenar's efforts to boost his motivation failed, and with another sigh, he stacked the papers in neat piles and put on his coat. *I hope mother isn't still up,* he thought. She also worked too hard, but Adenar planned to rise high within the Meritocrat Party, so he could support them both. His dream was to be on the council itself, aiding whichever king that ruled. All the hard work he put in now had to pay off some time. After all, that was what the Meritocrats believed.

He dreamt of better days when he wasn't some lowly assistant with barely a toe inside the party. He'd never have an assistant like him. Instead, the work should be done by those appointed it—their own personal responsibility. He relished the thought, until realizing he'd actually gotten the job *because* someone allowed for an assistant just like him, though he didn't know who that 'someone' was.

Amidst his deep thoughts, he placed all the papers in the correct drawers, and readied to begin the final part of his assignment. He stared out a window on his way, looking at the endless rain hitting the cobblestone. His reflection stared back, and he let out an exasperated breath at seeing the growing stubble on his chin. *I need another shave soon,* he thought. *If I'll ever have time.* He ran his fingers over his strong chin and marked cheekbones, which his mother said he'd gotten from his father, but he didn't know who he was and his mother sure wouldn't tell him. It had led to countless heated discussions between them, but her resolve was strong.

"Alright. Let's get this over with." He went out the open backdoor of the headquarters into the pouring rain, walking the long way to the gate.

"Of course you're still here," the gate master said from inside her hut as she noticed Adenar.

He smiled at her and lifted his eyebrows. "Are you even surprised, Venna?"

"No. They work you too hard, they do. Are you hungry?" Before Adenar could answer, her hands rummaged around in a bag at her side. "I've got apples, bread, some cupcakes . . ."

"It's fine," he said, despite being hungry. Venna still found some bread with thin slices of steak on them, something he couldn't refuse. "You're a lifesaver," he said, taking large bites of the delicacy.

"Well, someone's gotta help you when you help everyone else."

Adenar chuckled. Despite her age, she was sharp as a needle, which made her a great gate master. The gate was large, with a mechanism inside of her little hut to open it. Through great struggle, or with the help of one of the two soldiers standing guard, she could use the contraption, and today was no exception: one guard was already on his way over, his plate mail clanking and clinking.

"Good, good," she said, dramatically falling back on her chair. "What would I do without you, Cleverus?"

Through the guard's vizor, Adenar spotted yet another tired man. "Ask Veredar," he scoffed with a thick voice, placing his hand on the lever and rotating it.

"Has anyone told you how clever you are, Cleverus?" Venna asked.

"More times than you can imagine," Cleverus answered.

Venna laughed, and Adenar felt a little better not being alone constantly. He tucked the last of the bread into a pocket before waving Venna and the guards goodbye.

Even though the rain still poured, many people roamed the streets, making him feel safer and not so disconnected from the world. In a city of nearly a million, there was bound to be a lot of nightly activity. Some bakeries and other shops awaited wares, others prepared their stores for the next day, and some just liked the peace.

A tall man wearing a large black coat passed by him, and shortly after, something crawled over Adenar's shoes. He looked down to see a pack of gnurgles running across his feet, following the tall man. Adenar always wondered if people kept gnurgles as pets or used them for their amazing sense of smell.

Despite being an adjacent district, the route to the Warborn District was long. Adenar walked towards a carriage, hoping he wouldn't be gone for too long. The castle in the middle of all four districts rose like an enormous pylon, and he faintly dreamt of going inside—until the lanky carriage driver with thinning hair asked him where to go for the third time.

"Oh," he said, snapping back to reality. "The headquarters in the Warborn District."

"Alright then," the driver said, whipping his horses into a trot.

Adenar fell back into his thoughts the moment the wheels started turning. *Callan better not have more work for me in the morning.* The coronation was still a month away, and the galas would only get larger, something he dreaded. Everyone talked about the insane amount of work during the last month, but he was already exhausted.

The carriage slowed as they exited the Meritocrat District and entered another gate into the Warborn District. The cobblestone roads were dirtier, and some areas smelled quite bad, despite it being a prosperous district. The sanitation was simply not as good as in Adenar's district. Here, everyone carried weapons, and most industries relied upon forging armour and crafting weaponry.

As the carriage barrelled on, Adenar's head sunk into the headrest, and he drifted into sleep. Adenar snapped awake as the door opened. "What?" he asked, dazed.

"That will be four silver chips," the driver said.

Adenar shook himself awake, found the correct amount of chips, and paid. "I'm sorry," he muttered. "Long night."

"Tell me about it," the driver said, climbing back into his seat as Adenar stepped outside. The horses sprang into motion, and the carriage disappeared. Adenar faced the giant headquarters of the Warborn District. Great banners, sodden with rain, displayed their red colours with the party's official emblem on them: two crossed axes with a sword in the middle.

"Hello," a creaky voice said from below and Adenar jumped back as something tugged on his coat. It was a trasher, standing up to his knees. "Hello?" the trasher said again, pushier this time.

"Hello," Adenar said, kneeling before the ragged creature with a long nose and giant ears. Its hands and arms were full of warts with long dark hairs growing from them, but Adenar didn't care. He'd been around trashers before, and found them fascinating. He ran his hand over the creature's head, and it leaned against his hand, relishing the petting.

"What is it?" Adenar asked.

The trasher adopted a troubled look on its face and circled its stomach. "Me hungry. No give food." It wore a garbage bag over its body and its arms and legs were meagre.

"Here," he said, giving it the bread and meat.

The trasher slowly put its fingers on the bread, treading with care.

"It's okay," Adenar said. "Take it."

"You nice. I thank very much."

Adenar rose, but the trasher gave him a concerned look.

"What?" Adenar asked calmly.

"Can I go?"

"Yes, but eat quickly, so you don't have to share."

The trasher rubbed his knee once, which they sometimes did as a form of thanks. "I eat now. Is mine." Then it scurried off across the street and into an alley, stuffing the food in its face. Adenar chuckled at the curious creature waddling away to its cousins.

After that, he could neglect the large building no longer and approached. Adenar frowned upon discovering no soldiers guarded the gate, and it was open. The Warborn usually had four guards outside at least, as everything had to be as 'militaristic' as it could. This was unusual, but also nice, as he wouldn't have to waste time getting through the gate at night and get those forms faster.

He couldn't deny he felt some excitement at these peculiar discoveries, though, it probably proved to be nothing, as it always did with such things. Nevertheless, he walked through the long courtyard, filled with swords, spears, shields, and halberds neatly placed on countless racks, and up the small staircase. A few rats sat further down the steps, looking for food. Adenar felt he'd seen a lot more vermin in this district lately, and even in the Meritocrat District.

Discovering the main doors to be locked, he hammered on them with his fists. No answer, and not a soul in sight. *Even more peculiar. There's always someone to open the door.* He started to round the great structure to the smaller entrance at the back. This wasn't his first time doing night visits to different district headquarters, so he knew about the unusual entrances too. He frowned when no one met him at the back either, the only sign of life being an open window higher up with lantern light streaming out of it.

He found the smaller wooden door and knocked. No one came to open, so he knocked harder. Still nothing.

"This is just my luck."

Against his better judgement, he tried pushing it open, and to his surprise, it worked. He exhaled in relief, really needing those papers and forms. Closing the door behind him, he still found no one inside. During the day, several hundred people occupied the building, and at night, at least someone should be there.

Adenar knew where to go to find the reception, where he hoped the papers would be. He went down the long hallway that led to the large hall, where the reception was straight ahead, and he actually heard some rustling. He strolled to the counter, where an older dark-haired woman frantically searched the shelves for something. She wore a tattered yellow dress, and didn't seem to notice him.

"I've come—"

Her sharp, startled scream cut him off, and she turned in an instant, revealing an eye patch over her right eye.

"Sorry," Adenar said, holding his hands up disarmingly. "Didn't mean to scare you."

She composed herself quickly and turned back to her search.

Adenar frowned. "I've come for the attendee forms regarding the next Meritocrat gala."

The woman just kept searching the shelves, going through countless books and binders, almost sounding like she was on the verge of crying. She had to be too old to be a receptionist, but she was also the only one around. He coughed to get her attention.

She waved a finger at nothing in particular. "Maybe over there."

Adenar sighed and took to searching himself. He quickly found a pile marked 'Callan,' and flipped through the papers, discovering they were exactly what he needed. The woman suddenly snatched a book from the shelf and ran out of the room, not sparing Adenar a glance or explanation, gone the same way he came.

He wanted to know what that had been about, but didn't have the time or energy to investigate. The Warborn Party had spread all kinds of rumours about a coming war with Brattora, and perhaps he could learn something about it to expose it as just rumours, but it was too late now.

He readied to leave, looking at the different statues of generals proudly presented at each end of the desk. Above hung a banner with their slogan: 'Conquer, or be Conquered'. Times were peaceful and the city prosperous, so he'd always wondered why conquering would be necessary. Warborn people always put him on edge with their politics, pushing for an aggressive military front. Ashbourn was at peace with all adjacent kingdoms, so their political strategy felt like poking a sleeping wretcher. The thought of the Warborn winning the coronation gave him shivers. He hoped their rumours of war were just a political weapon, and nothing more.

He closed the back door of the building and went back into the pouring rain. *At least it's not cold,* he thought, trying to focus on the positive aspects of the incredibly long night. Light still streamed out of the window, but now shadows danced in the glow. Faint voices sounded through the pitter-patter of the rain, and they cleared as Adenar walked closer.

"We have come to put a stop to this," a raspy, but strong voice said aloud. Adenar stopped beneath, curiosity blossoming. Maybe he could learn something valuable.

"So I can see," a female voice answered calmly. He'd heard that voice before, but couldn't place it. "I did expect this from you, old man. I knew you'd break eventually, giving in to your primitive ways."

"Silence!" the male voice shouted. "Your father would be ashamed." This seemed serious. *Maybe I should go?*

"Yes, of course you're right," the woman said again. "He would not approve of this, but he never approved of anything I did."

"You're mad," the man accused. "You always have been. He knew it. We know it."

"Mad?" she asked. *Where have I heard that voice before?* "I guess by your definition, that's true. However, under your leadership, the Warborn have grown stale and complacent to be ruled by others."

"We have followed the King, as we should! Though we didn't crown him, Koradin won the last two coronations fairly, and we are devoted to him."

"Such an honourable man you are. And for twelve years you've been chained under his rule. No wonder you lost your teeth. Something has to change, and I have brought it. You've grown roots and become familiar with the way things are. Many wonder if you're changing sides."

"Changing sides?" the man asked aghast. "We're one nation, all on the same side."

"See? Weakness. We don't hold the ideals of those lesser than us. The other parties are weak, and now is the time for a strong hand to lead the way. Koradin had his time, but stronger steel is required."

"This is treason!" The familiar sounds of several swords unsheathing rang through the pouring rain, and Adenar's heart pounded hard. *What is going on?* He constantly debated whether to stay or leave, and curiosity won.

"Treason?" the female voice said, laughing. "We are long past treason."

"What you're doing is unnatural!" the man shouted. "And it ends tonight! Form ranks, men!"

"You've always been brave, general," the female voice said. "I'll give you that."

General? This is General Toran, the King's highest-ranking military officer?

"But I'm afraid it's your bloodline that ends tonight," said the woman. Her name was at the tip of his tongue.

"You're not worthy of the title 'Ironword'," General Toran said, and the woman's identity fell into place. *Eranna Carner, of course.*

"You are a worthy sacrifice," another, new, dark and heavy voice reverberated through the night, unnaturally deep and mighty, causing fear in his heart. The voice felt like a gut-punch, and the skin all over

Adenar heard a most terrible sound before screams and gut-wrenching sounds filled the air, followed by what could only be blood and guts splashing to the ground. The horrendous screams turned into wet, gurgling noises. *What have I gotten myself into?* His heart raced.

"Anyone else?" Eranna asked as the room stilled. "Anyone else feels the need to stop our progress?" Nothing was said, and the metallic clanks of swords falling to the ground rung through the air. "How wonderful. But you've already proved your loyalty and will follow your dear deceased general soon. Seize them!" An enormous cluster of disjointed competing sounds spilt from the window; swords clashing, men dying—and, in the cacophony of noise, Adenar fled the scene, hoping he would escape alive.

CHAPTER 1

The Eyes of the Dead

Raindrops pooled on leaves, before dropping to the moist ground. The sun slowly rose from behind distant mountains, sharp sunlight shining into Ara's closed eyes. A slow breeze rustled her clothes, setting the branches of the trees to languidly wave in the wind. Morning had arrived, and as usfual, Ara's eyes shot open. She looked around the small campsite, noticing she wasn't the first one to rise. Despite Topper sleeping soundly next to her, Khendric was nowhere to be seen. *He'll probably be back soon,* she hoped, worrying for him.

It had been two days since they left Cornstead, and despite the beautiful morning, her mind drifted to thoughts of how it all ended. Not only that, but she had become aware of another peculiar . . . ability that had grown stronger since the deadly nightmare. Besides the strong arm, she'd been feeling Khendric's dark thoughts. Not what they were, but she could tell where he was from the pressure his thoughts exerted on her mind. She sighed, looking at her veiny arm, remembering Martyn's hot blood flowing through her fingers. She'd killed him, and it felt both great and terrible. Knowing that she was capable of killing felt both frightening and empowering. Martyn still haunted her dreams, and yesterday she had awoken feeling immense guilt. Talking to Topper had helped, as he put it in perspective, reminding her that he truly was a monster. Telling herself over and over again lessened the guilt bit by bit. Overall, her mood slowly improved.

Because of the newfound ability, she knew Khendric was nowhere near, as she'd feel him. His mind was still riddled with darkness and hadn't changed at all since leaving Cornstead.

Wanting to break out of her thoughts, she rose and gathered the camp's defences, a routine she hadn't missed. She grimly thought back to Cornstead and wondered if it was her fault Khendric had become this hollow man. Had she not prodded on how she survived the venom, maybe he be alright. *I can't think like this,* she commanded herself and pushed towards better memories.

A faint smile spread across her lips when remembering Robert. That joyful old man lived a better life than he could imagine because of Ara. She missed him, and wished him all the best from afar. There had been no last goodbye, but he would understand. The whole population of Cornstead also had their lives because of her, Khendric, and Topper, saved from that wretched tentacled blob, even if they didn't know it yet. Maybe they would understand in time.

Topper slowly woke as Ara mounted the great varghaul heads onto his horse.

"Oh," he said, voice sluggish. "You're done . . . great. Where's Khendric?"

"He's somewhere," she said, faintly feeling something coming closer on her mind. It had to be Khendric. She hadn't told them of her ability yet, unsure if she should worry them. It became so much more real if she revealed it, instead clinging to the comfortability of them not knowing.

Not too long after, Khendric appeared from the forest, walking up the steep hill to their ledge. He looked tired, with dark bags under his eyes. Topper ignored him, continuing preparations to leave.

"Where were you?" Ara asked, feeling him strongly in her head. It didn't hurt, but was annoying.

"I couldn't sleep," he answered curtly, got up on his horse, and provided no further explanation. Ara sighed, wanting to help, but she didn't know how.

After the small camp was packed up and all defences accounted for, they trotted further away from Cornstead on their horses.

The sun shone strongly, the moisture from morning evaporating rapidly. Far away she heard the terrible singing of a treehowler. Apparently, these tree-climbing creatures sang like that to attract females. Ara couldn't understand how the horrible noise could attract anything, sounding like two grown men screaming at each other.

During these two days of little conversation, amidst all of her plaguing thoughts, one thing kept her mind occupied: the red book. She brought it forth from a satchel on Spotless.

Doombringer

Known location: Bound to no location.

Type: Destroyer

Rarity: Extremely rare

Weakness: Lack of metal

If you're reading this page because a doombringer is near and you need information on what to do, in short: RUN AWAY.

No one has successfully studied a doombringer, because as the creature expires it's also reduced to dust.

Doombringers plummet from the sky, looking like a moving star. On impact, they erupt the earth around them with earthquakes, before starting their destructive rampage. As far as survivor stories go, they have a humanoid shape made of living metal. A farmer described it as "layers upon layers of thin metal wires constantly slithering over the body."

I've seen one briefly myself and the farmer left out the worst part: the face, or . . . the lack of one. They have no eyes, no mouth, no ears. Instead, it's just a churning, blistering hole. Through this "mouth" they both consume metal and release energy. Doombringers somehow attract or suck materials into their hole with the help of incredible wind, or some other magical force. Any metal in their vicinity is consumed, building an unstable exploding energy. The energy is released back into the world in a terrible inferno gushing from the same hole, burning and smelting everything in their path like a beam. The more metal engulfed, the stronger the inferno.

The doombringer is either stopped by lack of metal or consuming too much, seeming not to know their limits. Of the two options, the former is preferred, to avoid an enormous explosion matched by nothing else imaginable. Historically, cities have perished, gone in the blink of an eye.

If doombringers lack metal, it smoulders into metallurgic dust that decays rapidly. Some believe they have some divine aspect to them, stemming from the moon, but that is most likely old superstition. This was introduced

by the native people of the Iceblood clan, who revered the
moon, thinking doombringers were sent from their god to
punish evil. But we don't know why they appear, and
men will always try to explain what they cannot grasp.

- Alec

Ara hoped never to come close to such a beast. Reading felt good while riding down a quiet road in the gleaming morning sun. She embraced the simple sounds of nature: trickling water from a hidden stream, birds chirping, and leaves blowing in the wind, feeling thankful no treehowlers tried finding mates nearby anymore.

Khendric trotted up beside her, his posture slumped, head hanging low. "I need to talk to you about something," he said with a tired voice, his mind plagued.

"What?"

"After everything that happened in Cornstead, you've proven many things to me. You're strong, of mind and body. Your willpower must be made of steel, after everything you've gone through. At the start of Cornstead we talked about getting to Ashbourn so you could become a nurse."

She frowned, feeling the slightest knot form in her guts. "Yeah?"

"You don't want that, right? You want to be a beast hunter?"

"Yeah," she chuckled, relieved

"We want to make you into a real beast hunter. As we have done until now, we want to teach and train you ourselves, teaching you everything we know. If that arm won't lose its strength, you have a serious advantage over most opponents and beasts. Foes will underestimate you because of your size." His thoughts seemed to lighten, which made her feel better too. His proposition was exactly what she wanted, and she sort of thought it obvious after Cornstead.

"I see your smile," Khendric said. "You need to think seriously on this, though. Being a beast hunter is nothing of glory. Yes, you save people, but many times you fail. Innocents will die, and sometimes, it may be on your hands. There will be hard times and difficult choices. You'll have to do foul things, like with Martyn. These experiences will form scars, and you'll carry them with you forever—but hopefully, you save a life here and there, too. The choice is yours, but choose carefully. I'll give you some time to think it over."

He was right, good and bad things had happened in Cornstead. Deep down she already knew her answer, but she had to come to terms with the cost. The thrill of discovering clues, solving mysteries, helping Robert, and bonding with Khendric and Topper, felt great, but there would be pain, death, and helplessness. Topper had been killed, proving how dangerous it could be. She'd almost been hung, beaten by dwarves, had the nightmare of a lifetime—and it had all shaped her. The good and the bad gave her life meaning, much more than anything before it. She loved mysteries, itching for a new case already. Whatever pain would come, she would take it or die. Whatever sorrow would fall upon her, she would deal with it or perish. Sometimes she would help people who ended up condemning her, like the people of Cornstead, but she could be that saviour, knowing in her heart they were all safe. *What I did to Martyn might have been wrong, but I did it. I'm going to own up to it, so I can leave it in the past. No more feeling uncertain about it. That decision is a part of me, and I cannot change it.* From here on, no more thoughts would be wasted on him. She looked to Khendric, grabbing his arm.

"I want to," she said with a wry smile.

"Absolutely certain?"

"More than I've been about anything in my life."

"Don't colour me surprised," he said, grabbing her arm. "I'd like to officially welcome you to the team, not that it's necessary." They shared a beautiful moment where all negative thoughts seemed to vanish, and all the pain of her past put to rest. Cornstead had been her rebirth, and she liked who she turned out to be. They were her family now, and the glow and warmness returned. Memories of her mother and father returned, but not to cause her sorrow, but to remind her of her roots, and how far she'd come. Perhaps her father would even be proud of the things she'd done. She missed her mother greatly, and that stinger wouldn't disappear any time soon, but at least she was surrounded by good people who cared for her. Water culminated in her eyes as Khendric let go of her arm, and she looked toward the sun with joy.

* * *

The next days consisted largely of three things: riding, fighting lessons, and endless questions about countless beasts. Khendric taught her how to wrestle and fight using her hands, showing her simple techniques for punches, jabs, and dodges—and where to hold her arms to keep her guard up.

While she focused on Khendric's teachings, Topper sat on nearby rocks with the red book in hand and asked her questions. Paying attention to both things was next to impossible, but that was the whole point. When she answered Topper's question, Khendric got through her guard, but when she successfully warded him off, she got Topper's question wrong, or didn't hear it at all. They insisted this was the best way to learn, though she had her doubts, but it helped Khendric's mind clear, so she let them work on her. His thoughts still fell into dark spirals when they rode, but they cleared when he taught her, making the bruises worth it.

After four days of trotting through thick forest, they reached the border to the Sangerian Grasslands, which would have gone unnoticed to Ara the landscape didn't change so drastically. The forest ended abruptly, giving way to green pastures, faraway mountains, and hills as far as the eye could see. Rivers snaked their way out of the forest behind them, delving through the green land before them, splitting it apart. She'd never seen such beautiful, clean nature, and leaving the damp forest behind felt amazing.

"Was hoping for that," Topper said with a smug voice as he rode past her, tapping her chin, making her realize her mouth had fallen open. "The Sangerian Grasslands is a beautiful kingdom. There's no denying that."

They rode until the forest disappeared behind them, and stopped for supper. Khendric and Topper had packed a lot of supplies, and they ate pretty well. After the meaty meal, Topper found the red book and Khendric motioned for her to stand.

"You're getting good with punches and routines," he said. "Today, we're going to spar." Quickly, Khendric came at her, lightly punching her torso. "When sparring, we pretend to fight, but with little force behind blows. We're not actually trying to hurt each other."

"Alright," she said, growing a little nervous. She threw some punches, but they never landed, as he blocked them and toppled her to the ground with his foot. This repeated several times until her back turned red.

"You're not using your feet enough," Khendric told her.

"You could have said that before." She dusted off her leather armour, breathing heavily.

"Nah, you needed some pain for the lesson to stick."

She rolled her eyes.

He jabbed at her, but she blocked his fist.

"How do you know which gender a katanor is?" Topper asked.

"What?" Ara asked, not ready for his question and received a light punch to the guts, staggering back. "Ouch."

Khendric shrugged his shoulders with a mischievous smile.

"How do you know the gender of a katanor?" Topper repeated.

"Uhm, if it has spikes it's a male," she said, ducking to no use, as Khendric adjusted his punch and struck her head. *How does he know everything?*

"That would've hurt," he said, casting a smile.

She chuckled helplessly and stood back up.

"And what do you do if it's a male?" Topper continued.

Khendric assaulted with a flurry of attacks, and she blocked the first two, but took every punch after that. He didn't hit hard, just enough to make her understand what would have happened in a real fight. When it was over, she could finally answer. "You do nothing. It's the female katanors that are dangerous. They're aggressive and extremely protective."

"Correct. "Topper seemed pleased and turned a few pages.

Let's see if you're ready for this, she thought, hatching a plan.

Khendric tip-toed around her, before punching into her guard and ducking quickly around her with incredible—almost unnatural speed, wrapping his arm around her neck, locking her in a chokehold. "Now you're dead," he said, whispering victoriously into her ear, "there's nothing you—"

Ara gripped his elbow with her strong arm and ripped it aside, throwing him around her, sending him tumbling to the ground.

"Oh," she said, triumphantly. "There's something *I* can do."

Khendric stood back up, spitting out some grass with a smirk. He nodded respectively and fell into stance. "Shouldn't have done that."

"And why is that?"

"Now I'm going to have to firmly kick your ass," he said.

In a flash, he ducked forward. Ara tightened her guard, but he threw himself at her feet, causing her to stumble forward, crashing to the ground. Khendric grabbed her normal arm, twisting it so she couldn't move and placed his knee on her back. "That arm is amazing," he said. "But now you can't reach me."

Ara tried, but he was right, and released her.

"I'm going to teach you manoeuvres like that. And we're going to spar more often." He dusted off his shirt and looked at the sky. "With our pace, we're about four, maybe five days from Ashbourn. I'll teach you a lot by then, even some sword training."

"So we're still going to Ashbourn?" Ara asked, happy at the prospect.

Topper perked up from his stone. "Why?"

"A great city like that provides a lot of opportunities," Khendric said. "It will be good for her. Great housing, usually a surplus of cases too, often simple ones that pay well. There are great areas to teach her how to fight as well."

Ara couldn't dispute him—those were good and fun reasons, but something hid behind his eyes.

Topper rose and walked up to Khendric, staring into his eyes.

"What?" Khendric asked.

"Stay still," Topper said, narrowing his eyes.

After a tense moment, Khendric deflated, breaking eye contact. "It's not—"

"Oh no," Topper said. "Not again, Khendric. You split for a reason."

"What?" Khendric exclaimed, arms out innocently.

"Don't try to fool me with those eyes. You want to go to Ashbourn because you believe Darlaene is there."

Khendric sighed with a foolish grin on his face. "I heard in Kalastra she might be there. Do you remember Harry, the bartender?"

"Eric's father? Of course."

"He told me she'd gone to Ashbourn, after we solved his case."

"He said he didn't know," Topper said.

"He lied, afraid we'd run off too."

"Who is Darlaene?" Ara asked, intrigued.

Khendric walked away from Topper. "The most fantastic woman in the world."

"She's Khendric's on-again-off-again muse," Topper explained.

"You're in love?" Ara asked, eyes wide in shock.

"So very much."

"Why haven't I heard of her before? Why isn't she here?"

"Yeah, why is that, Khendric?" Topper asked.

Khendric sighed. "She's a beast hunter too, but with no magnificent abilities, like me, Topper, or you."

"She's also a beast hunter?" Ara asked.

"But a fragile one," he said. "So, whenever we're together, I can't stop worrying about her, to the point where I want to lock her up to protect her. So we had to go our separate ways."

"Not that she would be locked up," Topper said. "She's as stubborn and unrelenting as the ocean."

Khendric looked to the sky. "That's what I love about her."

Topper rolled his eyes. "She's also incredibly . . . practical."

"What do you mean?" Ara asked.

"Oh, come on," Khendric protested.

Topper looked at him with a hopeless look. "Every time we're with Darlaene, I die so much more."

"Why?" Ara asked, frowning.

"Let me put it like this," Topper said. "To Darlaene, I'm some expendable item that never runs out. She always sacrifices me, throwing me into harm's way, just for an easy getaway."

"I think you're exaggerating," Khendric added.

"She threw me to the wretchers," Topper quickly said, counting on his fingers. "I was beaten to death by the trollman, cursed by the witchtrolls, beaten to pieces by the gorewing. The narworm incident, where I was bait—"

"You didn't die that time," Khendric said.

"I was eaten by the octinara, the most painful experience I've ever felt. And that other time morilmen drowned me, and every time because it was easier to let me die than try to save me." Topper breathed heavily after the outburst.

"Well," Khendric said, nonchalant. "Maybe you die a little more when she's around."

"A little?" he replied, agitated. "A little more?"

"But you come back," Ara said.

"Are you kidding me?" Topper shouted. "So I'm just to be wasted into harm's way, no regard for the physical trauma I go through?"

"I promise," Khendric said. "I'll do my best not to let that happen this time."

Topper's answer was a flat stare. "If she's in Ashbourn, I don't think we should go. Khendric is clearly letting his personal desires impact his decision, and that isn't what might be best for you—which I think should be our top priority."

"You're absolutely right," Khendric flatly admitted. "But I don't see why Ashbourn isn't a good place for Ara to be and learn. Darlaene won't see her the way she sees you, and chances are, the cases aren't particularly dangerous either."

"Darlaene wouldn't have rushed to Ashbourn if there wasn't something serious. She's attracted to danger."

Khendric's attitude changed, his eyes falling to the ground, his thoughts worsening. "Well, I can't let the trail go cold. What if I never see her again? I need her. I'm going to Ashbourn, and it's your choice if you want to come or not."

Topper and Khendric glared at each other.

"I'll go to Ashbourn," Ara said, stealing their attention. She wanted to see the city, and Khendric's earlier arguments about housing, training areas, and small, simple cases provided a secure and good basis for her. She also wanted to meet the woman that had Khendric spellbound.

"I am not happy," Topper said. "But if it's what Ara wants. Fine." He pointed his finger scoldingly at Khendric. "You'll keep that promise. Tell her not to expend me like a bullet. And don't try to hide her next time,"

"I will do my best," Khendric assured him.

Topper took a firm hold of his arm. "I mean it."

"Yes, yes," Khendric said dismissively. "It's time to get going again."

They climbed onto their horses and started moving. Khendric's thoughts weren't as bad. The darkness still clouded his mind, but not as intensely as before. *Maybe it helps to think about her. Or doing other things that forces his mind away from whatever haunts him.* Whatever it was, she was glad for it, and excited for what Ashbourn had to offer.

"I need more blood," the phantom voice in her mind since the nightmare whispered. She huffed and tried ignoring it, not letting it ruin the beautiful scenery.

* * *

Night approached and darkness fell upon them, but as always, their defence was up. This had been a better day since Cornstead, with less dark thoughts and some smiles.

In the clear night, a million stars shone down on her, as she laid with her head on a log. Topper already slept, but Khendric sat awake, stirring the dying campfire. He occasionally shook his head to divert some dark thoughts that circled his mind. She almost asked what had happened to him, but sleep rolled over her; her eyes almost falling shut.

In the distance, with blurry vision, she spotted two small red lights moving in the forest with constant speed. Her eyes shot open as Khendric put his hands over them, waking her abruptly.

"Did you see the eyes?" he said with a sharp voice.

"What?" she asked, trying to move his hand away.

"The red lights in the forest."

"Yes, but I thought they were just in my mind."

"They're not. And if you want to live, do *not* look back into those red eyes. What lurks in the forest ahead . . . is a deathwalker."

"A what?" she asked as he slowly removed his hand.

"Don't look at it. From here I can't tell which way it's facing. Deathwalkers are harmless, unless you lock stares with them, then you're dead."

Ara tried not looking in its direction, but curiosity was a strong force.

"Wanna go look at it?" Khendric asked.

"Won't that be dangerous?"

"Just don't look into its eyes."

"Well, yeah. I want to check it out." She rose, trying to look for it, but not at it. Khendric wrapped some cloth around a burning stick, making a makeshift torch, and grabbed her hand, leading her deeper into the forest—towards the deathwalker.

As they neared, Ara heard a humming sound, accompanied by faint whispers. Khendric's flickering torch revealed their positions like a lighthouse at night, but he didn't seem bothered.

A figure appeared in the darkness, the torchlight illuminating black, tattered robes. With no red eyes visible, she guessed it faced away from them. It lacked a lower body, floating in the air, somehow.

"If it turns," Khendric said aloud in the eerie forest. "Close your eyes." The creature was barely visible, its spectre clarifying as they stepped closer. It moved peculiarly, hovering in the air, undisturbed by the terrain.

"It can't hear us?" she asked.

"No. Can't even sense us."

A whisper sounded in her ear, too low to make out what was said.

Thin, bony, mangled arms became visible, with only remnants of skin remaining, producing a ghastly sight. The creature moved abruptly, yet smoothly, further into the forest, before coming to a stop a few feet away. Khendric followed, and she followed him. The creature still had its back to them.

"How is it flying?" Ara asked.

"I don't know. Magic? It might turn rapidly. If so, close your eyes. Place your hands over your eyes and look to the ground. Then, carefully look for the flying robes, before raising your head." Ara nodded in understanding. She wanted to see its face. This close, the whispers were more frequent, but still too faint to make out words. They *must come from the deathwalker*.

"Why can't I look into its eyes?"

"As far as we know," Khendric said. "It's oblivious to its surroundings. They just drift around. Why they keep to forests is unknown. I don't think they can see, except for when meeting eye to eye with someone."

The creature slowly turned away from Ara, towards Khendric.

"I don't even think they're really here," he said. "I believe they're here and . . . partially in some other world, or partially grasped by death. You can't even touch it. Your hand goes straight through. They're dangerous at night, because many look into their shining red eyes in the darkness. If you lock eyes, you become visible to it, and it soars towards you, ripping your intestines out. I've seen it once, a long time ago. A man named Erolan looked into the eyes of a deathwalker. It charged him with lightning speed, tearing his stomach open, continuing to drag his entrails out. Erolan's hands couldn't touch the deathwalker, so he couldn't defend himself. It was terrible, and as his heart stopped beating, it turned dormant again." Ara's calm heartbeat had been replaced by a quick pulse, fearing its gaze. It slowly rotated towards Khendric, who looked at it sombrely, before he closed his eyes as its vision brushed past him. "Tell me when I can open my eyes again."

From the side, the deathwalker's skull became visible from under the tattered hood. This had clearly once been a human, and only bone remained, but no jaw. Red, mesmerizing smoke slowly coalesced within its sockets, creating the emanating glow.

"You can open your eyes," she said.

Khendric did as he had explained before. The deathwalker kept turning towards Ara and she closed hers. Just knowing its gaze washed over her made her uncomfortable, a female whisper growing barely audible in her ears.

"You can open them now," Khendric said, and she followed his example. The creature floated away from them in a slow manner, passing through a tree.

"Are we going to kill it?" Ara asked.

"We can't. At least not right now." He followed, stepping closer to inspect the fabric of its clothes. "I think this might have been a dress at one point, probably belonging to a woman."

Ara frowned. "This used to be a person?"

"Yeah, a very unfortunate one."

Another whisper rang in her mind, almost loud enough for her to hear.

"You see," Khendric continued. "This woman was killed by a voreen blade. Anyone murdered by such a blade turns

into a deathwalker, destined to roam the woods . . . forever.
A terrible curse."

"A what-blade?"

"A voreen blade. It's an almost dead culture, surrounded
by mysticism."

"I've never heard of it."

"There are few voreen left, and they are solitary. Meeting
others of their kind, or others of any kind, usually ends with
blood. They're so violent and incredibly dangerous, we're
lucky they're nearly extinct."

"So she was killed by one of these voreens?"

"She must have gone too far into the forest and met one.
Poor woman. We don't know much about their culture.
They didn't have a written language, and human records are
mostly speculative."

"Could it be close to here?" Ara asked, anxiously, feeling
deep sorrow for the creature floating before her.

"I don't think so. She could have been killed hundreds of
years ago by a voreen blade. I've always wanted to see such
a blade."

"Why?"

"They're said to be enormous, magical, and almost alive
as their green and black surface slowly churns around itself."

"Are the voreen also big?" she asked, as they slowly followed the deathwalker through the moist forest.

"No. They're like us, but with grey skin and spikes on
their heads, and they lift the blade as if it was paper, and are
incredibly strong and fierce, using magic, or so I've heard."

"If you kill one, can you take its blade?" she asked.

"Clever question. Kingdoms would be traded for them,
so no. Only a voreen can lift their blades. So finding one
often marks a grave, unless another voreen picked it up."

"And this poor woman was killed by one." They looked
sombrely to the ground. "And what about the whispers?"
she asked.

Khendric lifted his head. "The whispers?"

"You can't hear them?"

"There are no whispers."

"What? I hear them, coming from her." She pointed at the deathwalker.

"Really? You're certain?"

She nodded, feeling an unnerving sensation in her stomach.

"What do they say?" he wondered.

"They've been too low to make out, but grew louder the closer I got to her."

"Hmm," Khendric hummed, rubbing his chin. "Try stepping into her."

"What?"

"Try stepping into her. It's not dangerous." He waved his hand through her being. The deathwalker turned towards her, and she closed her eyes and did as he said.

Nothing. Only the rustling of the wind on the leaves, until a scream shot through her being as clear as day, "*My daughter! Has anyone seen my daughter?*"

Ara reeled back in shock and fell to the forest floor, opening her eyes. The deathwalker loomed right above her, menacingly staring into the forest ahead.

"Close your eyes!" Khendric shouted. She did so and waited. "Okay, you can open them. It moved away. Are you alright?"

"I think it's searching for its daughter," she said. "I heard a woman screaming."

Khendric looked at her in disbelief, extending his arm. "This is peculiar. I've never heard of this." He stepped into the deathwalker too, listening, but he shook his head.

"Is something wrong with me?" she asked.

"You don't need to worry," he said. "Yes, it's weird and not normal, but so what? I mean, you can hear her, but . . . nothing's happening to you."

"Yet."

"Yet," he said. "And if something does, you've got me and Topper to help you out. One might say we're experts."

She returned his half-smile, but the worry was still plain on her face.

"Maybe you're very gifted," he said, trying to lighten her mood.

"In hearing the voices of the dead? No thank you."

"They can be killed during sunrise and sunset, in the crimson light," he said, eyes on the deathwalker. "Nobody knows why. They materialize for a short time and a simple knife is enough."

"Really?" she asked. "Sounds too simple."

"Yeah. It's speculated those specific times of day have some profound meaning in voreen culture. Anyway, go back to the camp and get some sleep. I'll follow it around through the night and lay it to rest at dawn."

"I can stay," Ara suggested, but Khendric waved the offer away. *He is already so tired,* she thought. *He needs to sleep.*

"I'll manage."

"No, really I can—"

"Ara," he said softly. "I would like to be alone for some time, please?"

She sighed, not liking his idea, but nodded and headed back to the camp, leaving him alone with the red glowing eyes. She found the makeshift bed, rug and animal hide, and laid down. Topper still slept soundly, oblivious to what had happened. Listening to his heavy breathing, she relaxed and quickly fell asleep.

CHAPTER 2

Phantom Bandits

Ara awoke the next morning as Khendric approached the small campsite with bags under his eyes. She shivered from the cold night and tried getting the fire started again. Khendric sat down across from her.

"Did you kill it?" she asked, putting the wood in place.

He nodded solemnly.

The lumber was too cold and moist for her to relight the fire. "We don't need to take off for some time. You can get some rest."

"I'm fine. The quicker we get on our way the quicker we reach Ashbourn." Dark thoughts clogged his mind again. Being up all night, alone, with only the remnants of a poor, forlorn woman, had probably sent his mind into twisted shadows.

"I'm getting better at fighting," Ara blurted.

Khendric gave her a quick look of confusion accompanied by a frown.

Guess he wasn't expecting that, she thought. "I can't wait for today's session," she continued.

Khendric looked away from her, his grim expression returning. "We'll see."

Ara sighed. *Guess I'm trying this.* Her mind said "no," but her heart said, "don't be a wuss."

"Nah." She cocked her head. "Think I'm pushing the session up a bit earlier." She rose and brushed off her clothes.

Khendric looked puzzled, with a dismissive look. "Ara, this is not the time—" he rolled backwards to avoid Ara's fist coming at him in full swing. "Stop! I'm not in the mood."

Earlier, that would have worked. She'd obey him. But now, she dared trust her instincts. *What's he gonna do?* she thought. *Leave me in the forest?*

Ara threw her whole body at him, knocking them both to the ground.

Khendric didn't fight back. "Ara," he said in a tired voice.

She lifted her strong arm, loaded with power, and brought it down directly towards his face. She'd never seen Khendric truly terrified, but he seemed to realize an anvil was about to crush his skull. His eyes broadened and he ducked away at the last moment, rolling away from her.

"Are you insane?" he shouted, trying to stand.

Ara took a firm hold of his coat and sent him flying several feet skidding along the ground, dust rising in his wake. He rolled to his feet, looking annoyed as he felt the back of his head. Ara charged him, and he ducked, tripping her over him. She hit the ground hard, losing her breath.

"Alright," he said, cracking his neck and knuckles. "Think you're clever?"

Ara lashed her arm in a circle, striking his feet with full force. He didn't just fall; he flipped, crashing down on his face. Ara rolled close to him and got a hold of his coat before he regained control. This time, she lobbed him into the air, truly experiencing her awesome gift.

He landed somewhat gracefully, grunting. "Okay-okay, you little dirt stain. I know your one trick." His lip had been bleeding, but the wound had healed already.

Ara threw two punches at him, but he dodged them with ease, jabbing her stomach. She gasped, but his elbow struck her cheekbone, throwing her towards the ground. Before she hit the dirt, he grabbed her leather vest and lifted her back up.

"Tha—" she tried saying, but he planted his knee into her side. All air left her lungs, the pain unbelievable. "Stop!" she begged.

"Oh no," Khendric said. "There's no backing out now." Even if it was a bit sinister, he did smile, which took away some of the sting from the incoming lip-splitting punch. *My plan worked*, she thought, her blood flying into the air.

Khendric kicked her flatly in the chest, toppling her backwards. She scrambled to her feet, but Khendric's foot hit her shin and she fell to one knee. He towered over her and readied for a punch, but Ara used her momentum to rise and punch into his side with a good portion of her mighty strength. With a crunch, he flew several feet into the air, before crashing to the dirt, moaning terribly. *Oh no*, she thought, wobbling over to him as best she could with her injuries. To her surprise, he held a sickening smile through tears and blood.

"I think . . ." he said between heaves of pain. "I think you broke my kidney and back."

"What!" she said, panicked. "Sorry, I don't know the strength of this—"

"It's fine," Khendric said, panting. "I'll heal. A regular man would die though."

Relieved, she groaned and laid down beside him. She'd been beaten by her father, but that couldn't compare to this. Yet now she felt alive, instead of scared and alone. Khendric's dark thoughts were gone, for now.

"Are you done?" Topper said, trying to light the campfire. Ara hadn't noticed he'd awoken.

"Only if Ara says so," Khendric said, his wounds sowing themselves shut.

"We're done, please, I can't take anymore." Ara breathed desperately, trying to stave off the exhaustion. Fighting was truly tiring.

Khendric patted her on the shoulder as best he could. "Thank you, I think I needed that."

She couldn't help but smile, despite the pain.

While she laid in her misery, Topper got the fire going and heated breakfast: meat and bread. Khendric had fully healed and didn't even look to have a scratch on him. As the meat finished, he gave her some of his blood, which didn't taste nice, but she quickly felt way better.

The brawl had been good for her, too, giving her some real experience and perspective as to what she could do with this monster of an arm. It didn't look particularly strong or thick with muscle, making it a hidden weapon. The fight had the desired effect: Khendric's mind wasn't nearly as muddled with darkness.

"The book," the voice said again. *"Where . . ."* it trailed off. *A book?* Ara thought. This was the first time it said anything concrete.

"We're actually about four days from Ashbourn, I think," Topper said.

Khendric narrowed his eyes and gave Topper a suspicious look. "I've been thinking," he said.

"I'm impressed," Topper chuckled, not meeting Khendric's eyes.

"When Martyn killed you. You came back after . . . what, eight days? You rode a horse. That means your heart is somewhere around an eight days ride away from Cornstead."

Topper sighed.

"Admit it," Khendric pushed. "You've been here many times. I know they don't bury the dead in Cornstead or the surrounding villages."

"It's been long since I was in Cornstead last," Topper revealed.

"Well," Khendric continued. "I try not to let you die too often. So is it Marrowwood? Or maybe Hallowar?"

"You know I won't tell you," Topper answered, annoyed.

"Where's the trust?" Khendric asked, arms dramatically out to the sides.

"Well, if you piss me off enough, I might turn on you, and then I don't want you to know." Topper handed them some food.

Khendric scoffed.

"Eat up." Topper's body could have been a commander in the army. He was taut with muscle, broad, and had a strong face.

She consumed her meal and Khendric helped her pack down the camp.

* * *

Over the next couple of days, they continued practising. Khendric taught her to use a sword and how to aim with the pistol. She didn't get to fire, as he had few bullets. Khendric was a good and patient teacher, though his thoughts constantly swayed between better and worse.

As time passed, she correctly answered more of Topper's questions, and though Khendric didn't admit it, sometimes he struggled as they sparred. Her arm had so many uses, saving her time and time again. Of course, Khendric adapted and changed his techniques, but bandits or beasts wouldn't know.

No longer did the world seem so large and overpowering. Learning about and how to kill the beasts the common people feared took away the initial fright.

Khendric and Topper shared many stories of what sounded like fantastic adventures, though they probably painted them brighter than the reality. Ara guessed that as years passed, the stories became more and more heroic. *I also have a story now*, she thought. A good story too, with both pain and glory.

The landscape continued on and on with green hills and great pastures. Occasionally they saw a village in the distance or met other travellers. Khendric ended up talking to them, bargaining for rumours of beasts or simply socializing. One day he bought a black glove with a long sleeve off a travelling merchant and gave it to Ara. She'd been hiding her arm at every meeting, so putting it on was instant relief. The fabric was of good quality, perhaps part of a lavish outfit for a ball or a fancy party. It reached to her shoulder, where her shirt took over the job of concealment.

They entered a small hamlet called Greenleaf, consisting of three houses, and the group parked their horses. Far away Ara spotted two children running towards them through a gigantic field of corn.

"Probably excited to see customers," Khendric suggested, heading inside. Following Khendric, she discovered the house had one bar desk and a table for customers, but no bartender. They sat down.

"He'll be here soon," Topper said. "We've been here before, a long time ago. The bartender is also the farmer and it's all run by one family. The kids will probably inform him of our arrival."

"Oh," Ara murmured, hunger sprouting in her stomach.

"The last time we were here," Khendric said. "Were we coming from Cornstead?"

Topper nodded. "Yeah, after we dealt with the terronus, about four years ago. Nasty creature." Topper looked nauseous by his expression.

"Terronus?" Ara wondered.

"They're also called 'The Nightmare of Man,'" Khendric said. "Long bodies, thin arms and legs, and a small rectangular head, with four eyes and a nose. Their skin is sleek and black, almost scaly. On their stomachs are six mouths, placed evenly." His fingers drew the beast on the table, making it easier to visualize. "During the day, they're never to be seen, but during the night they make themselves visible to their victim in short glances, at the edge of your vision." He put his finger gently to the edge of Ara's eye. "People end up uncertain if they saw something in the corner of their eye or not. Usually, a corpse is found the next day, with six different bite marks on their back. It's a mess."

Ara's eyebrows lifted. "So, how did you kill it?"

"Oh," Khendric said. "Maybe Topper can explain."

"Of course," he replied, rolling his eyes. "Well, someone thought it'd be a great idea if I was eaten by this terrible beast, which was very, very painful. While I was getting eaten, Khendric and a . . . certain lady . . . swooped in and stabbed it to death. While feasting, they don't pay much attention to their surroundings."

"Oh," Ara said, excited. "Clever—"

Topper's expression darkened.

"I mean . . . oh, how terrible."

Khendric shook his head, chuckling. "See, even Ara sees your greatest use."

Topper opened his mouth to reply, but a middle-aged woman with a dirty, yet kind face walked to the counter. "Hello," she said, with a rather deep voice for a woman. On her shoulders rested what looked like two lumps of coal. "Sorry for the waiting time. My boy came screaming of your arrival."

"It's alright," Khendric said. "Have you got something to eat?"

The woman looked around under the counter, and the two coal-like lumps fell off her shoulders. She didn't seem to mind and continued looking.

Upon seeing Ara's curious face, Khendric whispered, "It's a pair of coalits."

"Coalits?"

Six small legs cracked out of the creatures and lifted it slightly. The coal-like body split in the middle, and long thin yellow tentacles rolled out over the counter, reaching the ground. "Afraid I got nothing warm," said the woman and rose with a frustrated look. "Some oatmeals, bread and the likes." She put one hand each on one of the coalits's tentacles and their small legs climbed them back onto her shoulders, closing their bodies.

"Everything alright?" Khendric asked.

The woman sighed audibly. "Actually, I've had to close shop and work full time on the farm. That's why there's no food here. And . . ." she trailed off as if considering whether to say more.

"I'll gladly have some bread and oatmeal," Khendric said. "We have a few slices of meat."

"That's good. Oh, and the name is Ellinor." She disappeared out the door. "I'll be right back with your meals."

"Why does she have coa-lits?" Ara asked immediately.

"They're great at finding mildwevers," Khendric said. "Which destroys crop with spores. We think it feels the mildwever's vibrations as it releases said spores, and tracks it down to eat it."

"So why were they on her shoulder?"

"Coalits imprint on someone from an early age. When they're not hunting, they want to sleep, preferably on their mother's shoulder."

"I wonder why they work the farm full time," Topper asked. "Last time, the husband complained about the house not being big enough for the bypassers."

Khendric had thoughtful eyes, but Ara didn't know what to make of it or why there was any reason to ponder it. Ellinor returned, carrying three bowls with stale, stark food in them, and some bread.

"If I may ask," Topper said. "Why have you closed?"

Ellinor opened her mouth, stammering slightly before talking. "You're beast hunters, right? I vaguely remember you. Well, not you, or you," she said, gesturing to Ara and Topper. "But I remember you."

Khendric nodded. "You're right."

Ellinor took a deep breath. "I had to close because I don't have the manpower to run both the inn and the farm anymore. You see, my husband, Morin, died." Her eyes flashed, and Ara sensed sparks of dark thoughts reverberating from her. "So now, I have the boys and my little girl working their fingers off because the king demands more wheat. Some riders came by, giving me the new shipment orders, saying something about many farms and villages stopping their supply to the capital. Even with Morin here, we'd have trouble supplying this ridiculous amount. Then, there's also talk of war."

"War?" Ara asked, anxious.

"Oh, there's always talk of war. Probably nothing to worry about." Ellinor waved her hand dismissively. "I need to tell you something. Do you remember Morin?"

Khendric frowned, nodding.

"He was the kindest of men, which is why this is so disturbing. You see, I killed Morin." Ellinor breathed tensely as she waited in silence for Khendric to say something, staring into his eyes. He simply gestured for her to keep going. Tears welled up in her eyes. "I killed him. I don't know what happened, but . . . he wasn't himself. I heard my youngest boy, Marian, scream at the top of his lungs. So naturally, I ran out to see what was the cause. Morin was chasing him with a knife in hand. I got his attention and I noticed he had changed—I could see it. His look was one of a beast, and I was prey. He came at me with his knife, eyes dark. He attacked me." Her voice trembled with anger. "I don't understand why. Why would he try to kill me? Anyway"—she wiped gruffly at her face—"I ended up piercing him with the pitchfork."

Khendric creased his brows; he was probably thinking the same thoughts as Ara.

"I'm not a murderer," Ellinor said. "I had to do it, to save my children."

Khendric put a hand on hers. "If what you say is true, what you did had to be done. Your children are probably alive because of it."

Ellinor smiled weakly through her tears.

What had happened had to be the same thing that happened to the crazed villagers of Cornstead. Her description had been spot-on on the symptoms. *That means we have good news*, Ara thought.

"Is there any place only your husband used?" Khendric asked. "Like a shack or an office?"

Ellinor frowned. "Well," she said, thoughtful. "He used to be the only one with the animals. None of the boys found any interest in them. It's just pigs and chickens."

"Right," Khendric said. "And do you use the farm now?"

"Yes. I have to."

"And have there been any episodes of light-headedness? Or times when you felt completely dull?"

Ellinor cautiously nodded. "Hmm, there was one weird incident, when I think about it. I don't remember much, but my boys, Marian and Davlin, told me I acted strange one night, shortly after Morin died. I hadn't answered them when they talked."

"Do you remember any of it?" Ara asked.

Ellinor shook her head. "I thought it to be the grief of the heart. I am heartbroken and the realization that I had to take care of the farm by myself loomed over me."

Khendric narrowed his eyes. "Topper, can you go to the farmhouse and check it out?"

He nodded and went outside.

Then Khendric told Ellinor what had happened in Cornstead—about the unknown tentacled beast nearly driving the village to madness, and Ara felt relieved he'd come to the same conclusion. After going through how the beast had infected people, even Ellinor thought it likely this had been the case with her husband. She looked troubled, despite Khendric's words of having killed it.

"It's good to hear that such a menace is dead," Ellinor said. "It's a small comfort."

Topper came back.

"So?" Ellinor asked, looking at him intensely.

Topper sighed and nodded. "I found traces of the spores."

"So it was this tentacled beast you talk of?"

"Yes," he confirmed. "The spores are almost gone. I don't think you have to worry about them, but just in case, you could give it another week."

"Oh, I've been in there lots of times," she said dismissively.

"Did any of the animals act weirdly?" Khendric asked.

"How do you mean?"

"Becoming docile perhaps? Or enraged?"

"Yes. Many of the chickens had to be put down because they didn't move. Day by day, they just stood there, staring into nothing, growing meagre."

"Just like Robert's dog," Ara said, breaking into the conversation.

"Yeah," Khendric said. "This confirms what we already were sure of, and the beast is dead."

"Good. Vile creature. I'll have to go back to work," Ellinor said and left them alone.

Topper sat down and finished his meal.

"So the beast must have moved through here then?" Ara asked.

"Your guess is as good as mine," Khendric said. "Or, and I hope this isn't the case: there are more of them."

More of them? Ara thought, alarmed. She hadn't even considered that.

"But we don't know anything for certain," Khendric continued. "Hopefully, there was only one."

"I hope that was the last we see of it," Topper said. "And I wonder what it is. When we get to Ashbourn, I'll head to the library to see if anything shows up. I like reading and hopefully, I'll stay far away from Darlaene."

Khendric raised an eyebrow. "I told you I'll talk to her about it."

"Sure, thanks," Topper said, smiling as if Khendric was a child.

Khendric sighed. "We should get going."

Ara was ready to get back on the road. The thought of the tentacled monstrosity infecting the farm nauseated her. They were back on horseback as evening slowly approached, behind skies heavy with rain. Ara felt sorry for Ellinor, having her life turned upside down like that.

Raindrops fell from the sky and Ara's mood soured. Khendric's mind worsened too, but Ara had no idea what to do this time. She'd played all her cards.

Topper rode beside her, looking ahead.

"You said you like to read?" she asked him.

"Yeah. Wish I had something to read now."

"You were good at reading in Cornstead too. Perhaps that is a core personality trait?"

Topper didn't break his stare, but let out a breath. "Maybe, but I think our attention is needed elsewhere." He nodded toward Khendric.

Ara had hoped a conversation with Topper might force her mind away from Khendric's distracting, emanating thoughts. He continued darkening, slumping in his saddle.

They entered an area with more trees than before, and hills cascading in the distance. The night slowly enveloped them, Khendric's mind declining further into darkness too. With no plan, and probably against her better judgement, she rode up to him. "Khendric," she said, not prompting a reaction. "Are you alright?"

"They're here," he whispered, voice shaking. Even his hands shook.

"Who's here?" Ara asked, looking around.

"Shh," he hushed her, looking at the surrounding hills with mad eyes. "Show yourselves!"

Ara scouted the area, alarmed and confused. Topper did the same. Khendric looked terrified, frantically scanning the trees, scratching his arm furiously.

Topper rode up. "What is it? What are you seeing?"

"Bandits," Khendric shouted and kicked his horse into a sprint, riding straight ahead.

"What!" Ara exclaimed, also kicking Spotless into motion. In the darkness, she barely spotted him, trying to follow.

Khendric abruptly stopped his horse and pulled out his pistol, aiming into the darkness. "Get away!" he bellowed, firing his gun. Startled, his horse reared, throwing him from his saddle. The gunshot flashed the area around them, but revealed no enemies. Ara searched desperately, getting off Spotless.

"No!" Khendric shouted, getting awkwardly to his feet. "I have to save them!"

He took off—off the road and into the woods. Ara ran after him, the moonlight barely enough to separate him from the trees. "Khendric! Stop!"

"Where are you?" Khendric yelled. "They're coming! The bandits. They're back!" Terror and dread filled his voice. He fell to the ground in front of her, curling into a ball. Ara and Topper caught up, his expression as confused as hers.

"Khendric," he said. "What's happening? There's no one following us."

"Please," Khendric begged, scratching his arm intensely, tears streaming from his closed eyes. "I can't go through the pain."

"That's the arm the tentacled beast infected," Topper pointed out.

Ara got down on one knee next to him.

"Be careful," Topper said. "I've never seen him this bad, and I don't know what he is capable of."

"Please . . ." Khendric begged, eyes distant, his tears falling to the cold ground. It was disturbing seeing him so vulnerable, and not his usual all-in-control-self. He was a rock, a mighty cliff weathering all the might of the ocean. But something in his past, something terrible, haunted him.

"Don't kill her," he murmured, rocking back and forth. "Mother, no . . ."

A stone sank in Ara's stomach. *So that's what this is about*, she thought.

Khendric's eyes fixated on Topper. He rolled to his feet and pulled out the gun. "Back, bandit!"

Topper raised his hands to the sky and stepped away. "Wow, calm down now."

"Get back, you monster!" His arm shook with fear. "I'll kill you this time!"

"Khendric," Ara shouted. "That's Topper! Your friend! You're on the road with him and me, Ara."

His eyes darted to her, then to Topper again, but he held his weapon aimed, grinding his teeth together.

"We just escaped from Cornstead and talked to that lady Ellinor in Greenleaf," she said. "You're among friends. You're safe."

"It's me," Topper said, slowly lowering his arms. "I'm no bandit, but your partner."

Khendric breathed heavily, blinking repeatedly, before finally lowering the gun and hunching over.

"Are you back with us?" Ara said.

Khendric nodded slowly and one last tear fell from his chin, blending into the fresh rain. "I am not back there," he said, his voice calm again. "That wasn't real. The bandits. The voices. Not even the laughter. Just a hallucination."

Ara wanted to ask, but suppressed her curiosity, and put a hand on his back.

He straightened. "I'm sorry. I heard familiar voices and smells. It took me back to . . . it's not important. Thank you." The darkness clouding his mind was gone, at least for now.

"For what?" Ara asked.

"I'm not sure. Just . . . thank you. That's never happened to me before. I really believed I was back in my early youth. It seemed so incredibly real. I saw them, the bandits chasing me with those horrible, rusted knives." He shivered. "We should get back to the horses and set up camp."

"Khendric," Topper said. "Are you sure you don't need to talk about this?"

"Yeah. The episode is over. I'm very sorry you had to see that."

It had been unpleasant for Ara. The frightened, shaking Khendric would haunt her for a long time, but more than that she wanted to help him. She thought him invincible, a man never to lose control and always ready to handle any situation, but this was something completely different.

"You scratched that arm furiously," Topper pointed out.

Khendric looked down with a considerate look. "It's itching. Which is an entirely new feeling for me. I don't itch."

Ara frowned, wondering how that would be. Did his blood even stop him from itching?

"This was the arm the beast latched onto. Maybe I'm not fully healed from its venom. But . . . Ara got a much larger dose than me."

A knot formed in her stomach. *Should I tell them?*

"And she doesn't seem to have any hallucinations like this." Khendric turned, examining her.

"I hear a voice," she said, praying they wouldn't think her crazy.

They frowned.

"It's the same voice I heard in the nightmare."

"What do you mean you 'hear a voice'?" Khendric asked.

"Sometimes, out of nowhere, this low, rustling voice talks in my head. It has no direction, it's just there."

"What does it say?" Topper asked. "Is it telling you to do bad things?"

Ara shook her head. "No. It once said it needed more blood, and another time something about a book."

"It's not using our names?" Khendric asked. "Or saying anything related to your location?"

"No, and I don't think so," Ara answered, feeling guilty for not having said anything earlier.

Khendric considered something, looking down at the ground. "Maybe there's more to this venom than we first thought. But, we have to get back to the horses. Let's pray they haven't run off."

* * *

They all helped set up camp off the road, a task difficult in mere moonlight. They grunted and worked, wanting protection from the beastly world. Ara placed the spikes for the duskdevils, but felt something else bothering her. She hadn't told them the whole story about the venom coursing through her veins, but why hadn't she? They wouldn't get mad, and secrets only made her stomach ache.

"Guys," she said, as the last spike had been thrust into the earth. "There's more than the voice, and the arm."

Khendric mounted the varghaul head on the spike. "What?"

"I also have one more . . . ability, if you can call it that."

"Another one?" Topper asked, sitting down as the camp was ready.

She nodded. "I've been able to physically, or maybe mentally, feel other people's dark thoughts."

Khendric's questioning frown was barely visible in the gloom.

"It has grown stronger, starting like an itch on my mind in Cornstead. It's like there's pressure on my brain, in the direction of the person having dark thoughts." Khendric and Topper shared a confused looked with each other. "I've been able to feel your thoughts all this time," she added.

His eyes widened in surprise. "What? Are you serious?" He rubbed his hands together nervously. "Could you read them?"

Ara shook her head, and he instantly looked relieved. "No, I can only feel where they're coming from, not what they are."

"Well," Khendric said. "I'd say that sounds pretty amazing. Impossibly strong arm and a partial mind reader. You're becoming very valuable, I must say."

Of course he'd turn it around to something positive.

"It's true," Topper agreed. "Have you felt any thoughts from me?"

"I don't think so."

"Hmm," he mumbled. "Maybe because I'm not human?"

Ara had thought the same thing, but lifted her shoulders to show she lacked an answer.

"This can be used in your favour," Khendric said. "If the pressure isn't weakened by walls and obstacles, you can basically see through structures, if whoever on the other side has specific thoughts. You said dark thoughts, but that is somewhat vague. Do you know which types of thoughts?"

"I'm not sure," she answered Khendric. "A young boy in Cornstead was envious, which I felt. I felt Martyn too. He was thinking about murder and felt resentment."

"So you can feel resentment, jealousy, murderous thoughts," Khendric said.

"And whatever you're thinking about," she added.

He nodded his head slowly. "And that."

It felt good having told them, and she laid down, tiredness washing over her like a wave.

Khendric looked up at the stars. "We'll learn more about it, but don't fear it. Tell us if something new happens or anything else you'd like to share, especially if the voice in your mind tells you to hurt anyone."

Khendric hadn't told her the origins of his dark thoughts, and he didn't seem inclined to do so either, but since his episode, his mind had cleared a lot and she detected no sinister thoughts from him. Maybe having the episode helped somehow. Whatever the case was, she was glad. *Let's hope it stays that way.* She quickly drifted off to sleep.

CHAPTER 3

Ashbourn

The sun felt burning hot on Ara's thighs and had done so all day. No winds cooled her down, and she hoped not to faint. Khendric and Topper had removed their coats, and it reminded her what kind of brutes they were, their arms and backs taut with muscle.

According to Topper, they should arrive in Ashbourn before evening. Ara couldn't wait to see the great capital. What adventures awaited them there? Hopefully a new case, not as deadly as her first one. *Something simple wouldn't hurt.*

The path expanded into a real cobblestone road and houses popped up here and there, proving they neared Ashbourn and Ara constantly, looked to the horizon, hoping to see it.

"You see that mountain?" Khendric asked, pointing at a large, nearby mountain.

Ara nodded.

"Just behind it lies the city."

Clouds hid the summit from sight, mist cascading down its sides, making it look magical.

"Have you heard of mountainherders?" Topper asked.

"No."

"That mountain has its very own mountainherder," he said. "A mountainherder is a stone giant that hibernates for somewhere around ten years at a time. When it wakes, it gathers stone from the ground or adjacent mountains, building the peak of its mountain higher and higher. Somehow, the giant beast fuses the stone together."

"Really?" Ara asked, shocked.

They both shared a nod.

"That's why it's so tall," Khendric added. "It wakes up and just keeps building and building."

Ara stared at the mountain and spotted movement. The closer they got, the clearer it became. Something large climbed down the mountainside, and she pointed at it. "Is that it?"

"By the craven's mother," Khendric said. "It's actually awake! Come on, we've got to see this!"

He kicked his horse into motion, breaking off from the road and directly towards the great mountain. Ara and Topper followed, Spotless having no trouble keeping the pace. The closer they got, the more the figure grew, Ara realizing exactly how massive the mountainherder was. Khendric halted a good distance from the foot of the mountain.

Cracks from the giant stepping down from plateau to plateau echoed in the air. The giant's body was formed from stone itself, and covered with moss and even some trees on its back and shoulders. It moved slowly, the sound of stone grinding against stone reverberating from its joints. It faced towards the mountain as it made its descent.

"Make sure your horses aren't standing on any rock," Khendric said. "Mountainherders revere stone and grow furious when someone steps on them. They suddenly spring to life, determined to murder anyone guilty of stone-stepping."

After reaching the bottom, the giant stone creature thrust both hands into the earth and dragged up a boulder the size of its chest, giving Ara a memory for life.

Its triangular head was small compared to its body size, with a sharp chin. The large square-like arms held the boulder and without hesitation, the mountainherder began the climb to the distant peak.

"That must take forever," Ara said, tired at just the thought. The giant carried the boulder on its shoulder, somehow keeping it in place with its hands, and they watched it climb for a long time. Its resolve would impress anyone, as it never took a break towards the far-away peak. Once the spectacle had vanished, they headed back to the road and resumed their ride towards Ashbourn.

"You're lucky," Khendric said, smiling at her. "You've seen a pharlanax and a mountainherder in your short time with us. These are incredibly rare beasts and most people never get to see either of them in their lifetime."

Ara thought back to that night when the pharlanax flew above them in the night sky. "I'll treasure the moments," she reassured Khendric.

As they rounded the mountainherder's mountain, a gargantuan city crept into view, with a castle rising to the sky in the middle, surrounded by a large city wall. Ara felt her heart leap in her chest.

Kalastra had been a large city, but this was something else, unlike anything she'd ever thought humans could build. Even with the massive mountain, the city looked impressive. A new adventure was about to begin.

After what felt like an eternity, they stood in front of the gates. Even as the sun crested the horizon with its crimson light, the gate teemed with life. People constantly tried entering and leaving the city: merchants and farmers with carts, men carrying sacks of grain, and countless others for unknown reasons.

As they stood in line, waiting to enter the city, Ara spotted a man on a small stage to the side of the gate, with a sizeable mass of people listening to him preach.

"You must not believe the peace will last," he said aloud. "War is coming! The king keeps this from you, knowing if you knew, he'll lose his throne!"

"Ugh," Khendric said, leaning closer. "Don't worry about him. He's a representative of the Warborn Party. They always preach that war is coming."

"The Warborn Party?" Ara asked.

"I'll tell you about it later," Khendric said, before giving his attention to the guard at the entrance. "We are beast hunters."

The guard expressed mild surprise before ushering them inside. "Here's your notice of arrival," he said, and handed Ara a piece of paper with their date of arrival, signed by a sergeant.

"I can take that," Topper said, and she willingly handed it to him, not wanting responsibility for a small piece of paper like that.

Stepping inside, her mouth fell agape. Buildings went on forever, divided by winding streets, creating a magnificent maze of unique structures. Marketplaces, fountains, statues, foundries, bakeries and everything else belonging to such a city sprouted forth. Trashers ran around busy streets even at nightfall. Some people gave them food while others ignored them, keeping their attention on their conversation. A pack of rabdogs were forced back into the sewers by guards, and a woman ran by yelling that a shiny had stolen her necklace. Ara felt a little at home, as she'd grown up in the chaos of a capital. Luckily, no heartflies swarmed braziers or torches. The city was marvellous. The busy street chatter between all kinds of folk enchanted her, and she felt calmer than in a long time

Khendric led them slowly through a stream of people following the main street. It had a wide berth, with shops, carts, and countless merchants selling their wares. They rode past a wide, massive building with an oversized sign that said 'The Museum of The History of Meritocracy'.

"This city is divided into four large districts," Khendric said loudly so she could hear. "Each one belonging to a political party. At the centre is the castle." He pointed in a direction, but buildings obstructed the view. "Just wait until you see it up close. We're currently in the Meritocrat District, but they all have different gates to enter the city through."

"And the man outside?" Ara asked.

"From the Warborn Party," Khendric answered. "Which lies leagues away over there." He pointed again.

Sitting atop Spotless was a luxury, lifting her above the hoard of people. They could have conversations and she could look around.

"They are heavily focused on all things war," Khendric continued. "So naturally, they've always been spreading rumours of war."

"But Ashbourn has a king," Ara said. "Why all these political parties?"

"A good question. Ashbourn is not like Kalastra, where the throne is inherited. Instead, here, a new king is crowned every sixth year by the people."

"What?" Ara exclaimed. "So, you can vote for people in the royal family?"

"No, the new king doesn't need to have anything in common with his predecessor, except that he has to come from a political party."

"That's absurd!" Ara exclaimed as Khendric led them into a side street almost as wide as the main street. "What are these four political parties?"

"Well, you have the Meritocrats, whose district we're in right now. Then there are the Warborn, the Passionists and the Royalists. The Meritocrats believe in an individual's hard work. That you should be paid for what you're able to produce. The Warborn believe in a strong military front. The Passionists believe all people should do what they're passionate about, and like this, there will naturally be enough bakers, blacksmiths, soldiers and so on. The Royalists believe in complete and total devotion to the king, in the sense that the king should share the wealth amongst the people and be in total control of everything the citizens are given."

"I see," Ara answered.

"They should be in the middle of the coronation process now," Topper added while trying to squeeze in beside her, but the moving crowd made it impossible. "I think in around two weeks, a new king is crowned."

"Who's the king now?" Ara wondered.

"Koradin Banner," Topper said. "He's been the king of Ashbourn for twelve years, meaning he's won two coronations."

"And he's from this district," Khendric leaned back and added. "So for at least another two more weeks, Ashbourn is under Meritocratic rule."

"Is that good?" Ara asked.

Khendric chuckled. "Some will say yes, others no. I haven't spent much time here, but I think Koradin has been doing a good job."

Before long, Khendric turned them down another, less crowded street, and pulled up to a building. Getting off their horses, a young lanky man walked up to them.

"Do you require the use of the stables?" he asked with a high-pitched voice. He couldn't be much older than Ara, with the same black hair as her, just curly and short.

"Yes," answered Khendric. "Three slots for an indefinite time."

"That will be three silver chips a day," the young man answered.

"Here's a golden one," Khendric said. "I'll give another when it's needed." The young man took it and the three of them walked through the door to the inn.

It was called 'The Just Lion," and inside was a grand room with a huge counter—tables and chairs everywhere, and it boomed with people. A bard sang a lovely melody, freezing Ara in her tracks. It was about his lost love, who'd turned out to be a luster. She didn't know what a luster was, but barely noticed Khendric telling her to sit down. The bard described the beast disguising itself as a woman, whom he cared for until she tried to claim his life. Then he sang of how he broke free of her bonds and slew her, completely captivating her with the wonderful atmosphere as his fingers glided over the cello.

"Have you heard music before?" Khendric asked.

Ara's eyes stayed on the bard. "Only briefly. Once when I was younger, I walked past an older man playing fiddle, but only for a second, before my father pulled me along."

The bard was tall and muscular, playing in just a leather vest and linen pants. He had long brown hair, tied behind his head in a ponytail. His fingers moved vigorously over the instrument, filling the room with playful notes, easily heard over the conversations. She had never enjoyed music before, and it touched her very soul. Tears ran down her cheeks, but she didn't care, taking it all in, letting it envelop her until the bard put his instrument down and joined some of his friends at a table.

"That was beautiful," Khendric said, drawing her out of her trance. "I've rented two rooms for now. Whenever you are ready, we'll go to sleep. Then tomorrow we'll either look for work or practice your sparring skills. It is up to you."

"I would love to look for work," she said with a very calm voice, still feeling the effect of the beautiful song.

"Then that is what you two will do," Khendric answered with a smirk. "I got some other business."

"I really hope she's not here," Topper said, sighing. "Are you going to 'The Troublesome Sailor'?"

Khendric tipped his head. "Among other places."

"It's an old fighting club," Topper explained. "Khendric always goes there when we arrive in Ashbourn, to listen to rumours, fight some sorry fools, and . . . it's Darlaene's favourite place to stay."

"Well," Khendric said. "I have a very good relationship with the manager. He lets me fight whomever I wish and tells me all the rumours he currently knows, all because I saved him from a trollman once."

"You killed a trollman?" Ara asked.

"I did," he said proudly. "The trollman skull is now on display, hanging majestically on the wall of the club."

"I helped," Topper added.

"Barely."

"Without that torch, you'd be dead."

Khendric turned to Ara with raised eyebrows. "Topper is trying to claim parts of the honour, because, in his drunken stupor, he flung a torch in my general direction, which I managed to dive for and use against the vile beast."

"Foolish is the man who forgets the tiny details of what saved his life," Topper said, leaning back confidently. Khendric looked at Ara with a flat expression, before they barked out uncontrollable, mocking laughter. Topper sighed once more, rolling his eyes.

"But wait," Ara said, as they calmed. "You fight people in a fighting club?"

Khendric nodded. "Hand to hand combat."

"Well, that hardly seems fair."

"I know," he agreed. "I'm better with weapons."

"I meant to the other guys."

Khendric just looked at her questioningly.

"Because you regenerate?"

"Oh, that. That might be why they call me, 'Khendric, The Undisputed.'"

Ara couldn't help feel sorry for those who fought against him. It would be like trying to fight the current, but she just smiled hopelessly. A waitress put some soup with bread on their table, which Khendric had ordered. Hunger sparked to life in her stomach, and she dug in. It was a wonderful moment and Ara blessed the way her life had changed. As her bowl was empty, her eyelids became heavy with sleep. Khendric made a leader's decision to go to bed. She didn't protest, and with a stomach full of food, sleep found her in minutes.

CHAPTER 4

The Scepticism of Beast Hunters

Dunk-dunk . . . dunk-dunk . . . dunk-dunk . . .

The sun streamed through the window, and Topper awoke to the familiar beating of his heart. He heard it anywhere and at all times, and was so used to it he barely even noticed. Instead, he heard the sounds of the city; carts rolling, merchants bartering, and bells ringing in the distance.

He sat up, rubbed his eyes, and noticed Khendric's empty bed. *Not wasting time,* he thought, knowing he was searching for Darlaene. Topper prayed he wouldn't find her, but if she was in the city, he would sniff her out. A pity, as he'd grown fond of this body. He moved easily, and it was strong, unlike the boy he inhabited previously. That vessel made him jittery and nervous. Topper even wondered if that nervousness was part of his true personality, which he hated thinking about. He had tried narrowing down his personality. It seemed simple: just take note of which character traits followed him through death. But it hadn't been easy at all. Every body made him act different, and the difference between traits blurred too much.

He got dressed and looked in the mirror, loving his great body, and intended to keep it. If Darlaene showed up, he could just work on his own.

He locked the door to his room and knocked on Ara's door.

"Yeah, I'm ready!" she barked through the wooden door instantly. *Of course you are,* Topper thought, scoffing.

She was out in the hallway the very next second. "Where's Khendric?"

"He's already gone, most likely looking for Darlaene."

"Oh," Ara said, deflating. "I thought we'd at least have breakfast first. Well, well . . . let's eat and then let's go!" She was halfway down the stairs before Topper even moved. She gulped down her morning meal, and Topper forced his down to satisfy her. He'd come to hate breakfast, or . . . maybe his body hated breakfast? He wasn't quite sure.

He couldn't remember if any previous vessels held a grudge against the early meal. After two hundred years of different lives, they all blended. *Stay focused.* Thinking too much about earlier lives had driven him to madness before.

"Where do we go first?" Ara asked, gesturing for him to hurry up eating the last piece of his meal.

"In front of the Meritocrat Headquarters," he began, mouth full. "There's a board where people put up jobs for us beast hunters and other trades."

"Great," she said with a bright smile. "Come on."

"You must be the most impatient woman I've ever met."

"I don't think you've met a lot of women," she answered, triumphantly. "And for being over two hundred years old, that's quite embarrassing."

Topper produced a flat look gesturing towards other people close by.

"Oh, sorry," she said, her triumphant look replaced by embarrassment.

"Come on," Topper said, leaving the table.

Together, they strolled down the cobblestone roads towards the large business street. The streets boomed with life, and Ara's eyes were glued wide open. Ashbourn had grown into a grand city over the last decades. Topper had walked these streets when they were just dirt, long before the castle and the four large political parties existed.

Vague memories of life as a shoemaker's apprentice circled in his mind when passing 'Malaren's Shoes'. *So that's why it's familiar,* he thought. He couldn't remember much from that time of over a hundred years ago, except for old Malaren's face, and felt happy that Malaren's shop had survived. After all, Topper helped start it.

He shook himself out of his reverie. *Focus. Don't dwell on the past, live in the moment. Lest you go crazy again.* It proved hard, as flashes of previous lives could spring to life from anywhere.

They passed all kinds of different people; merchants, street performers, musicians, and beggars, before reaching the large, wide, and clean main street, with a road for carriages in the middle. Ara did as expected: stopped at the start of the street, gazing upon the massive Meritocrat Headquarters at the far end. Even from here, it loomed over them, with enormous windows and terraces on all different levels. Beautifully carved statues rose proudly directly from the building's walls. A huge wall surrounded it, with an impressive iron gate in front of its courtyard.

"That has to be the headquarters, right?" Ara asked.

"Yeah, it's quite—"

"Spectacular," she interrupted. "Can we go inside?"

"After we check for cases, sure, but its charm is from the outside."

The pair walked down the busy street, finding the board across the street from the massive building. Ara searched eagerly for anything of value, but mostly it looked like people needed workers. After skimming through the different post-ers, Topper actually found one for beast hunters. He pulled it off the board and gestured for Ara to come over.

Beast hunters needed.

The Meritocrat Headquarters.

Be discreet.

That was it, with a weak stamp showing the Meritocrat's sigil: two hammers crossed over a shield. Topper frowned, but Ara's eyes lit up.

"That's great!" she said. "We get to enter the headquar-ters. Come on."

"Hold on. This is the most peculiar call for beast hunters I've ever read. There's no description of the problem—and no name." He considered if this was worth it, but when see-ing Ara's excited eyes, he had to yield. "Alright, let's check it out. But on one condition."

Ara halted once more. "What?"

"You don't get to decide if we take the case or not. By that, I mean: don't blurt out a 'yes, we're on it.' I decide, ok?"

"Sure," she agreed to his relief. "That makes sense."

"Good. Now compose yourself. Look professional. Not all *bubbly*."

She stood up straight, chest high, and walked with an el-egance he'd never seen. Suddenly, she grew up. They crossed the road and walked up the stairs to the iron gate.

To the left, in a small hut, sat an older woman. Two sol-diers in gleaming plate armour stood guards on either side, holding huge halberds. Ara walked beside Topper, awed eyes at the building in front, until she stopped abruptly, shifting her eyes intensely to the ground in front of her.

"What's wrong?" Topper asked.

"The voice. It spoke again, but clearer than before."

"What did it say?"

"'She's here.' You don't think the voice meant me?"

"Most likely not. What would the chance be—"

The old lady in the hut stuck her head out. "Are you just going to stand there?" she asked with a rasping voice.

Topper showed her the poster. "We found this on the board."

She grabbed it from his hands and put on some reading spectacles, studying the words for an eternity before shaking her head. "I recognize this handwriting, and I should probably turn you both away, but he'd find out and never forgive me." She handed him the poster back and waved for a guard to open the gate for them. Ara's spark returned to her eyes, and she ventured excitedly into the courtyard, forgetting the 'professional' part completely.

They walked through the neat and clean courtyard alone, passing beautiful fountains and statues of supposedly famous people. *Maybe one of them is me,* Topper thought, humming to himself. Together they walked to the two enormous doors forming the main entrance, and familiar office noises vaguely made their way through. Topper expected the headquarters to be busy so close to the coronation. The Meritocrats were probably up to their necks in conferences, speeches, and all kinds of political games to get their king crowned once more.

He pushed the doors open and it was as busy as he predicted; people running everywhere, waving papers around, yelling at each other. He felt relieved he was merely a beast hunter, where he got to kill beasts, not debate on whether this and that.

Ara followed him to a wide desk not far from the entrance. The young, dark-haired receptionist looked completely unaffected by the busy circumstances, filing her nails, their presence prompting one glance before looking back at her delicate hands again. "Meritocrat Headquarters," she said emotionlessly. "How can we be of service today?"

Topper showed her the poster. "We found this on the board outside."

Like the woman outside, she rudely grabbed it out of his hands, examined it and frowned before handing it back. "I've heard nothing of this." Her eyes fell back on her nails.

"What do you mean?" Topper asked, pointing to the official seal.

"I said: I haven't heard of anything we might need beast hunters for."

A head popped forth from a room just behind the large desk. "Beast hunters?" said a young man with blonde, short hair, leaning back on his chair to make his head visible. "You're beast hunters?"

Topper nodded and noticed Ara's look of confusion.

"Stay right there," said the strange young man before disappearing into his little room. His small office hid under a staircase, near the receptionist's desk. With a ruffled Meritocrat uniform and a scruffy hairdo, he exited his cubby and approached hand outstretched. "Very nice to meet you," he said with a smile, grabbing Topper's hand and shaking it firmly, before doing the same to Ara. He turned to the woman behind the large desk. "I'll take care of this."

Her raised eyebrows questioned the young man. "You're looking for beast hunters, Adenar?"

He chuckled awkwardly and gestured to Topper and Ara. "Follow me if you'd be so kind." He led them outside to a bench near the walls of the massive building. "I'm relieved someone finally answered my call." He sat down. "Please, be seated."

"You put this out?" Topper asked, showing the poster while seating himself.

"Uhm. Yes, I did. Sorry about the lack of context. I'm trying not to get noticed. I always put it up in the morning and take it down when I am done for the day, which usually isn't before nightfall."

"Why?" Topper wondered, noticing the bags under the young man's eyes.

"I am scared I'm being watched," he whispered, leaning closer. "That's why there's so little information on the note."

"Who would be watching you?" Ara asked in a whisper.

"I don't know if I can trust you," he answered with an apologetic look. "I mean, for all I know . . . you're not *truly* beast hunters."

That actually made Topper chuckle and he flashed his medallion.

"Can I see it?" Adenar asked and inspected it thoroughly after Topper placed it in his hand. "It looks good," he said and lifted his gaze to Ara. "And yours?"

Her eyes fell to the ground. "I don't have one."

"So you're not—"

"She's an apprentice," Topper said, unhappy at her apparent self-doubt. She wasn't wrong, though, still having much to learn when it came to bestiary knowledge.

"Oh, I see," Adenar said. "Congratulations on your apprenticeship." He turned Ara's lips into a smile.

Topper examined his deep blue, tired eyes, which hinted at a hidden intensity or persistence, perhaps. Was there more to him than met the eye? "So good enough? Going to tell us something?" he asked.

Adenar nodded carefully. "My name is Adenar and I'm an assistant at the Meritocrat Headquarters."

"I meant about the case. We already know your name."

Adenar chuckled. "I'm getting to it. I've called for beast hunters because of an incident that happened about eight days ago. How long have you been in town?"

"We arrived yesterday," Topper said.

Adenar narrowed his eyes. "Then you have a notice of arrival?"

It was a clever question, and Topper was minorly impressed. He found the notice of arrival Ara had given him and showed it to the young man.

Adenar looked at it and let out a relieved breath of air. "This is great. Actual proof that you arrived yesterday. I guess this is the best opportunity I'm going to get. Alright, I'm just going to assume you don't know much about recent events."

"Probably smart," Topper said, leaning closer.

Adenar scouted the surrounding area. "Seven days ago, a funeral involved the whole city. It was for the general of Ashbourn, General Toran. To our king and the nation, it is a great loss. He was a renowned member of the Warborn Party, so naturally, they arranged the funeral. The public has been told he died while out on a patrol mission with recruits, far up north at the border to Paradrax. The Warborn told us General Toran fell in a Paradraxian ambush, bolstering their claim that war is coming. But . . . that's not what happened, and I am the only one who knows the truth. I was at the Warborn Headquarters to gather some important documents sometime before. On my way out, I heard what really happened—through a window. General Toran was talking to another woman on their council, Eranna Carner, accusing her of treason. The room was packed with guards and swords were drawn. I think Eranna admitted she was treasonous. Then"—he paused, sighing—"a much deeper voice said the general would be a great sacrifice and . . . then the worst sound I have ever heard in my life followed. I heard the general's body be . . . torn apart? Or sort of like he exploded. It was horrible and I ran away." Adenar sat still, staring into the table.

"That's it?" Topper said.

Adenar creased his eyebrows.

"You didn't see anything?"

"No, I was below the window."

"Did you actually see a beast?" Topper asked.

"No, but I am sure that they killed him."

"Who?" Topper prodded.

"Eranna and her men," he said sternly.

"So he was killed by people?"

"I . . ." Adenar said, leaning back in understanding. "No, that sound . . . it couldn't have been a human."

"So this is based on a sound?" Topper wondered, shooting Ara a glance. Her eyes fell to the floor. *She wants to take the case anyhow,* Topper realized. *This would be a lesson to learn. don't get involved with humans against humans. You'll become someone's enemy.*

"I guess it's based on a sound, yes," Adenar admitted, leaning on his knees.

"And you are a Meritocrat?" Topper asked.

"Obviously," Adenar frowned.

"And the coronation is two weeks off?"

"Yes."

"And if beast hunters investigated the Warborn Party this close to the coronation, that would surely cause concern for all voters, something that could undermine the whole party if news got out."

Adenar glared at Topper. "That is not what is going on," the young man protested. "This really happened. He was murdered."

"Maybe," Topper said. "But this case could affect the coronation. Without further evidence, except for a sound, meddling in politics is something we avoid."

"Please," Adenar said grabbing Topper's hand as he stood. "I beg for your help. I've saved twenty gold chips, regardless of the outcome."

Twenty gold chips? Topper thought, impressed. Normally, a beast hunter charged five to six gold chips at most, and even that was rare. *But, if the Meritocrat Party backs this, twenty chips is nothing.* The young man seemed sincere though, his eyes unyielding.

"Listen," Topper said calmly. "We're staying at The Just Lion. If you produce more evidence, I'll happily reconsider."

Adenar's eyes fell on the table, his expression grim, but he let go. Ara mirrored his expression, but Topper gestured for her to turn, and they left Adenar.

Ara's pace felt so slow, Topper almost wondered if she'd been injured. "Maybe what he said was true?" she said as they walked through the courtyard. "He seemed honest."

"He *did* seem honest," Topper answered, urging her onwards with a hand on the back. "And I don't doubt he believes a beast is involved, but we can't work on only what someone heard one night, meddling in dangerous politics."

Though she still seemed displeased in her vacant expression, no more words sounded from her lips about the subject.

"We'll go to the Royalist District and look for work," Topper said. "And if nothing shows up, we'll spend the day sparring or going through questions about beasts."

Ara sighed dramatically, but Topper couldn't offer anything else. This hadn't gone the way she imagined. He guessed she expected them to find a case in the morning and solve it come nightfall. That wasn't at all how the beast hunter profession worked. Often, they'd go days or weeks without cases. Or, they became buried in cases and picked who would live or die.

The duo crossed the road and went to a carriage. Ara stared at the floor as Topper told the driver to go to the Royalist District, hopefully, to find more work.

* * *

Sitting on top of a bell tower, Khendric stared out over the city, evening colouring the landscape and buildings a deep red. He had searched all day for Darlaene, but she was nowhere. A knot formed in his stomach. What if he never saw her again? They always found each other, or so it seemed. He did his best to suppress the fear.

They had agreed it might be best not to meet, as their fear of losing each other greatly compromised the plans of their cases. But then again, it wasn't his fault she couldn't break out of the chain he put on her to keep her safe from the morilmen-riddled cave. That was on her.

He had one last place to check: The Troublesome Sailor, his fighting club in the Warborn District.

The long climb down from the bell tower would be insanely dangerous for regular folk, but he was afforded some chances and scaled down rather quickly, unfortunately slipping on a windowsill not too far above the ground. He crashed through a sheet of linen stretched over a lonely merchant's stand, smashing into his wares. Beads, necklaces, rings, and piercings flew everywhere before Khendric stopped rolling. It hurt, but nothing he couldn't deal with. The plump merchant with as much hair on his arms as Khendric had on his entire body looked bewildered.

"What do you say?" Khendric asked as he rose. "Ten out of ten?"

"What do you mean?" the merchant exclaimed with a thick accent, probably from across the sea.

Khendric tossed him two gold chips and turned.

"My wares are worth a lot more than two chips!"

"Your counterfeit wares are worth more than two chips?" Khendric asked, amused.

The merchant sighed. "Alright, fine. Go."

Khendric did so and ran up the short house wall in front of him, jumping from rooftop to rooftop to reach the club as quickly as possible. The wind roared in his ears and memories of his time spent in Master Yanavar's establishment surfaced. That was a good time, and had saved him after—he didn't let his thoughts wander there. Master Yanavar had taught him and the other boys—his orphaned 'brothers'—to skim across rooftops and fight, both unarmed and armed, and he often wondered what they did now.

"Did you see that?" a boy said as Khendric lunged over a small street, hoping not to start rumours of beasts on the roofs. He neared the club and climbed down, conforming to more socially acceptable ways of transport.

The Troublesome Sailor was packed with people, but Collem, the manager, still recognized him immediately as he passed the entrance and ushered him inside.

Collem hadn't changed a bit, with his shaved head, wrinkled forehead, and beardy chin, reminding Khendric of a handsome rat, if such was possible. He still wore the golden ring in his left ear for good luck, walking with his crouched back. "Ooh, Khendric, you are back, my friend!" he said with the same accent as the merchant, rubbing his hands together. "Finally, we shall have some quality fighting!" He laid his middle finger on Khendric's forehead, a sign of respect from his culture.

Khendric did the same. "It's good to see you again. I've been longing for a good fight."

"Yes, yes," Collem said. "I've got good fighters tonight." He led Khendric through the masses of people with a hand firmly on his back.

The entrance was on the second level of the building, with a gigantic fighting pit on the lower floor. On this level, there was a bar, tables, chairs, lots of inebriated people dancing and screaming, and a huge hole offering a view into the pit below—which the screaming was centred around, watching the contenders go at it.

"One question first," Khendric said, halting Collem. "Is she here?"

Collem narrowed his eyes. "Your fire?" he asked.

Khendric nodded.

"No, I have not seen her, not in a long time."

Khendric's frustration grew, but nothing like a good fight to keep his mind off her. "Alright, let's fight!"

* * *

After beating three opponents in a row, Khendric actually felt tired. The two locally renowned fighters had been easy, but the one as large as three kegs demanded more work. Khendric had tired him out, relying on his stamina and unfair healing abilities to sustain blows that would knock out a regular man.

"Khendric wins again!" Collem bellowed throughout the room as the monster of a man laid on the ground. The crowd cheered crazily for more, and Khendric raised his hand to Collem, signalling he'd do one last fight.

"He is ready to take on another!" Collem roared. "This time, he'll fight someone with a personal agenda towards beast hunters. He claims one killed his family!"

Khendric rolled his eyes, wondering what the story was here.

"Now he is on his path of justice! Where better to get it than in a fighting ring! Get ready to meet Cantar, The Hunter of Hunters!"

Khendric chuckled. *That's ridiculous.*

Through the crowd emerged a tall figure with no hair and thick arms and a broad chest. Half his face and all of his arms held swirly tattoo patterns. He removed numerous rings and piercings, and with anger behind his dark eyes, he stepped into the ring. "Are you a real beast hunter?" he asked with a thick voice.

"Yes, but not the one that wronged you."

"It doesn't matter."

Khendric sighed. Too many times people held grudges against all beast hunters for the actions of a few, seeming to forget how dangerous the profession was. Things could go wrong—*often* things went wrong. "I'm sorry for what happened to you," Khendric said. "Mistakes happen."

The large man bit his teeth together. "Are we going to fight?" he asked.

Fine, Khendric thought, tired of such ordeals. He closed his eyes and reasserted his mind to become a shadow. The demanding fighting technique was meant for training purposes, teaching students to dodge and deflect attacks, and only worked against one adversary, demanding absolute concentration. He blocked out everything in his mind, the screaming, the feet hammering on the floor, Darlaene. Years of practice let him enter a state of complete focus.

The bell rang—Khendric's eyes shot open. Only Cantar and he existed, his mind constantly assessing every movement made by the large man. Cantar stepped forward, guard at his temples. Khendric remained still. The large man stepped closer. Khendric spotted the muscles on the left side of Cantar's jaw tighten—a double jab. Khendric masterfully leaned back just enough to be outside the two quick punches.

The well anticipated right hook followed, which Khendric ducked beneath, circling Cantar, spinning out of the desperate, yet powerful, kick. Anger spiked within Cantar's eyes—and a flurry of punches thundered from the man. A duck, dodge, block, and a deflective hand, rendered all his attacks useless. Cantar roared and threw his body at him to close the distance. Khendric stepped aside, tripping him with his foot.

With a face full of dirt, Cantar found his footing and attacked, fueled by rage, until he panted wildly. Khendric breathed normally and exited the shadow stance. A kick into Cantar's knee threw him off balance. He tried a desperate grab, but Khendric snuck past his defence and placed Cantor in a chokehold, and like that, the bout ended. Cantar didn't give up before fainting, which Khendric admired, but it was over.

The crowd roared, and he welcomed the cheers, bowing graciously. Blowing off some steam felt great, and got his mind off of her. Nothing was better than some honest fights.

Well, they weren't really honest, but *they* thought so. Sweat, blood, and punches made him feel alive.

"That's it for tonight," Collem shouted. "Maybe we'll be blessed with such a show another night! Come back and see!"

Khendric went to the bar and ordered a drink, free of charge of course. A champion had privileges. He looked up at the old trollman skull Collem kept over the bar, only to find it gone. He frowned. *Collem wouldn't part with that.*

"I had to sell it," Collem said as he came and sat down next to him.

"You *had* to sell it?" Khendric asked.

He looked regretful. "Yes. Several months back, a bunch of large men came to the club, not to fight, but to buy the head. They offered a good price, but I told them the establishment had no trouble with money. The mood tensed and I felt danger loom in the air. I either take their money or their beating—they *would* leave with the head."

How bizarre, Khendric thought. Who'd be that interested in a trollman head? "Do you know who they were?"

Collem shook his head. "They wore dark clothes and made themselves untraceable in the night by splitting. I'm sorry."

"That's fine," Khendric assured him. "Better keep your head, than the head of a dead beast. Now let's have a drink."

***

Adenar had trouble keeping himself awake, which was reasonable. This was the sixth night he spent outside the Warborn Headquarters, spying on them. The Warborn hadn't buried General Toran the day of his supposed funeral, because after digging up the casket he found it to be empty. That had been the second most terrifying experience of his life, right after the night of the general's death.

The night's temperature felt comfortable, which made him even drowsier. He gambled on them not burning the corpse, in fear of a kindler rising from the body, which could be disastrous. So he stayed outside their headquarters every night, spying, in hopes of learning something.

The beast hunter from earlier needed more evidence, and this was how Adenar could get it, hoping they'd dispose of the body soon, not risking the smell of a dead body within their headquarters.

Just as his eyelids shut, sounds reverberated from the courtyard. Two people argued, followed by horses trotting on cobblestone. A large carriage pulled by two mares halted at the gate, right across the street from Adenar's hiding place. *Please*, he thought. *Let this be it.* The gate opened and the carriage moved toward him at a slow pace. No light shone through the carriage window, and the two annoyed men sat in the driver's seat, talking condescendingly to each other. As it passed, Adenar climbed onto the back of the vehicle, almost slipping, but got a firm grip, and prayed not to be discovered.

The carriage left through the main gate of Ashbourn and headed for the woods. After entering the thick and dark forest, they quickly came to a halt

"Shouldn't we go further?" a thin voice said.

"No," another voice answered—thicker, and authoritative.

"But she said—"

"We'll do it here," the strong voice commanded. "Nobody'll know."

Two thuds followed as the two men jumped down from the carriage. Adenar stayed put, not seeing a reason for them to check the back, yet he still trembled. What had he gotten himself into? He was merely an assistant, but now he was also a spy, trying to send beast hunters after the Warborn

Party. The doors of the carriage opened, and some tools landed on the ground.

"Hey, those are my nicest tools."

"Shut up. Help me get him out."

A loud crack sounded from deep within the forest, but luckily the two men's screams masked Adenar's yelp.

"What was that?" asked the first guy.

"Come on, let's get this done quickly. Who knows what kind of beasts lurk around."

The two men pulled something from the carriage, and Adenar used the moment to slide off the carriage and sneak a small distance away. Crossing the dirt road as silently as possible, he hid behind a large tree, made possible by the moon's light.

When behind the tree, Adenar leaned his head to get a look at them. They dragged something large into their dug grave. *That must be the general,* he thought. After a soft thud, the men buried the corpse. For once, Adenar wished they were further south in the Sangerian Grasslands, where the dead weren't buried. He sighed at having brought such a small shovel, attached to his belt, realizing he had quite the job to do.

The two men returned to the carriage and disappeared with haste in the opposite direction of Ashbourn. Adenar remained for some time in case they watched the area. Then, he emerged and went over to the poorly dug grave concealed under branches and leaves, almost making it look like a natural part of the vegetation. He got to his knees and started digging.

It didn't take long before he panted from the exertion. *What am I doing?* he thought. *Why am I so bent on doing this? Maybe I just want some dirt on the Warborn Party so they don't win. Or maybe I want to become the hero that discovered their dark secrets. Am I doing this for justice or egotistical reasons?* Several footsteps approached him rapidly and he jumped back, lifting his shovel defensively, expecting to die any second. A few feet away stood a curious creature with six legs and a barrel-shaped ribcage, reaching to his knees. Its skin seemed to be an assembly of differently coloured leaves, and its head resembled that of a dog. The two front legs were curved with a talon, while the others has some small claws. *Good job, Adenar, now you're going to die in the forest all alone.* It struck him how terrible a plan this was, and how foolish he had been.

The creature seemed to examine Adenar while slowly waddling toward the poorly dug-up grave. Adenar controlled his breathing, but kept the shovel upright. The beast started digging in Adenar's hole with incredible speed, taking its attention off Adenar completely, who then lowered the shovel slowly. Quickly it uncovered a large bag, digging it out perfectly. The stunned Adenar just remained by the side, trying to comprehend this encounter. The beast circled the large bag and nipped at it with its curved legs, until it managed to break it open. It lowered its head and sniffed the contents inside. With a screech, it turned its tail and ran away, gone in the night. Adenar stayed completely frozen for some moments, listening for *anything* else. The loud crack reverberated from deep within the forest again, prompting him to get a move on. He opened the large bag, and a ghastly smell struck him, almost forcing him to vomit. This had to be it. He gathered all his courage and looked inside hurriedly.

As suspected, he'd found the corpse of General Toran, but in a terrible condition. Surprisingly, it was in one piece, though barely. Countless differently sized holes covered it from the thighs to the neck, and the chest had been ripped open. Adenar closed the bag before he threw up. This was the beast hunter's job.

All that remained was to run back to the city, get hold of a horse and a cart, return here, bring the corpse through the city, and find the beast hunter—all before people woke up. He'd use the same gate the carriage had left Ashbourn through since it was free of guards, which was probably the

Warborn's doing. The carriage hadn't gone too far from Ashbourn, and with that in mind, he ran.

* * *

Khendric stood atop a tall building overlooking the Warborn District. The night drew to an end, and he still hadn't found her. He clenched his teeth, sat down, and dangled his legs over the edge. The passing wind usually made him feel better, but not now. What if she wasn't here? *No,* he decided. *I won't let this consume me. It's only the first day in Ashbourn.* He needed to stop worrying so much.

He shut his eyes. The night was beautifully calm and quiet. Except it wasn't a complete silence—one disturbing sound vaguely sounded in his ears: a horse and a carriage. He listened closely—the horse rode hard. *Someone's in a rush. And I'm bored.*

He rose and chased the sound across the rooftops, the previously comfortable breeze now howling in his ears. Few people could match his speed, as he vaulted over chimneys and lunged from roof to roof. The sounds of the horse and cart grew louder as he reached the main street, and stopped atop a building surveying the area. Not to his surprise, a horse with a cart pulled up at the far end of the street, coming from the entrance gate, probably. A man held the reigns, heading straight towards Khendric's building.

As he closed the distance, Khendric saw he was a young man, and on the cart was something quite peculiar: a blanket covering what looked *a lot* like a dead body, confirmed by a foot dangling off the edge in the free wind.

Khendric readied for the oncoming raider of the night, climbing lower on the building, and as the cart neared, he ran to match the speed as good as he could and jumped. He made a loud thud as he landed expertly on the small vehicle, making it wobble violently, and the horse whinnied. The young man turned in an instant, looking scared and in disbelief, pulling the horse to a stop, looking at Khendric with wide eyes.

"Pull into that small alley there," Khendric told him and pointed.

"Who are you?" the young man asked.

"Stay calm," Khendric said with a smooth voice. "First, pull into that alley."

The young man stared at him in confusion, before finally doing as told. The cart narrowly fit, but the young man handled his horse well, before turning sharply to Khendric. "I'm in a theatre group. This is a prop."

Khendric frowned, stifling a laugh. "You did a good job on the smell." He leaned down and lifted the blanket.

"Who are you?" the man asked. "You're not a guard, clearly. Are you working for the Warborn Party?"

"Would you want me to work for the Warborns?" Khendric asked with a sly smile. The young man stared deep into his eyes without saying a word. "I think you played a card too early there. Because, if I, in fact, was from the Warborn Party, my interest would pique."

"So . . . you're not?" Khendric shook his head. "But, then who are you?"

He ignored the young man's question, and went back to uncovering 'the theatre prop'.

"Stop! Alright, let me explain."

"What is your name?" Khendric asked before he could open his mouth.

"My name?" he asked, still confused. "It's . . . Adenar."

"Well, Adenar . . . I've seen many peculiar things in my life. So the truth will probably be best." Khendric knew this young Adenar was no killer. His eyes were too innocent.

"Alright," Adenar said, holding his hands up. "I'll tell you. Yes, that is a real corpse, but I didn't kill him, I swear.

He's been dead for days, hence the smell. I'm taking him to beast hunters."

What? Khendric frowned, and motioned for him to continue speaking.

"I think he was killed by a kind of beast, especially after looking at the corpse." Adenar climbed to the back of the cart, shielding his mouth and nose. Khendric stepped back, and Adenar removed the blanket.

Beneath—a ghastly sight. There was something peculiar about the corpse. Those holes were something Khendric had never seen before, like tendrils had pushed through the flesh. However, his facial expression remained motionless.

"So?" he asked, covering it up. "Will you let me go? I could never have done that to anyone."

"What did the beast hunters look like?" Khendric asked.

Adenar slowly lowered his hands. "I don't think I should say."

"Do you want to leave here alive?"

"One was broad, of average height with dark skin," he quickly recited, as if a switch had been flicked. "The other was a young woman with dark hair." Adenar stood completely still, waiting.

The lad was terrified, but Khendric couldn't blame him. He'd come crashing down like a doombringer on the poor guy. Now he towered over Adenar, and looked quite fierce. Khendric was having a great time though, internally chuckling to himself.

"You may leave," he said. "I would hurry, people will soon be waking." Adenar let out the longest breath Khendric had ever heard and tried backing his horse. Khendric jumped off and helped pull the cart out of the alley, before properly covering the corpse in the back. Then he disappeared into the night, leaving the startled Adenar alone . . . until they most likely met again.

CHAPTER 5

The Plan

Adenar drove the carriage with haste towards the inn where the two beast hunters stayed. His heart beat hard after meeting that man. If he *was* a man, seeming more like the embodiment of night itself: shrouded in darkness, deep voice, and an unnatural balance. Adenar shuddered. He'd never been so frightened in his life and thought for sure the stranger would end him. Even without authority, he exuded an aura of total dominance. Hopefully, Adenar would never meet that apparition again. His horse drooled from the aggressive trip, but luckily they drew close.

How will I get the corpse inside their room? I can't just carry it to their quarters. Just dragging it up on the cart was a real hassle. Adenar pulled the horse to a stop outside the inn and got off the cart.

Except for another large carriage rolling past, he was alone. A whistle sounded from the stables, which seemed integrated into the inn. It had been short, and he barely made out the shape of a man inside. His heart stopped and he froze in place.

"Bring it around here," a deep voice reverberated from the stables.

"Bring what?" Adenar said as nonchalantly as he could.

"There's no time," the man answered urgently.

Dawn loomed, so he knew time was of the essence. Adenar gritted his teeth and went back to the cart. A couple of trashers casually inspected the corpse, poking at it and grimacing from the smell. "Shoo!" Adenar said, and they quickly scattered. He tried lifting it off, but lost control and it slipped off the carriage. A loud thump followed as it landed on the ground, and he muttered a curse. His hands shook with excitement and fear. If anyone saw this, his life would be over. He tried dragging the corpse the short distance from the cart into the stables, but his feet slipped again and again.

"By the craven's mother," the voice from the stable said, and out came the male beast hunter from before. He hoisted the corpse upon his shoulders. Adenar felt rather foolish at this point. "Thank you?"

They went through the stables, leading behind the inn, where a window stood open. No light streamed from it, and they were luckily surrounded by buildings. From the window hung a rope—which the beast hunter tied around the body—and it rose into the air.

"Follow me," he said with a stern voice.

Adenar did as told, and they went back through the stables again. "How did you know I was here?" he dared to ask, but the beast hunter offered no answer. They went past the cart and through the actual entrance of the inn.

Only the innkeeper was up, not to Adenar's surprise. The broad beast hunter wasted no time and headed up the stairs and to the room, Adenar following like a dog on a leash. He shut the door, leaning against it, realizing how out of breath he was. *I can't believe I made it.*

Adenar had never done illegal activities. While studying at the university, he was quite conscientious, always on time and worked hard—harder than most. The other students went out drinking, dancing and flirting, but not him. What had happened to *that* Adenar? Now he went digging up corpses and he didn't understand himself at all.

Gathering his wits, he focused on breathing normally. He lifted his gaze to see the corpse atop a table, with the two beast hunters around it and—Adenar's heart stopped. The apparition that landed on his cart stood in front of him, barely lit by a candle.

"Ready to die?" he said with a look of absolute insanity.

Adenar's head drained of blood.

"Khendric!" the young female beast hunter shouted. "You're scaring him to death."

Just before Adenar's vision went dark, the man laughed aloud. "Alright-alright. I'm sorry, Adenar. No harm will come to you."

"What? But, but . . . but you said—"

"He wasn't serious," the young woman said.

"I just wanted to see the look on your face when you thought me an omnipotent being."

Adenar's heart was in his throat. "So, you won't hurt me?" he asked, realizing his fingers held around the handle of the door.

"Not at all. Now come over here."

Adenar moved warily towards them, and the man gestured for him to hurry.

They removed the blanket and examined the corpse. How they managed the smell, Adenar didn't know, but he wore his bravest face and tried not to waver in the face of their expertise. He stood between the two beast hunters from earlier, keeping a safe distance from the last one just in case he was insane. The ghastly sight of the corpse made his stomach churn.

"You did a good job bringing this here," the closest male beast hunter said. "I'm Topper by the way. This is Ara." He pointed to the young woman, who gave a short nod. "And you have already met Khendric."

"I apologize for the way we met," Khendric said and stretched out a hand. "I didn't mean to scare you, but people are talkative when they fear you."

"It worked on me."

"What are these?" Ara asked. She pointed to one of the many peculiar holes in the dead general's body.

Khendric stuck his finger into one, rummaging around in the wound. "There's no blood." He brought out a knife and cut open the general's forearm. "Not a drop at all."

Due to the corpse's pale skin, Adenar suspected as much.

"There is definitely something weird about this corpse," Topper said, looking contemplative.

"So, you'll take the case?" Adenar asked.

"That's not what I said," Topper answered. "For now, we're just examining."

"Sorry," Adenar replied, looking down at the horrid corpse.

Khendric chuckled. "Don't worry. We'll conclude at some point, we just need to determine if this is the work of some beast or not."

Adenar's stomach churned with eels. What if they still didn't believe him? He couldn't possibly find better proof. They seemed like nice people. He didn't know what to make of Khendric, but Ara looked kind. Her dark hair fell to her shoulders, partially hiding her face. She couldn't be older than Adenar, maybe not even in her twentieth year. Adenar was twenty-three, but felt fourteen when around these people.

"Maybe we can use the paratis serum?" Ara asked, producing deep frowns from the two other beast hunters. "What?"

"That's a secret of the trade," Khendric said, and she immediately blushed.

Adenar stiffened, looking terrified at Khendric. "I won't tell anyone. I don't even know what it is or . . . remember the name."

"You did get the wrong impression of me," Khendric said. "As I said: you're in no danger. Though, I would like you not to tell *anyone* what you're about to see."

Adenar nodded too many times. When looking at Topper, his eyes held a flickering, bright orange flame, the colour churning vibrantly inside his pupils.

"Don't raise your voice," Topper said calmly, and Adenar barely dared to breathe. Topper examined the corpse intensely. Occasionally, he'd lean and sniff different parts. "The wounds on his chest have a faint smell of metal residue," Topper whispered. "All of them."

"Was he clad in plate armour?" Khendric asked.

"My best guess," Topper answered.

"So," Ara said. "Whatever made these peculiar holes plunged through plate armour?"

In the following thoughtful silence, Adenar noticed how tired he was and left the thinking to the professionals. This was his eighth night without sleep, spying on the Warborn, and ultimately his exhaustion caught up to him.

"I can't think of anything that could do this," Topper said.

"Maybe a needler?" Ara proposed.

"Unlikely," Khendric answered. "A needler would have left the city long ago for the mud-lands. And a spiderling can't go through steel like that."

The holes were all over the corpse's torso, arms, and neck. Adenar had heard about spiderlings, but had never seen the arachnoids. A friend at the university had a dog that was killed by one, though.

"So we don't know?" Ara asked blatantly.

"Not yet at least," Khendric answered.

Ara frowned, looking at Khendric and Topper critically. "Are you still debating whether this was done by a human or beast?" None of them answered. "The body is *completely* drained of blood, and we don't know what weapon could make these wounds? I'm thinking whatever made them, also sucked the body dry. Can you give any reasons how humans could have done this?"

A burst of hope sprung to life in Adenar. She'd said what he dared not.

The two other beast hunters looked contemplative. "I've got nothing," Khendric said, bowing to Ara sarcastically.

She rolled her eyes. "I believe something's going on, and it's worth checking out."

"I do agree," Khendric said. "But whether we're taking the case hasn't been decided. I'm fairly certain this couldn't be done by man, however, this is a delicate scenario. The city is in the middle of the coronation and meddling with the Warborn during this time can be dangerous. Ara, you've already had a taste of human nature, and this could get worse than some village constables on our tail. The Warborn has plenty of resources."

"But," Ara said. "What if there's something sinister going on within a fraction of the party? If so, maybe they'd be inclined to help us?"

"You really want a case," Topper mused.

Ara sighed heavily, ending with a flat smile. "Yes, I do. But regardless, you can't dispute something's going on with this corpse, beyond what humans could have done. You tried dismantling the case, but could not."

Topper looked to Khendric and they both nodded to each other. "Yeah, you're exactly right," Topper said, inclining his head in respect.

"So," Khendric said, facing Adenar. "Who are you in all of this?"

That was complicated. Being from an opposing party, he must have looked biased in their eyes—and maybe he was. The Warborn had never been his cup of tea, with their brutal ways of solving conflict, valuing only strength, pushing for war, and only caring about military strength. Adenar enjoyed solving issues with words and insightful discussions like Ara just did. Sure, he'd held a sword a few times, but the quill felt like a stronger weapon. Under Koradin's rule, the military had remained strong, but as a defensive measure. If the Warborn won the coronation, Adenar feared they'd use their armies offensively. "I am just an assistant at the Meritocrat Headquarters."

"Assistant to whom?" Khendric asked.

Even more complicated, and with no answer. "No one in particular, really. Everyone loads their work on me it seems. I have a busy schedule, you might say."

"So you were hired to be an assistant to nobody?" Khendric asked.

Adenar nodded uncertainly. "Most of the employees— me included—don't know how I got the job. I just applied straight after I finished my studies and, to my mother's astonishment, was offered a job. On my first day, I was actually escorted around the building by Ponther Caein." A smile grew on Adenar's lips, but their faces revealed they had no idea who he was. "That was a true honour. He's the king's spokesman during the coronation and has been on the council for ages. After he showed me the headquarters, he provided me with a small desk beneath some stairs, and . . . I never saw him again. The first days, nobody bothered me, probably as puzzled as me as to what my job actually was. As time passed, people guessed I was the lowest ranking individual in the building, thus it became truth, and everybody exploited it."

"So," Topper began. "Why are you the only one who knows what happened to the general?"

Adenar exhaled. "Callan, another employee, charged me with the task of getting some forms from the Warborn Headquarters at night. When I got there, the gate was open with no guards, hence, I let myself in through the back entrance. I found the forms and when I was about to leave, I accidentally eavesdropped on a most secretive conversation, where the general 'discussed' with Eranna Carner, who's on the Warborn Council. I don't remember much of the actual conversation, but the general called Eranna's actions treasonous and unnatural." Adenar reheard the terrible sounds of the general's flesh being torn apart. "Then . . . a darker voice, rumbling like thunder in the distance, spoke. It said General Toran was a worthy sacrifice and after that . . . gut-wrenching sounds." He shivered.

"The voice seemed unnatural?" Khendric asked. "Too deep to be human?"

"I can't say for certain. But I think so, yes."

Topper noted down Adenar's words. "This will require a lot of investigation, as we're all uncertain regarding what caused this. Tell us about the Warborn Party."

Adenar considered where to begin. "The Warborn's only focus is war—"

Topper waved a hand. "Not about their politics. Specifics about the coronation."

"Oh," Adenar nodded. "Uhm, their Chosen for the crown is a newcomer, named Ronoch Steelbane. We don't know much about him, other than he's from Brattora."

"The Chosen?" Ara asked.

"The Chosen is the one who's crowned king if their party wins the coronation."

"That makes sense," she said. "And Brattora?"

"The capital in Paradrax, one of the neighbouring kingdoms," Adenar explained. "Ronoch claims to be from Brattora, but we haven't been able to confirm it. At least not as far as I know. I'm not told much. So, the Warborn's main point is that Brattora is getting ready for war, which I think isn't true. Ashbourn has great trade agreements with the city, which benefits both kingdoms."

"What do you trade?" Khendric asked.

"Well," Adenar said, not wanting to delve into that. "We sell them armour and weapons and in return, we get clothes, food, and beverages."

As expected, all three beast hunters frowned.

"So," Topper said. "You're arming them with weapons in return for clothes, food, and beverages, and this stranger comes along from the city you're supplying with said weapons, telling you the city is getting ready to invade you."

"I know it sounds convincing," Adenar snapped. "That's why so many people are falling for it, but I don't think it's true."

"Maybe you don't want it to be true," Topper suggested.

"Of course I don't want it to be true," Adenar answered, raising an eyebrow. "Who would want it to be? But that's beside the point: people are forgetting that Brattora is already at war with another one of their neighbouring kingdoms and *that's* why they need a heavy supply of weapons. Also, Paradrax isn't rich in ore, so they couldn't have produced a sufficient amount on their own. Koradin has also said numerous times again that he talked to the Brattoran ruler, who states time and time again that being knee-deep in one war is quite enough."

"Of course he would say that," Topper said, sitting down in front of Adenar. "Who would want to admit to such claims?"

"Koradin investigated the issue," Adenar said, feeling annoyance bleed into his voice. "During a speech, he said Brattora doesn't have enough resources to pose a threat to both kingdoms, and since Ashbourn is already an important benefactor to their ongoing war, it's highly unlikely they're also planning to attack us."

"I guess that makes sense," Topper said, leaning back. "Sorry for putting you under pressure, but I wanted to engage your emotions to see how you reacted."

"What?" Adenar asked.

"So, this Ronoch," Khendric said, stealing Adenar's attention. "Did he just waltz into the Warborn Party, and is now their Chosen?"

"No. We don't think so. Some sources say he worked for the ruler in Brattora, but left the kingdom to warn us of war. If so, the Warborn naturally picked him up, as he would help further their cause. It would have been foolish for him to not join the party, as they're the only party who believes him."

"Those are reasonable arguments for both sides," Khendric said. "Not that we would indulge in politics, but I don't see why Brattora would risk war against yet another kingdom."

"I think it's rumours," Adenar said.

"Do you think so because you don't want it to be true because it would weaken your party in the coronation—or do you truly believe it is just rumours?" Khendric asked.

It made Adenar consider his stance. "I'd like to believe it's just rumours. I'll tell you this much: if the rumours are proven to be true, beyond doubt, I'll either welcome Ronoch as the new king or try to change the Meritocratic stance."

Khendric cocked a questioning eyebrow.

"I mean that," Adenar said. "I want what's best for the city. I don't care about being right."

Khendric slowly nodded his head. "I believe you."

Relief flooded Adenar. He fought with his life, desperately trying to get them to take his case.

"And there is something fishy about this corpse, something I can't explain," Khendric said. "Which means we don't know what we're potentially dealing with and those cases are more demanding, as you probably know, Ara."

She nodded.

"But, we have to conclude." Khendric strolled over to the corpse.

Adenar tapped his fingers nervously, feeling more anxious than ever. Even more than those hectic days after the murder of the general.

"I say we take the case," Khendric said after an eternity. Adenar almost jumped with joy. "But," he quickly added. "We're going to make a plan *and* some conditions."

"Of course," Adenar said, mind racing. "We'll make a contract!" He knew how to do that. In fact, he was pretty good at it.

"Sure," Khendric said. "But first we have to hear what my 'lesser' companions have to say?" He gestured for them with a devious smile.

Ara rolled her eyes again. "I want to help."

Adenar wanted to hug her, noticing in the light of the lanterns how pretty she was.

"Let's do it," Topper said.

Khendric stretched an arm out, and Adenar clasped it soundly. "Guess we're in business, at least for a time. How much can you pay?"

"I've saved up twenty gold chips," Adenar said.

Khendric examined him. "You're telling the truth, aren't you?"

Adenar frowned. "Of course."

"Usually there's a fair bit of haggling involved."

"Oh. Maybe... it was just ten chips."

Khendric and Ara both laughed. Adenar felt so tired he had trouble keeping his eyes open, and barely revealed a tiny grin.

"Here's how I want to go about this," Khendric said. "We work on this case for a week. After that, if we can't find proof of something sinister, we're allowed to drop the case, unless we're close to a trail or reasonably sure that some beast is in fact behind this. If we then decide to drop the case, you pay us ten chips. Does this sound agreeable?"

Adenar wouldn't get a better deal, and after everything he'd gone through, he would pay them the full twenty for a day of investigation. "Yes."

Ara yielded a look of excitement as her eyes lit up and she sat up straighter.

The sun found its way through the windows, announcing morning's arrival, and Adenar sighed heavily, as he would soon have to find his way back to the headquarters for a full day of work.

"We need to make some sort of plan," Khendric said. "Would you say I'm wrong with our primary suspects being Eranna and this newcomer, Ronoch?"

"I think she is the main suspect," Adenar said. "And then there's that deep unnatural voice."

"My best guess is that, if the voice came from some kind of beast," Khendric said. "It was a conscious one, with an unpredictable nature, unlike a wretcher, which all behave the same way. Conscious beasts are especially tricky, as they adapt to different scenarios. If the voice was indeed a beast, it's probably working with Eranna to help her fulfil a purpose."

"Like winning the coronation," Adenar said.

"Maybe," Khendric said. "How do we approach this? We need to see these people, get close to them, or my favourite: sneak into their houses." He chuckled, feeling right good about his sentence.

"Breaking into their houses?" Adenar asked. "That's . . . illegal."

"We often must—how do I put this—*bend* the law," Khendric said. "We don't hurt anyone unless we have to, but a little break-in here and there comes with the job. If we're discovered, this emblem may protect us." He showed Adenar his beast hunter medallion.

"If you say so," Adenar said, debating whether this had been a good idea or not. "I mean, I would want you to do everything in your power to stop this potential beast."

"That's the spirit," Khendric said.

Adenar followed them downstairs and Khendric kindly bought him breakfast. It helped keep him awake, but the drowsiness got worse by the minute, but just before his eyes fell shut, he remembered something. "Later today, Ronoch is holding a speech in front of the castle."

"Great," Ara said. "We can go and listen to him, right?" She looked to Khendric, who nodded with his mouth full of bread. "Maybe we can discover something useful from the speech, or follow him afterwards."

"We'll explore the options when we get there." Khendric swallowed the bread and looked at Adenar. "Anything else happening that could help us?"

He tried to think of other events, but his mind wasn't functioning, the dread of having to get new forms from each of the districts for the next gala plaguing his mind. He frowned as a possible idea sprung to life in his mind. *Would that be possible?* At first, he thought no, but, he *could* probably make it work. "The day after tomorrow, there's a large political gala, where all the important politicians, nobles, and wealthy people will attend. These parties are common leading up to the coronation, where the elite arrange deals, discuss politics and such."

The beast hunters narrowed their eyes conspicuously.

"I want to get you into this party. Hopefully, I can get all three of you in."

"I mean no offence," Khendric said, leaning back. "But you said you were a lowly assistant. How can you clear entrance to such a party?"

Adenar huffed a smile. "Well, these parties require *a lot* of paperwork, and being the lowly assistant that I am, I'm destined to get all the tedious tasks. In short, I'm in charge of making all the tickets and filling out the forms for each attendant. I'll easily add three more guests, as long as we make up decent backstories."

They seemed impressed, and Adenar felt his stomach flutter in anticipation.

"Alright," Khendric said. "If you can do that, I think we have a pretty good start. You seem like a nice guy, Adenar."

"I appreciate that," he replied. "You're not as scary anymore."

"I was hoping this meal would help."

"Make it three more, and I guess I can forgive you."

Ara chuckled, to his happy surprise.

"Pleasure doing business with you," Khendric said, stretching out his hand, and Adenar grasped it tightly. "No, go to sleep in our room. You need it."

"I can't."

"Adenar, close your eyes for a second and listen to me," Khendric said.

"But there's a corpse—"

"Just listen to me. Close your eyes and open your ears"

Adenar sighed and closed his eyes—falling asleep immediately.

CHAPTER 6

The Calm Before the Storm

Khendric had taken Ara to a small sparring area in the Meritocrat District, where anyone could practice for a small fee with blunted weapons. Several others trained too, some soldiers, while others looked like regular folk. Some boys a few years younger than her beat at each other, their cries often ringing through the air. Each sparring area was marked by poles and fences, and a tremendous rock wall surrounded the whole area.

Topper left after the plan had been concocted, and Adenar fell asleep straight after eating his breakfast. Khendric had carried him to the bed, and that's where they left him. Adenar had been exhausted; she was amazed he'd been able to stay awake the whole meeting.

Ara lowered her training sword as Khendric swung from below, stopping the blow with ease. Matching Khendric's strength with her dark arm was almost effortless. He swung once more—Ara stepped back and parried the blow. Khendric advanced, and Ara stepped back again, hitting a pole. Her stance broke as she grabbed the back of her head in pain.

"That is an important lesson," Khendric said triumphantly. "Always watch where you're going and be careful not to give too much ground. At some point, you'll have to counter my attacks and halt my advances."

Ara grunted and nodded, annoyed she'd fallen for such a simple trick. How embarrassing would it be to die because you stepped into a wall? She raised her simple one-handed training sword—it felt good in her hands, more so than axes and other weaponry.

Khendric seemed to master every kind of weapon with ease, which annoyed her more. *Why is he so good at everything and regenerates.* It was quite unfair.

"This time," he said. "I'll swing left, and you parry it, quickly closing the distance and grabbing my arm. Then knock me in the face with the elbow." He mimicked the motion against an invisible opponent. "Most attackers assume that a sword fight is just that, a sword fight. You'll take many by surprise by getting in close and using other body parts."

"Alright," Ara answered, excitement bubbling in her blood.

Khendric did the pretend swing. Ara parried and awkwardly grabbed his sword hand before he could retract it and put her elbow to his chin.

"Great. From here, you can twist my hand, forcing me to drop my sword."

Ara did so and it worked surprisingly well. They practised this motion several times before moving on to other nifty manoeuvres. She loved this: the fighting and sounds of swords clashing together, the grit and the dirt. Besides, being beaten up felt strangely therapeutic. It cleansed her of hidden anger, like taking a bath, but for your mind, washing away accumulated dirt.

Often her mind wandered and thoughts of her family surfaced, and she felt a little guilty for doing so well. She missed her mother, and thought she would be proud of her. It would be immensely fun to have her sister by her side through all of this, and she'd be so embarrassed when meeting Khendric and Topper for the first time. But they were dead, and through sheer luck, she was not.

"I meant to ask you," Khendric said, panting, stealing her attention. "Did Adenar have any dark thoughts as we laid our plans?"

"No," she answered and engaged in the next disarming exercise. "Actually, not at all."

Khendric's sword fell to the ground yet again. "That's good. He seemed earnest, but it's good you can 'check.'"

"He did seem earnest," Ara agreed, picking up his sword, but he didn't take it back. Khendric acquired two new blades from a nearby rack.

"My body withers," the familiar voice in her head said. *"More . . . I need . . ."* But it faded, and Ara ignored it, as usual, concentrating on the sparring instead.

"You look good holding two of those," Khendric said, swinging his own two blades. "So let's practice that."

She smiled, the wooden handles comfortable in her grip. His words had to be true, because wielding the swords made her feel powerful and fierce. Hopefully, she looked the part.

Khendric ran her through some ways to parry and strike with two swords, and different manoeuvres to disarm the foe or to both block and strike at the same time, and she got a grip on it pretty quickly.

"Great," Khendric said after a while. "Now let's do some light sparring."

"Really?" Ara asked, wide-eyed.

"Very easy and light," he said. "Is that clear?"

"Yeah-yeah," she answered, eager to start.

Khendric started with straightforward blows that she parried with ease, and she swung her sword back, but he parried. Trying to land strikes on Khendric felt impossible. He stepped aside and dodged so fast, but she had a lot of fun.

In a flurry, she attacked. He smiled, cocked his eyebrow, and took every strike on his blade. Their swords clung together and he spun around to her flank and tapped her on the back of the head with one sword.

"Hey!" she exclaimed.

"Why don't you step it up?" he said with a taunting expression.

Ara swung low. He parried easily. She also swung with the other arm—he blocked that too, and Ara realized she was completely open. With longer legs, Khendric firmly placed one foot on her chest and shoved her back. She stumbled, but kept her balance. They had many more engaging bouts, but Khendric parried, dodged, or disarmed her *every* time.

"They say you learn quickly when fighting an invincible opponent."

"Who says that?" she asked, raising an eyebrow while gathering her sword from the ground.

"They!" Khendric retorted. "I don't know. Topper, probably."

She chuckled and readied herself. *So, you think you're invincible?*

They engaged again and she swung her blades here and there, luring Khendric into raising his sword in a simple parry against her too obvious blow—with her enhanced arm, she put *all* her strength into the swing. It accelerated swiftly. He had no chance to react in time, and the swords clashed, breaking apart instantly—a crunch sounding from Khendric's wrist. He roared in pain and fell to one knee. Ara studied her broken blade. *That worked really well.*

"What was that?" Khendric demanded, eyes watering.

Ara tapped the back of his head. "Got you," she said, smirking.

"You *broke* my wrist!"

Ara stacked the swords on the rack. "You'll heal," she said dismissively. "Mister Invincible."

"That's not fair. And breaking the wrist is really painful."

"I think the blow to your pride is more severe."

Khendric shook his head as he carefully wiggled his fingers, followed by twisting his freshly healed wrist. "I'm not going to fall for that again."

"I hope you do. I'm a one-trick-pony." Her arm had amazing potential, and if she learned to use it properly, she'd be a dangerous foe.

* * *

Topper wandered up to the imposingly tall Warborn Headquarters, almost alone in the courtyard. He wasn't wearing his usual attire, but instead a blue shirt with a black vest. Looking formal couldn't hurt in a place like this, and he always felt it was easier to lie and spy when in unfamiliar clothes.

He wasn't convinced of the beastly nature of this 'case,' and a thorough check wouldn't hurt. He strolled up the steps to the main door, hoping that anyone could enter. Sure, Warborn guards stood posted both in front of the gate, at the doors, and just inside, but probably to scare off those weak of mind, and Topper was *not* weak of mind. After living for hundreds of years without going insane, he deemed himself 'pretty tough.' Well, he'd gone insane a couple of times in the beginning and killed himself to start anew. He tried not to think too much about past lives lived, as it only interfered with the present. Anytime a memory from a previous life began to lurk, he pushed it away.

Both Ara and Khendric had accepted Adenar's story quickly, without considering one vital fact: none of them knew what General Toran looked like, or if he was even dead for that matter. Typical Khendric, trusting his guts too much, and Ara just wanted a case.

It was up to him to add some scepticism—and where better to look than the Warborn Headquarters? He stepped inside the massive structure, which wasn't as busy as he had expected. No receptionist waited to aid him, instead he found differently labelled offices. Three offices were dedicated to military recruitment, one for general affairs, another for trading, and lastly trading military stock. Topper passed the other offices and stopped in front of "General Affairs." He knocked and a male voice told him to open the door. Inside sat a large man, wearing . . . chainmail? Topper frowned and was met with a frown as well.

"What?" the man asked. "I have to wear this. Please sit." He had a strong face, with a trimmed beard and dark hair. This was a soldier, not an office worker, probably forced into office duty.

Topper sat on the chair, noting posters of different people with slogans on them hanging on the wall, most with the words of the Warborn: "Conquer, or be conquered."

"What can I do for you?" asked the guard.

"Answer a few simple questions," Topper said nonchalantly.

"Alright." The burly man grabbed his quill. "Name, please?"

"Gerdon."

The man noted his name, date and time. "Alright, Mr Gerdon. How can I be of service?"

"I just arrived," he said, comfortably leaning back on his chair. "And want some news confirmed: General Toran is dead?"

The dark-haired man gave Topper a questioning look. "Yes? That's the talk of the whole city."

Topper knew as much, but he wanted to hear what *they* said about it. "I've learned to confirm such matters by reliable sources," he said.

The man wrote down something on his sheet of paper. "Well, it's true."

"And how did he die?" Topper asked.

The man ran his eyes up and down Topper's figure, exhaling shortly. "I'm not allowed to answer those questions, as people could print anything I say and twist my words. I'll find someone who can answer." He stood up, chainmail clinking, and walked out the door behind him.

"Excuse me," Topper said sharply, stopping the large man. "Do you have a painting of the general somewhere?"

The man pointed out in the hallway. "Right outside. On the wall, there's a large painting commemorating him. He's in golden armour. Wait there." Then he shut the door quickly.

Topper didn't like his hasty departure and left the office too. The painting was enormous, putting the other paintings to shame—and confirmed without a doubt that the corpse was the deceased general.

"Excuse me," a female voice said. A slender dark-haired woman approached him, hips mesmerizingly rocking back and forth with each step. "Mr Gerdon?"

Topper cleared his throat. "Yes."

"You found the painting," she said, gesturing at the great piece of art.

"I did."

"What a loss," she said, crossing her arms. Her eyes narrowed, studying the general. "It doesn't do him justice. You wanted to know how he died?"

Her eyes pierced him, as if she searched for something within his eyes. "I heard rumours that he died in an ambush, but I thought it best to have it confirmed."

She didn't answer, tilting her head, her lips curling upward ever so slightly. Topper broke eye contact, shuffling his feet under her imposing confidence. "Mr Gerdon," she said, lingering on his name. "What do you do for a living?"

"I own some estates to the south, close to Cornstead."

"Aah," she said, turning back to the painting with a devious smile. "Where, *exactly*?"

"You may not have heard of it," Topper answered, trying to sound earnest.

"I will have."

He felt sweat form on his forehead. "Close by the river lies a small port, named Darrelbane, which I own. It's a small community, with some farms and acres of grain."

"And your purpose here in Ashbourn?" she asked.

"Am I being interrogated?" he asked, feigning a chuckle.

The woman didn't even stir. "No. I am merely trying to judge who you are."

"Well, I best be on my way," Topper said, feeling a bead of sweat run along his cheek.

"Truly," she said sharply as he turned to walk away.

"What?"

"Who are you, *truly*?"

He turned to find her eyes staring him down. "And who are you, truly?" Topper asked with a foolish grin, trying to divert her.

The woman exhaled. "I am Eranna Carner," she said smoothly.

Eranna, Topper said in his mind, the blood draining from his face. *The woman Adenar said was in the room the night of the general's murder.* He realized the situation he was in, but how much could she know? They'd never met, and she had definitely not heard of him. But that knowing stare of hers was unsettling.

"This is a different attire," she said, slowly circling Topper, examining his clothes.

"Different attire?"

"Yes," Eranna said. "Different from the coat you wore in the Meritocrat Headquarters."

Topper tried not to swallow audibly. "Yes, I was there yesterday, but on entirely different business."

"That . . . I *do* believe," she said, leaning closer.

Topper fought to not shy away.

Eranna sniffed his vest and produced a wide grin. "Smells like this has been at the bottom of a bag for some time."

"I have many vests with me," Topper answered.

"I'm sure. And many coats as well?" Her devious smile curled her lips once more. His heart beat fast. Should he walk away? Perhaps a quick suicide would surprise her?

"You see," she said, facing the painting. "The Warborn are charged with the security and safety of Ashbourn. I do like to know who enters, and when I get word that three beast hunters arrived, I pay attention. I get reports of two beast hunters meeting with someone from the Meritocratic party. Not a high profile person, but, the very next day, one of those beast hunters blunders into my quarters, asking questions about the general's death." She turned to wipe away a bead of sweat from Topper's temple. "It does make me wonder: why come in with a fake name and a poorly made-up backstory?"

She glared at him and Topper couldn't stop feeling like a fool. How could he not have thought this through? *If* there was something about Adenar's case, Topper had just single-handedly warned one of the main suspects. He breathed heavily. "Why—" he croaked. "—would you be interested in beast hunters?"

"Why?" she asked. "Beast hunters are valuable in a large city like Ashbourn. Knowing where to find you could be vital and is part of my job as head of security. "

Topper turned away and walked out the door, waiting for her to order him to stop, but she said nothing. Even in leaving, he didn't feel in control. He stalked out of the courtyard, contemplating what a fool he was. How would he ever live this down? At times like these, he just wanted to kill himself and start a new life, but he cared about those people. Shamefully, he got into a carriage, trying to sort his thoughts.

* * *

Ara and Khendric entered the inn, Ara moving with care so as not to feel all her bruises at once. She'd asked Khendric to 'lend' her some blood, but after her display of power, he said "no chance." They sat down in a booth, their stomachs hungry for nourishment.

"I need his blood," the deep phantom voice said in her mind, reminding her of the deadly nightmare in Cornstead. Hopefully, these phrases were merely after-effects from that, though the voice seemed clearer than before.

A waitress strolled over. "What can I get you?"

"Salted mutton chops," Khendric said. "With bread and soup." He eyed Ara critically, before his expression melted into a smile. "She can have the same."

She scribbled their orders down. "And I regret to tell you this," she said. "All meals and beverages are twice as expensive for the time being. Is that a problem?"

"What? Why?" Ara wondered.

"You have to ask Skren, the innkeeper."

"I see," Khendrid said. "We'll still take the meals."

"Great." In a blink, she disappeared into the kitchen.

Khendric glanced at Ara. "Let's go find out why."

They approached the innkeeper, Skren—a plump, grey-bearded man, wearing a white tunic. His hair was ruffled, but he still maintained an air of elegance in his work, every glass and mug looking pristine.

"Charging double today?" Khendric asked.

Skren sighed heavily. "Unfortunately," he said with a rough voice, cleaning another glass. "Our shipment of supplies didn't arrive. Thus, I'm forced to use the emergency storage."

"Any idea why?" Khendric asked.

"I don't know much." Skren placed the clean glass on a tray. "No words of any attack. Instead, it seems no shipment ever left the village that usually supplies me."

"With no words of why?" Khendric prodded.

"None. I think only three out of seventeen caravans arrived in Ashbourn. If this persists, food will become scarce." Ara and Khendric frowned, and she felt worry come alive in her stomach. However, no dark thoughts emanated from Skren, and his nonchalant attitude calmed her somewhat.

"Almost all villages that help supply Ashbourn mysteriously failed to send their planned shipments?" Ara asked.

"It would seem so," Skren said. "Although, I think an extra caravan came from Cornstead. Perhaps the king sent an emergency letter. I just pray the next shipments arrive on time."

The casual manner in which Skren talked about Cornstead felt awkward to Ara. She'd been there and saved it. It shaped the woman Ara had become, yet to him, it was just another village. Khendric frowned deeply, as he placed the payment for the meals on the counter.

Skren gathered them with a sigh. "Hopefully, it won't last. I don't feel good charging this much."

"Anything else out of the ordinary?" Ara wondered.

The young waitress from before placed the meals they had ordered at their table.

Skren rubbed his chin. "Actually, there is something. Though I'm not sure it's worth mentioning."

Khendric put a silver chip on the counter, which prompted a chuckle from Skren.

"Take your silver back. I could never charge you more after those meals."

"Ah, I misunderstood," Khendric said, pocketing the chip.

The innkeeper leaned closer, pointing to a table close to the entrance. "See those three huge guys over at the table? They're just drinking water, and serve as my security. Crime is rising. It started in the Warborn District, but has spread to this district too."

"A rise in crime?" Khendric asked.

"Yeah. I fear harsh times are coming, but hopefully I'm wrong. Let's hope the Warborn's words don't come true. Famine and war don't mix well."

"What kind of crime?" Ara asked.

"All kinds," the innkeeper shrugged. "Street robbery to house robbery. Even inns have been targeted. That's why I hired muscle."

"You seem like a clever man," Khendric said.

Skren chuckled and shrugged again. "That might be. At least I'm clever enough to learn from other's misfortune."

"Might save your life someday," Khendric said. "Thanks for the words."

They turned and sat down to eat. A trasher climbed through the window in a hurry and jumped down on the table. The small, ragged, and thin creature looked uncertainly at both Ara and Khendric before it lunged towards Ara's bowl.

"Food!"

Khendric quickly grabbed it by its makeshift clothes and pulled it away.

"Hey!" Skren yelled. "Just throw it back out again!"

Khendric examined the meagre creature. He picked up a sausage and gave it to the trasher, which regarded it with reverence, its eyes growing big.

"No sharing," Khendric told it. "Okay?"

"No sharing," the trasher repeated, eyes locked on the prize. It ate it like a starved wretcher, before grabbing his finger with his small hands and shaking it. It ducked out the window in a hurry as Skren hurried over, stomach wobbling up and down, wagging his washcloth angrily.

"Sorry about that." He leaned over Ara and closed the window. "That's been happening more and more recently too." He went back behind his counter, telling his goons to watch out for the small creatures.

"Thank you for giving it some food," Ara said.

Khendric smiled. "It felt right. If we're going to run short on food, it'll hit them twice as hard."

He was a good man, except for when his mind was shrouded with dark thoughts. Then he was . . . sort of . . . murdery. Luckily, those thoughts had vanished. She didn't know why and was just happy he was alright.

"It is enough," the voice said in her head, but she suppressed it as before, trying to ignore her building anxiety.

***

A hoard of people surrounded Ara and Khendric, and the crowd was growing bigger. Ara couldn't take her eyes off the enormous castle in front of her. Despite its tall wall, it rose high into the sky, countless large round towers drawing the eyes ever upward. The far-away castle in Kalastra couldn't measure against this. Never had she seen such a marvellous feat of humankind. *There must be thousands of people inside*, she thought, understanding why people would want to be elected king.

The building had many different oval plateaus as it rose upwards serving as terraces, and Ara thought she spotted people leaning over the edge, but couldn't be certain.

The crowd stood before a wooden stage. They didn't have a plan for this encounter, but Khendric said he'd improvise. He had told her she was *not* allowed to improvise, but he'd never even seen her do it. Maybe she was a natural improviser.

The crowd swelled, filling the large open area and the connecting streets. Sneaking anywhere would prove difficult. Close to the stage, three large carriages in the red colour of the Warborn Party approached. From the front and back vehicles emerged soldiers, forming a tight perimeter. Clad in heavy plate armour, with shields, spears, and swords, it would take a lot of courage to try anything wild.

A man and a woman exited the centre carriage. Ara couldn't see any details as the soldiers surrounded them. *That must be him,* she thought. On the stage, emerging from amongst the guards, strode a tall man with completely black hair in a ponytail. His angular face, strong build, visible confidence, dark tabard with the red emblem of the Warborn, revealed that this was Ronoch. Beneath the tabard was a pompous deep purple shirt.

The crowd cheered, whistling and screaming, hands raised to the sky. Ronoch lifted his chin and narrowed his eyes, raising both hands in salute.

"Do you see anything?" she asked, as the cheers died out.

Khendric shook his head.

"It is good to see all of you!" Ronoch bellowed from his stage with his deep voice. "So many more have awoken and see the truth!"

Khendric pushed through the crowd to get closer, and Ara followed in his wake.

"Ashbourn faces a threat!" Ronoch continued. "And only with your help can we defend this magnificent capital. Our beloved King Koradin has been a great king for twelve years, but he has grown soft, refusing to see the truth! In his time, Ashbourn has been prosperous, gathering extraordinary trading agreements that have kept our city wealthy. This is no secret, not to us and certainly not to other kingdoms. Naturally, others want what we have, and a growing threat is inevitably advancing unhindered into our kingdom. The king's refusal to see this has claimed lives! The lives of soldiers, of our villagers, and if we continue to do nothing . . . your lives!"

The crowd booed, and Ara had to admit, he got her heart to pound. She felt the energy of these inspired souls eating his words. It could all be true, too. What he said made sense, and she felt some doubt about the case she'd pushed hard for them to take.

"Just recently"—Ronoch's voice shifted from inspiring to one of mourning—"it claimed a very important life, one many of us held dear: General Toran."

Various cries reverberated from the crowd, some blaming the king. To Ara, the words had the opposite effect. *Right,* she told herself. Knowing more than she should, this confirmed that the Warborn *were* hiding something about the general's death, fuelling the flames in the hearts of the citizens for their cause.

"It is truly a great loss for Ashbourn, an enormous blow to our military, and a personal blow to the Warborn Party. I vow to you, crown me your king and I *will* see Toran avenged!" The crowd went wild again, cheering for war.

A wave hit Ara's mind, causing her to stagger and lose balance. She let out a shriek as she sensed someone's dark thoughts pressing overwhelmingly everywhere on her mind. Her head felt like it was about to implode—and it was gone. Her vision cleared as Khendric lifted her back up on her feet.

"What happened?" he asked, concerned eyes drilling into her.

"I don't know," she uttered, no trace of the wave on her mind. "I was hit by something as the crowd cheered in the same way I can feel dark thoughts."

"Are you alright now?"

She nodded.

Khendric set her down in front of him—probably to keep an eye on her. "I was hoping I could get hold of some armour and sneak aboard one of those carriages," he said over her shoulder as Ronoch kept preaching. "But I think security is too tight, even for me. I don't know what else we can get out of this. Any ideas?"

Infiltrating Ronoch's garrison would prove challenging. "No, I've got nothing. Maybe the best thing to do is to listen to his speech and see if we can get anything from that."

"Brattora," Ronoch said, "has launched numerous attacks on us, and it's affecting you. Brattoran forces have successfully ambushed most of the caravans coming to the city. If this continues, we will have to resolve to use the city's food storage or starve. What's an easier target than a city crumbling from the inside?" His passionate voice rung through the crowd. "Unless we recognize this threat and deal with it, which we are currently *not* doing, this city will fall. Three days ago, four out of eleven shipments arrived. Two days ago, two out of nine and today only three out of seventeen. If this is allowed to continue, we will suffocate quickly! Yes, King Koradin does investigate this, I will admit as much. But the time for investigation is long gone. Now is the time for action!"

The crowd roared as he waved both hands to them. "I thank you for your time, great citizens! It is good to know that you see the truth for what it is! Remember: conquer! Or be conquered!" The crowd went wild one last time, cheering their throats dry as Ronoch disappeared into his carriage, guards surrounding him at all times. The vehicles drove away and the crowd dispersed.

"That was . . . boring," Khendric said.

"Let's hope the gala turns out better," Ara said.

They walked back towards the inn from the Royalist District. The four different districts met around the castle in a circle, so walking between districts took a fraction of the time near the centre of Ashbourn. The district was dirty. Rats, rabdogs, and other rodents ran across the streets, and heartflies buzzed around lanterns in alleys.

"The thing . . . or wave," Khendric said. "What was it?"

Worry returned to her troubling mind. Something was definitely wrong with her.

"I grow stronger," the voice coincidentally said in her head.

They got into a carriage and Khendric told the driver their destination.

"I don't know," she finally answered. "A wave crashed over me. The same kind of pressure I usually feel, just . . . all over my mind. Like my head was about to crumble."

Khendric narrowed his eyes. "And then suddenly gone?"

"Yeah, and the voice inside my head is talking more frequently. I don't know whether it's concrete or not. Just now it said 'I grow stronger.' Do you think it means anything?"

Khendric sighed, looking troubled as he stared out of the small window. "It might be, but let's say some beast out there is getting stronger and you have a sort of connection to it. What would be the chances of it being here—in Ashbourn, I mean?"

"That's true. Though the voice is clearer than before."

"Good and a frightening point. I'll tell you what we'll do. Get a quill and notebook from Topper, and write down everything the voice says."

Ara would do so, feeling the worry lessen somewhat. She removed her long-sleeved glove—which she wore almost all the time—and studied her arm, hating those hideous dark veins covering it like vines up a stone wall. She was disappointed at the day's findings, but hoped tomorrow would shed more light on the case. *A gala!* She dared to smile. It was both intriguing and terrifying. She'd never dreamt of attending something so grand, and she was to socialize with the wealthiest and mightiest in all of Ashbourn.

CHAPTER 7

Assassin and Corpses

The day passed slowly as Ara prepared for the party. Evening finally approached; darkness loomed over Ashbourn. Earlier, they'd been at the market and visited a beast hunter store to restock on all serums. While there, Khendric decided it was time for Ara to gear up, and they used quite a few chips on a dagger and a sword. Never had anyone bought her something of such value. Her new dagger was attached to her thigh and concealed nicely in a comfortable sheath.

After a couple of swings with the sword, Khendric told her it was a good and durable weapon. It was laced with silver, making it possible to kill certain beasts weak to the element. Some of the larger ones, like nightwanderers, required a complete silver sword, but her sword would harm it. Cool runes had been carved into the blade, apparently standard for real beast hunter swords, to protect against scribbler magic and the likes.

They bought some other items too: trollman hair, because it had a euphoric effect with no downsides—or so Khendric said at least. A scentless salve made from something called a hinlarva. It neutralized scent and odour, leaving the user untraceable for many different beasts.

Khendric wanted a wretcher's talon too, but the store was empty after someone came and bought every single one some time ago, and they took forever to stock up again. They hadn't bought anything specific regarding this case, as they had no idea what they were dealing with. Hopefully, they changed that tonight.

A wave of dread and excitement washed over her. *I can't believe I'm doing this.*

"I am stronger," the voice rang in her head, clear and taking her by surprise. She noted it down as Khendric said she should.

Khendric opened the door to her room, motioning for her to follow. She should probably tell him, but afraid it would overshadow their original party plan, she didn't.

"Adenar has arrived," Khendric said as they entered his and Topper's room. "With our fake personas."

Inside the room, Adenar laid some clothes on the table, together with various sheets and some small paintings. He greeted her with a shy nod and she awkwardly returned the gesture. Topper sat on a chair, staring out the window, looking paler than usual.

"So," Adenar said nervously. "This is actually happening? I'm assisting in the infiltration of a political event held by my party, giving trained killers access to the most important people in Ashbourn." He exhaled slowly.

"Killers of beasts," Khendric corrected. "Though some politicians are beasts." When no one laughed, his foolish expression deflated. "Not even a laugh from Topper?"

Topper barely turned away from the window, bobbing his knees up and down nervously.

"What?" Khendric asked. "Oh, by the stonepudders, what did you do?"

"Something foolish," Topper wheezed out. "I went to confirm General Toran actually looked like the corpse Adenar brought us."

That didn't seem foolish to Ara. She felt embarrassed she hadn't thought of it.

"I can confirm the corpse definitely is General Toran. I went to the Warborn Headquarters, and bumped into Eranna Carner."

"By the craven's mother," Adenar said, slumping in his wooden chair. "What did she get out of you?"

"She knew three beast hunters had entered Ashbourn," Topper said.

"How?" Khendric asked.

Ara swallowed dryly.

"She said the Warborn were in charge of the security of the city, my best guess is—"

"The guards at the gate," Adenar interjected. "They answer to her. She probably instructed them to report of anything interesting, like beast hunters entering the city."

"That implies she has something to hide," Ara said. "Right?"

"Actually," Adenar began. "It's not uncommon. It's important to know where to locate beast hunters."

"But she had Ara and me tracked," Topper said. "She knew we met with you at the Meritocrat Headquarters, though she did seem uncertain of your name."

Adenar paled. "Why did I get myself into this?"

"Oh, stop your pouting, it's not bad yet," Khendric said, standing. "So what did you give away?"

"She knows beast hunters are asking questions about the general," Topper answered. "Though I'm fairly certain she doesn't know what either you or Ara look like."

Khendric shuffled around the room, deep in thought. "She definitely has something to hide. As you did confirm we have the general's dead body, who is supposed to be buried in the city."

"She was clever," Topper added. "Cunning, asking all the right questions, putting pressure on all the right words, intimidating without obvious threats."

"She will recognize you," Khendric said. "Is there anyone who conceals their faces at the party?"

Adenar considered, frowning, shuffling through some papers on the table, running his finger down one column. "Yes, Sherazeru, of the fourth Kha, is attending. He's an emperor from across the sea, from the desert lands of Sun's Reach. They pride themselves on glorious robes and cosmetics. He brings a lot of servants and beautiful women to every party. The male servants wear orange robes and hide their faces to not steal attention from Sherazeru. That is a deadly sin where he's from. And what luck, they have dark skin, just like you."

"All you have to do," Khendric said. "Is subdue a servant and steal his clothes. We have just the right serum for that." Topper raised his finger and opened his mouth, but Khendric silenced him. "No-no! You got yourself into this mess. Consider this your punishment for revealing us."

Topper grew red-faced, but sat down.

"I reckon Eranna has some faint descriptions of us then," Khendric continued. "And I bet it's my beautiful face."

"Tell me you're not putting on that stupid nose," Topper said grimly.

Khendric pulled it up from one of his sacks. "You know I am. Ara, we should colour your hair too."

Change my hair colour? She thought excitedly. How would she look?

Adenar brought forth an overwhelming number of papers from a folder. "Right," he said. "It took time, a lot of research, and *all* my imagination, but I think I have made some believable people for you to be. Thirty-two years ago, a landlord from a smaller eastern city of the Grasslands, Irnathar, died of old age. His name: Eris Lordemure. Irnathar

118

also elects their leader, but not for another two years. It's then natural for the deceased landlord's next of kin to take control. The official records state the next of kin is Aviana Lordemure. I did some research and found Eris Lordemure was exiled from Ashbourn to rule over Irnathar as punishment for something, and he resented the king of Ashbourn, vowing to never return—at least that's what the records say. The real Aviana is not attending the party, which gives us an opportunity."

Ara began to understand and nervous excitement rumbled in her guts.

"So that will be Ara?" Khendric asked.

"Yes. I thought it natural for the heir to show an interest in the capital. At least, I don't think anyone will dispute it. Irnathar is a small city, not visited often by nobles unless they have to. And since the Lordemures haven't been in Ashbourn for decades, I'm fairly certain nobody knows what Aviana looks like."

"Excellent," Ara said, nodding. Adenar's nervousness was obvious, his fingers were trembling—and he wasn't even attending the party. She felt nervous too, but tried suppressing it, trying to focus on the intriguing part: becoming another person.

"It's good you think so," Adenar said. "As for you," he nodded to Khendric, "you will be her husband, Ravon Lordemure. On these two sheets of paper, I've written down important details for you to memorise. Read them well and know it all. You will be asked questions. Someone will wonder what the new lords of Irnathar are doing in Ashbourn so close to the coronation."

"And what are we doing in Ashbourn?" Khendric asked, sitting relaxed in his chair. "If anyone asks."

"Right," Adenar said and found another sheet of paper. "These are the nine cities in the kingdom. They all have a say in who's to rule, or rather their people have a say. But the truth is: the people almost always vote for whoever their lord favours. Hence, you're at the party to decide who you will cast your vote to, which will influence Irnathar's voting greatly."

"I like it," Khendric said. "That means we have an excuse to talk to anyone from any party."

"That's true," Adenar agreed. "Your objectives are Ronoch Steelbane and Eranna Carner. You just do whatever you deem necessary to find something we can work with."

"*If* there is something," Topper said. "I'm not saying there isn't, and there is definitely something peculiar about this, but it might not be bestial."

"Let's hope it's not," Adenar said. Khendric and Ara frowned, and Adenar noticed. "What? I don't *want* a beast involved. I contacted you because I'm convinced there's something out of the ordinary going on, but I still don't want there to be."

Khendric gave Adenar a short smile, nodding his head. *He likes him,* Ara thought.

* * *

Ara's excitement had been murdered. After the briefing, Khendric gave her the sheet of paper with her persona and told her to read it *fifty* times alone in her room! She'd gone back to her room, and she knew every letter on the boring paper. *I'm married to Ravon Lordemure. We have no children. My father's name was Eris, and he was exiled by King Roran of the Passionist party. I was born ten years after my father was exiled . . .* and she almost fell asleep again, too ready to become Aviana Lordemure.

Laying on her bed was the beautiful, silver-lined gown Adenar had brought, with dark ribbons and gorgeous white patterns. Ara put it on and her eyes widened at what she saw in the mirror. It was magnificent! She'd never fixated on clothes, and especially not when with Khendric and Topper, but this spoke to a side buried deep within her. The gown twirled in the air as she spun around, and she couldn't help but giggle. It fit perfectly with her long-sleeved glove, too. Tears pressed behind her eyes and immense gratification rained over her.

She went to the others, and Khendric, Topper, and Adenar gaped.

"Well, look at that," Khendric said. "I guess you're pretty after all."

Ara stuck her tongue out at him. Adenar looked stricken, mouth agape and eyes glued at her, which made her smile the goofiest smile.

Khendric, of all people, applied some makeup on her to make her appear older, and looking in the mirror her heart felt like it stopped for a moment. *Woah, I'm beautiful,* she thought, running her fingers over her cheek, almost letting a tear spill from her eye.

"I'm too good at that," Khendric said, examining her the same way a painter would examine his work.

"Th-thank you," she stuttered, stunned. They looked at her as if she was a new person—and she was. She was Aviana Lordemure, tall, proud, and ready to be drilled with questions about her upbringing.

*　*　*

Ara and Khendric arrived in a carriage at the Meritocrat Headquarters, in a long line of other carriages. He wore a black vest with a deep-blue shirt beneath. Khendric was quite handsome, but with the fake nose, she had trouble not laughing. Topper had left hours before them, needing to acquire the outfit off of one of the servants of Sherazeru and enter the party with him. Ara prayed he had been successful.

Their carriage stopped outside the building. All around, weak dark thoughts emanated from people in all directions. She tried to suppress it, hoping it was just politicians with their ploys and such.

They exited the carriage, following a long line of people, with more propping up behind them. Countless braziers lit the large courtyard filled with attendees for the party, dressed in lavish robes and gowns. Besides the braziers, torches burned a faint blue light, looking magical, while chatter and laughter spread through the slowly moving crowd.

Khendric held his elbow out for her. "Let's go, wife. Or lady. Whatever you wish to be called."

Ara raised her eyebrows and exhaled visibly. "Just call me Aviana," she said, grabbing his arm. Together they joined the slow crowd towards the entrance.

The most influential people in Ashbourn were more fashionably dressed than she thought possible, with stylized hair, elegant gloves, and shoes seeming otherwordly to her, with their expensive leather or greenish scales. Even the way they carried themselves distinguished them from commoners, like her.

"I feel a connection," the dark, trembling voice spoke clearly in her head.

"See that blue flame?" Khendric asked.

She nodded, trying to push away worry.

"The torch is burning octinara blood, which for some reason burns a blue flame."

The blue torches marked the path to the entrance and gave the place a magical feeling in the dark of night. Or perhaps it should feel magical, but all the dark thoughts around her buzzed in her mind. They emanated from countless people, despite them smiling and seemingly enjoying themselves.

Ara and Khendric climbed the stairs and found a man with a list at the top. Two guards stood posted outside. Another scrawny man came and felt both her and Khendric up.

"So sorry," the man said. "We have to search all guests."

His quick hands almost made her yelp in shock. Luckily, Khendric and Adenar had talked her out of strapping the dagger to her thigh.

The tall and broad dark-skinned man with the list wore a strained vest with a shirt underneath so tight a sudden flex of any muscle would rip it open. "Names?" he said with a dark voice.

"Who are you?" the voice inside her head asked, plaguing her.

"If you please, your excellency," the large man asked when she didn't answer.

"Lady Aviana Lordemure," she said, shaking the voice off and keeping her chest high. She had been told that's what noble ladies did and tried her best to radiate confidence. Beneath the charade, she trembled with nervousness. "Lady of Irnathar. This is my husband, Ravon Lordemure."

Khendric bowed to the large man, who wasn't looking anyway. With his quill, he quickly did two strokes.

"Welcome to the Meritocrat's party." With a kind smile, he gestured for them to enter.

They stepped inside, and Ara's nervousness turned to excitement. They were guided by lanterns down a corridor and up a large staircase made from white marble, with gorgeous railings made from stone.

When they entered the massive ballroom, Ara's eyes opened wide. The walls were a beautiful white colour, with tremendous windows everywhere. The floor had intricate patterns of black and white, and was almost clean enough for Ara to see herself in. The early night's breeze rolled in through grand archways, revealing huge terraces outside where people got fresh air. The globed ceiling was painted, depicting kings, queens and various beasts. Blue and orange lights danced near the ceiling, and with a squint, Ara spotted several small birds producing mystical light as they glided through the air. Their grace calmed Ara down a little, and for a moment she forgot why she was here. An orchestra played music as sweet as she'd ever heard, and she could feel tears welling up at all the extravagance. It flowed so beautifully, accompanied by dancers on a stage with the utmost elegance.

Khendric urged her onward, as she kept other people from entering.

In front of the orchestra was a large space for nobles to indulge in dancing. It looked fun and perhaps she could . . . *no,* she reminded herself. *You're here on a mission.* Adenar had shown them two small paintings of Eranna and Ronoch, but with so many people, how would they ever find them?

"Excuse me," a voice said, breaking through the haze of amazement. A lanky old man stepped up to them, wearing a green robe with white ribbons across his shoulders. "Lady Lordemure of Irnathar?"

"Yes," she said, presenting her hand.

He clasped it with both hands and shook it. "I am Councillor Elrich Obarum. I worked a lot with your father, before his . . . accident. I was afraid we'd never get the privilege of having a Lordemure present in Ashbourn again." Ara didn't know how to respond, and Elrich seemed to notice. "My condolences. Your father had the will of a wretcher and a true bone in the nose."

"A bone in the what?" she asked.

Elrich merely chuckled. "It's an expression here when someone is tough as a boulderbeast. What brings you to Ashbourn?"

"After father passed, it was clear Irnathar had been outside of the political spectrum for too long. My father's knowledge is outdated. I'm here to make up my mind on these matters."

"Naturally, naturally," the older man said, producing a smile. "I'm sure you know, but your father was a Passionist." After Ara nodded, he continued, "I am the Chosen of the Passionist Party and will be king if we win the coronation. I would gladly welcome your support. It would be a great way to honour your dear father."

"I'm sure," Ara answered. "Yet I would do Irnathar a disservice if I supported the Passionists only to honour my father. I'll engage with the other parties as well."

Elrich kept his smile. "I wouldn't have it any other way. If there is anything I can do, please ask."

A trained politician, Ara thought. She produced a smile and staggered back—a strong wave of dark thoughts coming from the staircase into the hall attacked her mind.

"Are you alright?" Elrich asked.

Khendric held her tight as she regained her balance. The occasional dark thoughts were nothing compared to this, emanating from one source. Ara glanced in the direction, seeing a woman with dark hair.

"Ah, yes," Elrich said, following Ara's eyes. "Eranna Carner, a woman most vile, if you ask me."

"Really?" asked Khendric, with an exaggerated pompous accent. "How so? Is she not on the council of the Warborn Party?"

"She is. And to most, especially the citizens of Ashbourn, she's renowned as a great woman. But, I believe it merely a facade."

What kind of thoughts could Eranna have to radiate this strongly? Eranna strolled into the hall, joining a conversation of strangers, the pressure luckily abating somewhat.

"A facade?" Khendric asked, innocently. "If we're to decide on who to vote for, your word on this would be greatly appreciated."

"Her father was a great man," Elrich said without missing a beat. "A true general, whose name was Erranar 'Ironword' Carner, for it's said he never told a lie and acted his whole life with honour. His daughter, Eranna, is nothing like that. She's cunning and devious."

"That is a serious accusation, sir." Khendric frowned.

Elrich leaned in closer and lowered his voice to a whisper, "She had a brother, Eric, but he died. The circumstances of his death were peculiar. He fell from a cliff while hunting with Eranna and became paralyzed. His mind never became the same either, but tradition saw to that he still became a councillor . . . until he was poisoned and died. Next in line, Eranna became a councillor the very next day. The culprit escaped, but many believe Eranna pushed him off the cliff and later poisoned him. Maybe if Eric's mind wasn't shattered, he could have told us what happened. Anyway, the Warborn Party fairs well in this coronation, through rumours of war that can't be confirmed. And there is talk of their Chosen, Ronoch Steelbane. Out of nowhere, he rises through the ranks and is their Chosen. I have some reports which claim he joined over two years ago, but they've not been confirmed."

"This Ronoch," Khendric said. "Is he here?"

Ara stood by herself again, her posture reclaimed.

Elrich scouted the area. "He should be at Eranna's side, but as usual I don't see him anywhere. Sometimes he shows up, sometimes he doesn't, which is also something to note."

"A girl... ?" the trembling voice asked in her head. *Not now.*

Khendric excused them from Elrich, who politely rejoined some other members of his party. She had to tell Khendric the voice was getting more frequent and specific.

"Another wave?" Khendric asked.

"No. Eranna has a *lot* of dark thoughts. I think they flared to life as she entered the hall. Because it hit me like an arrow."

Khendric frowning. "I will do what I do best." They strolled through the room. "I'll try to find Ronoch. It puzzles me that he's not at these parties. Seems like they're important. My guess is this is not a time he wants to be visited, so that's exactly what I'll do."

"Oh," Ara said, growing uncertain. "What will I do?"

"Keep on talking to people, try to dig up some dirt. If you dare, try to get into a conversation with Eranna herself. Oh, and by the way, see over there?" Khendric pointed over at a dark-skinned man in lavish orange robes, followed by his mass of servants.

Sherazeru, of the fourth Kha, Ara thought.

"No, not him. Look at that awkwardly moving servant over there. That's Topper."

All except one servant moved elegantly in unison with their master, tracing his steps, except for Topper. Luckily, he was at the back, wearing a costume that would shame him forever. The tight orange tunic-like piece of clothing threatened to snap at the shoulders. In contrast, a loose orange pair of silk pants fluttered around his feet. A large ball-shaped mask with various patterns, a painted mouth, and two holes for eyes hid his entire head.

He looked pathetic compared to the trained servants who did this every day. His steps moved too slow, his posture weak, and he looked like a kid forced to perform a chore he didn't want to do. They both stifled laughs and Ara did feel safer, knowing he was close.

"Tell whoever asks," Khendric continued, "that I fell ill and had to retire." And with that, Khendric disappeared down the staircase, telling everyone he passed he was on the verge of puking.

I swear that man has no shame. Ara did her best to look confident; chin and chest high, trying to push the voice's words to the back of her mind. *I should talk to Eranna,* Ara decided, steeling her nerves.

"Wine?" a lanky, handsome, young man with slick, combed hair held out a silver plate in his hand with glasses of wine on top.

"For me?" she asked.

"Of course."

"And I can just take one?"

He smiled. "This one is the best." He handed her a glass and continued doing his job. It tasted bittersweet, and Ara couldn't understand why the nobles loved this stuff. Still, she knew how expensive it was, and to just be able to grab a glass off a plate—unreal. Another woman approached her hurriedly, with long red hair and a slim face.

"Who are you?" she asked, bluntly. Dark thoughts emanated from her.

"I am Aviana Lordemure," Ara said, the practised phrase easily rolling off her tongue. "Lady of Irnathar and—"

"No, you're not," the woman said, teeth clenched and an intense stare into Ara's eyes. "And who was the man you were with?"

"My husband?" Ara asked after a short silence, almost stuttering.

The woman let out an exaggerated breath and grabbed Ara's arm, towing her into a hallway, out of sight.

"What are you doing?" Ara asked, voice low to not cause a commotion. A few people noticed, but none interfered.

The woman pushed Ara up against a wall and pulled a dagger out from under her skirts, putting it to Ara's neck. "What were you doing with him?" she asked.

Ara found some courage in her unimpeded enhanced arm, but could she react quickly enough? "It is my husband," Ara said, voice strained. "He had to leave. He got sick."

The woman narrowed her eyes. "He doesn't *get sick*. He doesn't get food poisoned. He doesn't even itch."

Ara's eyes widened. *She knows.* How could she know? Ara desperately searched for words.

"Darlaene," Topper said from the entrance to the hallway. "She's with us!"

This is Darlaene? Ara thought, forgetting the knife. She was gorgeous, with a slim build and curvy hips. Her angular face was strong, and the intensity in her eyes frightening.

"What do you mean 'she is with us'?" Darlaene asked.

"I mean"—Topper blundered over in his awkward clothing, the ball-mask under his arm—"that she's working with Khendric and me on a case. And you've got nothing to worry about."

After a moment, Darlaene lowered her dagger, concealing it. "Good to see you, Topper." She turned to Ara. "My apologies. I got jealous and . . . acted irrationally."

Ara exhaled as the woman released her.

"I'm Darlaene."

"Nice to meet you," Ara said ironically, holding her hand on her neck, wondering how she had gotten the dagger through security. "I'm Ara."

Darlaene turned to Topper, "What's she doing with you?"

"Working a case."

"She's a beast hunter?"

"Ara is working on becoming one."

"How did she end up with you?"

"Maybe she could tell you," he said.

Darlaene turned to her with a piercing look.

Ara bit her lip. "My family was killed. Khendric and Topper saved me. They realized I had nothing left and . . . I joined them."

Darlaene's glare softened—the dark thoughts of jealousy faded. "Oh, I'm so sorry. That's terrible."

"Khendric has been looking for you for days," Ara said. "From when we first arrived, he's searched the whole city looking for you."

"Really?" she asked, a sly smile sprouting to life—similar to Khendric's stupid grin. "Well, that does brighten my mood. What's your case?"

"I don't think we're discussing that with you," Topper said. "And we should get back inside."

"Oh, come on," Darlaene complained. "We might be able to help each other."

"I don't want to die," Topper added and nudged Ara to walk back. "Again."

Darlaene followed. "I promise I'll try not to use you," she said. "I'm investigating Ronoch Steelbane. You?"

Ara turned sharply, and Darlaene raised her eyebrows.

"Told you we could help each other," she said.

Topper sighed and walked forward.

A most peculiar sight awaited them inside of the great hall. Everyone kneeled, except for one extravagant, huge, blond man. Topper quickly pulled Ara down too.

"What is going on?" she asked.

"I don't know. It just seemed like the right thing to do."

"It's King Koradin," Darlaene said. "It's not usual for him to attend these parties, but if he enters, everyone kneels."

"For how long?" Ara wondered.

"Until he says otherwise."

Ara turned her head to see the king walk up a small staircase, to a beautiful golden chair, obviously made for him. "Your backs and knees must be hurting from all this kneeling!" the king said loudly. Nobody reacted. "That means you can stand."

A murmur of chuckling reverberated through the room and they rose.

As clear as day, Eranna's dark thoughts spiked when looking at the king—quite bothersome, for Ara.

The king was an older man, probably close to his fifties, with blond and long hair running down his shoulders. Despite the hair, he looked like a battle-hardened general, with his strong face and muscular build. His armour must have been for show more than actual defence, made of a silvery metal, glimmering in the light with golden embroidery.

"His name is Koradin Banner," Darlaene said as she snatched a drink for a servant.

"We know," Topper said. "Ara, we should get back to the case."

Ara nodded, and tried to bolster the courage to talk to Eranna.

"She is in danger," the deep voice said in Ara's mind. *"An old servant has been summoned."* An old servant? The words sounded important, but meant nothing to her. Besides, what could she do here?

"My target, Ronoch, didn't show," Darlaene said. "So I might as well tag along."

Darlaene seemed helpful. Perhaps they *should* share information, and Topper obviously let the fact she always got him killed cloud his judgement, which might be fair on his part.

"The voice in my head said something," she muttered to Topper as he put his stupid ball back on his head. "I don't think anything will happen, but something might be coming. Do you know what an old servant is?"

He shook his large head. "An old servant? I've never heard of it. Darlaene?"

She elegantly turned her head with a playful look. "So you want to team up?" she asked with a sly tone. "I don't know what an old servant is either, but you're sure she's not got a case of the crazies."

Ara couldn't blame her for thinking so. The people talking about a voice in their heads weren't usually alright.

"But," Darlaene continued, "in case she is not crazy, I'll stay close."

The music resumed and people started dancing again. Further away, the king joined a conversation. Ara and Topper walked closer to his high chair, her heart pounding. She'd never been close to royalty in her life.

Darlaene strolled close by—but not too close. With a smirked lip, she politely rejected anyone who wanted to start a conversation.

"I have to get back," Topper said and worked his way back into Sherazeru's flock of servants.

Ara steeled her nerves. Seeing Eranna nearby, surrounded by people, talking about the apparent ambushes by Brattoran forces, made the hair on her arms raise. She awkwardly stepped halfway into the circle, earning a few glares from two older men.

"Oh!" a plump woman said, motioning towards Ara. "Lady Aviana Lordemure!" Her high-pitched voice cut through the air. "That is you, right?"

Ara almost didn't find her voice. "Uhm, yes."

The plump woman clapped her hands together, bobbing up and down happily. "How exciting! I was hoping we would be able to talk."

She turned Ara into the centre of attention. They all examined her, Eranna's eyes sizing her up. Luckily, no dark thoughts sprouted from her, and Ara begged she wouldn't recognize her.

"Would it be terribly rude," the woman continued, "to assume you're here to decide whom to vote for?"

Ara swallowed in an attempt to bolster courage. "That is correct."

"Well, how exciting! I am Rosenna Olina, First Scribe of the Royalist Party." The plump woman bowed, and Ara followed suit.

"I am Ser Ellin Mardarian," an older bald man with a great white moustache, said. "Royalist Advisor, first in line to become a councillor." He curtly bowed.

"I am Nirala Banner," a young woman said. "Firstborn to the king." Nirala bowed perfectly as if she practised one too many times, her beautiful silver-lined gown barely touching the floor. Ara couldn't believe she stood mere inches away from the King's daughter.

Eranna's thoughts intensified when Nirala spoke. "I'm Eranna Carner. Supreme Councillor of the Warborn Party and Chief Advisor to Chosen Ronoch Steelbane." She also executed a perfect bow, without even a hint of a smile.

The two last men introduced themselves too.

"Are you not yet decided?" Nirala asked.

"Not yet," Ara answered, trying not to let her voice vibrate so much. "I'm trying to make up my mind, instead of relying on my father's political views."

"Clever," Eranna answered. "As you know, Irnathar is the first city one usually encounters when coming down from Paradrax."

"Yes," Ara said, not too sure about that.

"That means *your* city will be targeted by Brattoran forces," Eranna said. "For them to successfully invade the Sangerian Grasslands, they need the foothold that Irnathar provides, potentially single-handedly bringing our kingdom's demise. How large are your armies?"

Ara swallowed as dryly as ever, feeling her heartbeat quicken. "Around five thousand strong," she gulped, a complete shot in the dark.

"Too small," Eranna said. "It will never withstand a siege for more than a few days, and it would take us three to four days to get to you. Should Brattora bring their forces, they will conquer your city. I can promise you one thing: vote for Ronoch Steelbane and I shall personally see to it your army is doubled and our response time reduced."

How could she say no to this? Those arguments were rock-solid.

"Well," Nirala broke in. "That's if war really *is* coming."

Eranna tightened her jaw, a devious smile slashing across her face, as darkness pulsed from her head. "What makes you doubt it?" Eranna said, no reproach in her voice.

"My father's words. And he *is* doing a thorough investigation."

"Our general was killed by Brattoran forces," Eranna snapped. "And you're denying it happened?"

"Not denying," Nirala answered, actually smirking. "Just questioning. My father said he knew of no reason—or orders—given that would incline General Toran to venture that far north."

"The general doesn't need permission nor orders for such a simple task."

"I think if our generals travelled far away from the city, the king *should* be notified." Nirala feigned a short laugh and took a sip of her drink.

Wow, Ara thought. *These women are good. And not scared.*

Eranna's dark thoughts arose with the intensity of the conversation. Ara wanted to scream out what she knew about the general's death, how he hadn't been far north, and how Eranna had tried to hide the true burial of his corpse—but they didn't have enough information.

Nirala said, "All I'm saying, is that Lady Aviana should hear from more than you and me, and make up her own mind." She shared a warm smile with Ara, that seemed real, but could also be well practised.

Ara realized how insufficiently prepared she was for the party. These women made an art of saying one thing and conveying something different. Ara didn't have to answer as they dove into a discussion about the rise in crime in the city.

A wheezing, continuous whisper sounded in Ara's mind, coming from behind her. She turned and saw a man made purely of black, magical smoke swirling violently around his body, flickering like fire. He held a tray with glasses of wine in his hand—like a servant—and no one seemed to react.

Ara yelped, drawing the attention of all the others. They looked at her awkwardly before the conversation forcefully resumed.

Darlaene looked at her with a bewildered look. "What?" she mouthed.

Ara pointed at the shadowy man, but Darlaene frowned in confusion. The wheezing grew louder as the creature walked closer. Darlaene searched intensely with her eyes, but didn't seem to see anything out of the ordinary. Ara's heart pounded, and she pointed covertly again as he slowly moved towards the group. Darlaene disappeared into the crowd, leaving Ara alone.

The shadow-waiter was mere steps away from them.

Darlaene returned with Topper in hand. They moved closer to Ara, trying to act inconspicuously.

The waiter entered Ara's circle of people, offering drinks, and no one did anything, yet Ara saw a swirling mass of concentrated smoke and shadow, culminating around a human-shaped being. Some grabbed more wine, others declined, though it was hard to hear voices over the oppressive wheezing in her mind.

The being let go of its plate, letting it fall. Darkness warped around his hand forming a black dagger, smoke following its fast movements.

The assassin stabbed at Eranna.

Instinctively, Ara reacted quicker than she thought possible and grabbed the assassin's arm, arresting it with her immense strength. The assassin turned its dark head towards her. Gushing smoke, she saw now facial features—just blackness and churning smoke.

Immediate screams emanated from bystanders. "Assassin!" someone barked.

"You are of him," a multi-layered whisper, laced with hatred, sounded from the assassin.

It quickly formed a new dagger in its other hand and stabbed at her. She stepped backwards, saved by an inch, but it followed. Darlaene kicked Topper with all her might, sending him flying in front of Ara.

"Oh, not again!" Topper said mid-flight before the dagger buried deep into his chest, and he fell to the ground.

"I will never follow you again," the assassin said, and took off running towards a terrace.

"What is that?" someone yelled, its true form revealed to others.

Ara got down to one knee and turned the dead Topper over. The dagger slowly vanished.

Darlaene grabbed her arm. "He'll be fine. Follow the assassin."

Ara rose to pursue the killer—too valuable to get away—but met eye to eye with Eranna. She studied her and Topper's lifeless body before a most devious smile grew across her face. Ara sidestepped her and ran—a worry for another time.

She ran to the terrace the assassin fled through, leaving a vanishing trail of smoke in its wake. It wasn't far to the ground, and Ara scaled the balcony through a haphazard combination of climbing and falling.

Screams resonated from the front gate of the courtyard and Ara ran as fast as her feet could carry her in the direction, identifying the assassin in front of her. It neared the gate, where the eight guards formed a human wall, determined to stop it.

The assassin launched vicious attacks on the guards, slicing magical weapons with great speed, moving masterfully, dodging and striking with unmatched ferocity. Ara caught up, but the assassin turned and spotted her. Its movements turned from gracious to desperate, hacking and slashing wildly, taking more attacks to its seemingly incorporeal body. A spear pierced the dark figure's thigh and black smoke gushed from the wound. It didn't stagger, breaking through the line of guards with a mighty spin, killing three guards instantly. Ara shot past the guards in pursuit as the entity fled.

The assassin left a thicker trail of smoke than before, parts of its hand releasing smoke too—seeming to vanish. It rounded a corner into a small alley and Ara followed, ignoring her building exhaustion. She would *not* let it escape. She ran through the alley, jumping over crates and ducking beneath pipes. The gown slowed her, so she grabbed it with her strong arm and tore it apart, running up the stairs the assassin used and jumped over a wall. She stumbled when hitting the ground, awkwardly rolling up on her feet.

What would she do if she caught the creature? With no weapon, she'd be no match for it.

She came close as it climbed a fence, readying her arm to grab it. Some of its head evaporated into black smoke too, its right arm almost completely gone. Its foot tilted over the fence, just out of her reach.

"Damn it," she said, breathing heavily. She put her hand on top of the fence and, in a single manoeuvre, launched herself over, landing on the other side, only scraping her knee. *Woah,* she thought.

Ahead, the assassin slowly dissolved into smoke as it crossed a larger street and ducked into a smaller alley full of obstacles, barrels, crates, planks, and other rubble. Ara crossed the street too, almost trampled by several horses in front of a carriage. Her heart wrenched as grim thoughts of her sister sprung to life, traumas halting her next to the alley. In it, several anxious people moved back to their barrels with fire inside, trying to keep warm. Further ahead, she saw the assassin leap over obstacles.

Snap out of it, she thought and pressed on. The assassin had scared people out of the way, so Ara stormed through the alley. Ahead, it ran up a staircase, jumped to another building, and climbed to the roof. Ara had not come this far to chicken out. She ran up the stairs, jumped with all her might, and slammed her hand into the wall, breaking the stone, granting her purchase. Her feet rested on a window-sill. *This arm is really something,* she thought amidst her exhaustion.

The assassin scaled the wall above her, but her arm made it easy to ascend quickly and she was on its heels as they rolled onto the roof. It vanished faster than before, thick smoke pouring from its being as it leapt to a nearby building.

Ara followed, landing hard on the roof in a run. They jumped to the next building, the last one on the street. The assassin ran off the edge, falling far to the ground below. Ara slid along the rooftop, coming to a stop at the edge. The assassin evaporated into smoke as it fell, gone before reaching the ground. Ara laid down on the roof, breathing heavier than ever before. *Damn it,* she thought angrily, wondering what that thing was.

* * *

Khendric climbed the fence surrounding the great estates belonging to Ronoch Steelbane. Countless directions from strangers and he was finally there. The massive villa had a garrison, guard towers, and a fence. *High profile guy,* Khendric thought as he easily snuck forward.

Before reaching the building, Khendric crossed a garden. Having smeared himself with odour-neutralizing hinlarvae salve, no dogs or screamers smelled him. He remembered being bitten by a screamer—the bite itself wasn't so bad. But the small, blue, translucent reptilian beast somehow made its victim scream uncontrollably until fainting from lack of air.

He tore an arm off his nice shirt and tied it around his head, hiding his nose and mouth. *Time to intrude.* Silent as the night itself, he easily scaled a wall and climbed onto a guardsless terrace. He easily picked the lock and went inside.

Huge staircases led up and down several levels and the rooms were larger than most commoner houses—but next to no furniture. No paintings hung on the walls or flowers rested on windowsills. Khendric tried not to ponder too long and readied his paratis serum, elevating his senses to inhuman levels. He'd hear guards a long time before they heard him.

A foul, acidic stench seeped through the house. *Interesting. What is going on here?* For a quick moment, a voice whispered inside his head, but so low he wondered if it was simply his imagination. He snuck down a staircase—the stench growing stronger. Another smell mixed with the acidic one—rotting flesh.

Khendric stepped into a large hallway after taking the stairs from the second level of the house, searching for the source of the smells. Though strongly overpowered by the acidic scent, they both danced around each other, seeming to stem from the same place.

Low chatter reached his ears from a room far to his left. *So, I'm not alone*, he thought, happy he used the paratis serum.

Sneakily, he followed the smell, ending up in a kitchen. The guards's armoured footsteps rung around the house, but none headed his way. The smells of foods paled in comparison to the acidic one, which led straight into a wall. Khendric creased his brow and looked around. The smell didn't disappear *into* the wall, but exuded from under it, where a small vent hid, airing the acidic smell. *Close to the ground*, Khendric thought. *Must be from a lower level.*

Ronoch's villa was massive, with rooms everywhere, large and small, but he hadn't seen any stairs leading down. Khendric was in a smaller living room, having easily gone unnoticed by the guards, who weren't doing a good job, with slouched postures and an inattentive eye. Ronoch should invest in better security.

Different smells mixed in this room, like rubber and the odour of different human skin, almost drowning out the acid smell. He strolled about the room, trying to catch the individual scents. After a while, smelling yielded no more information, and he put his eyes to work—and saw it immediately. A thick blanket of dust covered everything inside: the tables, chairs and other furniture. The dust blanket also covered the floor, except for where people had been walking, and for some reason, *a lot* of people had walked to a wall beside the fireplace.

"Oh, how I love this serum," Khendric whispered. A small torch above the fireplace lacked dust on its holder compared to its companion. Khendric wiggled it back and forth, and with a soft click, the wall moved slightly. A push revealed a narrow circular stone staircase going downwards. Khendric went down, leaving the door behind him almost shut. *Wouldn't want to get trapped down here.* It was time to find Ronoch's secrets.

A metal door met him at the end of the staircase, lit by one torch. Hissing sounds emanated from behind the door together with bubbles popping? The effects of the paratis serum waned, and he saved the last dose in case he needed it. He slowly slid the metal door open.

The well-lit room revealed people dressed in white coats, wearing long dark gloves and masks, putting body parts into acid vats. The countless tubs filled with acid bathed the room in a green hue. Arms, heads, fingers, feet, bowels, hands, bones, an entire human body laid in the green sludge. Or, everything that had once made up *a lot* of human bodies.

On the walls hung large hooks holding too many corpses for Khendric to count. Some beheaded, others missing limbs, all young men and women. The sickening sight made him feel ill, mixing with anger. His eyes watered in response to the strengthening acid in the air. *What is going on here?*

"Who are you?" a voice asked. "Intruder!" yelled one of the masked men.

Khendric drew his pistol, ready for what he needed to do. This was why he hunted beasts: they followed their nature. Only man could perform cruel acts like this.

The men grabbed swords and cudgels. Khendric's dark soul returned, an unstoppable wraith of vengeance. His first attacker got too close, striking downwards with a cudgel. Khendric shifted right and jammed the gun up into the man's chin. Blood and bone sprayed from his head as the bullet carved into his skull. The next assailant in line for Khendric's brutality stabbed with a thin-bladed flaying knife. In a flash, Khendric unsheathed his blade to block the blow, leaving them at a standstill. He fired a bullet into the man's chest and redirected his blade into his neck. *Next*. He fired a bullet into the thigh of the next foe, the force shattering his leg sideways. Khendric kicked him backwards and into a vat, his agonizing screams drowned as acid flowed into his mouth.

Due to increased sensitivity from the paratis serum, Khendric's eyes watered heavily, his vision blurring. He tried to blink the tears away while parrying a blade slashing towards his head. A second sword entered his guts with an icy fire. He went down on one knee, not able to clearly see the second attacker, quickly firing into the one visible opponent.

The sword pulled out and re-entered his stomach. "Now, just relax," the man said, towering over Khendric. "You'll die soon."

"You'd think so." Khendric spat blood, the first wound already closing. Like lightning, he brought his blade into the man's thigh. "But I'm pretty stubborn."

He fell to the ground, leaving the weapon in Khendric's abdomen. Khendric groaned as he pulled out the sword. His eyes still watered, the paratis serum making the environment stressful.

"What are you?" said the man on the ground.

Khendric had to get out of here and pierced the man with his blade.

He examined the room, finding only tools to dismember the unfortunate souls in the acid vats. If he stayed too long, he'd faint, and headed for the door. He wouldn't hurt the guards. They probably didn't know about the hidden passageway.

He rushed up the stairs and burst out of the door, making too much noise, but he needed fresh air. The living room was empty and he ran into the hallway, hearing voices shouting through the manor. He leapt through a window and landed on the ground, escaping under the cover of night.

There was something fishy about Ronoch, that much was certain. Khendric thought of beasts that would need heaps of bodies, and in thinking back he noted there hadn't been the smell of blood coming from the dead. *Something that needs blood then*, he guessed.

* * *

Ara's breathing returned to normal as she lay on top of the square building. The assassin had said she 'was of him'? She wondered what it meant, removing the glove and looking at her tattered arm. *What is it I don't know about you?* she wondered, studying the black veins beneath her skin. *Couldn't you just be awesome power with no side effects?* The voice in her head had clarified lately too. Could the servant it mentioned mean the assassin? Whatever the case, she'd have to return with no information.

The roof was messy, with dirty sheets, blankets and pieces of wood everywhere. This whole part of the district had a quite unpleasant, far too familiar odour. Ara rose, surveying the area, and she was right—a slum. Several people crowded around burning barrels for heat. Ara used the stairs to get down, putting her glove back on and making a makeshift hood out of a piece of the torn gown.

Something had changed about her: fear didn't control her. She didn't feel as scared as she used to in the Rundowns. It was still there, but greatly dampened, her arm making her feel safer.

A group of men laid eyes upon her, and she steeled her stomach. The men's eyes grew wide and they gasped, scattering like frightened rabdogs. "She's back!" one yelled. Others looked towards her, and the same reaction spread. "The Dark Lady," a dirty boy shouted. "She's back."

The whole street cleared as if she was a doombringer. *Dark Lady?* she wondered, completely perplexed. *What are they talking about?* Uncertain, Ara made sure her dark arm stayed hidden. *It can't be that? How can they know?*

She kept on walking through the abandoned street, trying to remember the way out. Heartflies buzzed around lanterns, and she felt deeply sorry for the inhabitants here. In a staircase sat a shivering, older man, wearing ragged clothes, with hair as white as snow and dirt on his face. She stopped, looking at the poor fellow.

"I know you are there," he said, trying to hide his obvious fear. "Dark Lady. Have you come for more?"

"Why didn't you flee?" Ara asked.

"I'm blind. Nobody helped me get away."

Ara sighed heavily, feeling so sorry for him. "I'm not here to hurt anyone. I don't know why everyone is gone."

"So, you're not the Dark Lady?" Though blind, Ara saw his gaze lift.

"I don't think so. I'm certainly not here to hurt anyone."

"Oh," the man said relieved. "I thought for sure I wouldn't escape this time."

"This time?"

"Yes. Everyone fled because they were afraid to be taken. Some time ago, the Dark Lady and a lot of men came and kidnapped so many of us. I think she took twenty of the homeless here."

Ara sat down beside him, and he laid his hands upon her, feeling her face.

"My name is Ara, and I'm here because I chased an assassin, but lost its trail on a nearby rooftop. But tell me more about this Dark Lady."

"She came again, claiming even more of us. Her men brutally beat us, dragging us into wagons. No one knows what has happened to them, but none have returned. The woman wore black clothes and hid her face under a hood. She came back again and again, taking more, until . . . she stopped."

"When did she first appear?" Ara asked.

"Over a year ago, I think. She stopped after a month or two. But we fear her greatly, as you probably noticed."

"Yeah. How many did she take?"

The blind man considered her question. "Must have been around a hundred, at least."

"Do you know why?"

"No, and it's not like we can go anywhere."

Ara felt bad for the old, blind man. She had one gold chip on her and handed it to him. "This is all I have. It's a gold chip."

The man cupped it in his hands. "For me?" A smile spread along his lips.

Ara nodded, but remembered that he couldn't see. "Uhm, yes."

"Thank you, dear. Thank you so much. I'll try not to have it stolen. I think it's best if you leave now. The others might come back, and since you're alone they might hurt you. I'm not sure if they'll listen to me."

"Thank you. I'll do that. Best of luck to you." Ara hoped she could help these people, knowing too well how they lived, and how helpless she would have been in the Rundowns if this happened. She picked up her pace, leaving the slum behind.

* * *

Darlaene remained at the disastrous party. After the shadowwalker had tried to stab Eranna and had killed Topper, it all turned to chaos. Though the assassin was gone, people still fled the building as if in grave danger. Darlaene took it easy, sipped her drink, and tried to locate Eranna instead. She spotted her leaving through an exit on a balcony, her countless bodyguards following closely.

Darlaene didn't aid Ara in pursuing the shadowwalker as it would blow her cover. Hopefully, to Eranna it had looked like Darlaene simply tried to help another woman up. But she might very well have blown it too—why else would she kick one of Sherazeru's servants to save the girl? Of course, Eranna didn't know Topper was an expendable source of human bodies.

Darlaene felt so jealous Khendric had a morgal, and she desperately wished to acquire one of herself—one a little more welcoming to the dying part. She pushed through to the balcony Eranna left through. From it sprouted a stone walkway leading down to the courtyard below. Despite being crowded with people, Darlaene easily spotted Eranna in front of her.

She followed, not quite managing to appear frightened. The shadowwalker probably wouldn't return, but if it would, Eranna was its target. When nearing the ground, Darlaene dropped from the walkway, rolling on the ground, destroying her pretty dress. *This better be worth it.* She pressed through a crowd hurrying to get away, toward the large hall housing the carriages to the most prestigious people of Ashbourn— like Eranna. Taking advantage of the chaos, Darlaene climbed onto a beam in the ceiling positioned over Eranna's carriage. She'd been lounging on top of the same beam before the party as well to eavesdrop on Ronoch. Elrich wouldn't be pleased about her lack of intel on him, but what could she do? As she had foreseen, Eranna stormed into the hall and to her carriage.

"—they must be dealt with," Eranna's voice said as she came within earshot.

"Yes, Councillor," a male voice said—one of her goons.

"That was the female beast hunter that entered the city, I'm sure of it," Eranna continued, stepping inside her vehicle. "They're staying at 'The Just Lion,' in this district. We can't have them on our tails—it's too dangerous."

"Should we use the guards?" the man asked, remaining outside of the carriage.

"Are you daft? Of course not. How would it look if War-born guards stormed an inn and murdered beast hunters?"

"Then what—"

She silenced him with a quick hand out of the vehicle. "Perhaps this problem should not be dealt with by someone as simple as you. Perhaps *he* can do something instead."

The door shut and the drivers whipped the horses into motion. The poor goon scratched his head and shrugged, before leaving too.

That was good, for Darlaene had to get to the inn quickly to meet Khendric—*no-no*, to warn them of the coming threat. And also to meet him again. She wouldn't let a feeble woman like Eranna hurt her property—Khendric. Darlaene dropped to the ground, ready to work.

CHAPTER 8

Connecting Dots

Back in her room at the inn, Ara tried processing all the crazy things that had happened. She sighed thinking about the assassin escaping, but what would she do if she caught up?

"I will deal with her," the voice said.

Please don't let 'her' be me, Ara thought as the door opened and Khendric entered the room. Relief flooded her and she laid down on the bed.

"How did it go?" he asked casually as he took off his coat and hung it over a chair.

"There was an attempted assassination," she answered. "But I stopped it."

"There was a what?" he asked, wide eyes fixated on her.

"An assassination attempt."

Khendric frowned and sat wearily down on the chair. "Who was the target?"

"Eranna," Ara answered. "The assassin was—"

The door burst open, Khendric shooting to his feet and flipping his pistol out of its holster—aiming at a female figure with big, red, curly hair.

Darlaene raised one eyebrow at him and smiled smugly. "Like you could ever kill me."

"You're barely warm-up," Khendric countered. "Before fighting a sickly, starved boy."

Laying stunned on the bed, no words escaped Ara's mouth. *This is how you greet each other?* Ara expected Khendric to leap into her arms, embracing like long lost lovers.

"Anyway," Darlaene continued. "We don't have time for weak insults putting even Topper to shame."

"He's not dead, is he?" Khendric asked.

Darlaene sighed and nodded. "Eranna knows where you're staying and is sending *something* your way."

"How does she know?" Khendric asked. "I never met her."

"Ara revealed herself," she answered, making Ara blush. "You can stay with me in the Passionist District, come on."

"Where?" Khendric asked. "I want to leave a note for a young man. I'll tell you more later."

Darlaene wrinkled her brows, minorly annoyed. "Close to the Passionist Headquarters, and make the note vague. Now, come on."

Ara had no time to feel any shame as Khendric quickly packed their bags, led the horses from the stable, and paid for their stay—and just like that, they left. Darlaene led them into dark, small alleys, and after going through countless twisting turns, they finally emerged and walked into a broader street.

"Give me more blood."

"The voice in my head just said 'give me more blood'," Ara said, forgetting how crazy the words sounded to Darlaene. Khendric frowned, and offered no comforting words. They kept walking, Ara guiding Spotless through the street. She felt a storm brewed, as if something was coming for them. Some shady people hung about in the streets, and a nearby tavern echoed sounds of drunk people, but otherwise, it was empty.

"What are you doing here?" Khendric asked, finally breaking their silence.

"Not now," Darlaene said, halting and pointing to guards ahead.

"So?" Khendric raised an eyebrow.

"Who do the city's guards belong to?"

"The king."

She glared at him.

"The Warborn," he admitted, letting out a breath.

"And Eranna controls them. Best to avoid them."

They tried walking inconspicuously, looking like regular folk leading horses through the city at night. *"I have her scent,"* the voice spoke.

Pressure suddenly assaulted Ara's mind from all around her, clear like pyres in the night. "Something's happening," she said, clutching her forehead. "I can feel a lot of people with dark thoughts, and they're all coming closer."

Khendric looked in every direction, unholstering his pistol. Shadows in the night emerged from alleys, houses, and taverns. Khendric drew his blade and gun and Darlaene found her dagger as nine men approached with rusted weapons, surrounding the beast hunters. Ara put her hand on the hilt of her blade, trying to control her breathing, though it proved difficult.

"What do you want?" Khendric demanded, but none answered. Their eyes looked feral, holding their weapons toward Ara.

"What do you want?" Darlaene asked.

Ara couldn't speak out of sheer fear. The criminals didn't seem to notice Khendric or Darlaene, looking past them with distant eyes. They twitched and snarled, growling like hounds.

"Get back!" Khendric shouted, but the vagrants slowly walked towards Ara.

A group of guards ran down from their posts, having spotted the situation. Clad in armour and wielding shields and pikes, the noise they made would have caused normal people to turn, but these men didn't.

"What is going on here?" one demanded, probably the commander.

The criminals did not stop circling in on Ara.

"Stop!" the commander ordered. "Or we will stop you."

No reactions from the dark men.

"I don't think they're going to listen," Khendric said, pointing his pistol at the closest one, who didn't even flinch. "I don't even think they're going to acknowledge you."

The insane man snarled at Ara. "It is you!" he shouted, spitting.

Khendric cocked his pistol. The criminal lunged, head exploding as a bullet shot through his head. The gunshot sent the rest of the thugs into a flurry of violence. Khendric cut the stomach of one running past him with a swing. Darlaene stabbed another through the chest. Guards rammed spears into the backs of several on the command of their leader.

Khendric slashed a rusty dagger from an assailant and kicked him crashing into one on his way toward Darlaene. She seized the opportunity to stab both of the criminals in turn.

One broke through and Ara unsheathed her blade in time to parry the dagger coming for her thigh. The long spear of a guard rammed through his back next, ending the feud.

The commander rubbed his chin, puzzled. "What just happened?" The guards mirrored his confusion.

Khendric lunged into a heavy discussion with the guards about the peculiar manner in which the criminals acted. He talked loudly, engaging them all. They sounded as astounded as him, wondering why the criminals hadn't reacted at all to their presence.

Darlaene tapped Ara's shoulder and motioned for them to continue walking. They slipped past the guards without interrogation, something Ara felt thankful for, still shocked after the encounter. Not long after slipping out of sight, Khendric caught up with them.

The rest of the walk was uneventful; no more phantom voices or dangerous encounters. In the Passionist District, they approached a large building. *That must be the headquarters,* Ara thought. Darlaene led them through a gate into a neighbourhood. They went around a house and Darlaene helped them tie their horses. A fence surrounding the building shielded them from sight. *A good hiding spot.* There was water and hay for the horses too.

Darlaene led them to a trap door down into a cellar beneath the house. She unlocked the large lock and they entered a wine cellar with countless bottles stacked up against the walls. Darlaene quickly pushed past and opened one final door.

Inside was the perfect hideout; pushed over chairs, a table filled with stacks of paper, newspapers laying all about, a chalkboard written to the fullest, and other general messiness. Darlaene comfortably sat down on one of the chairs.

"You hungry?" she asked, gesturing in the direction of the pantry.

Still shaken from the encounter, Ara thought eating would do her good, and found so much salted meat it left her in awe. Khendric joined and together they concocted a glorious meal. "So," Khendric said, mouth full. "What are you doing here?"

"Investigating this Ronoch-guy," Darlaene answered. "You doing the same?"

"Somewhat the same," Khendric said. "We're investigating him and Eranna. Who are you working for?"

"Councillor Elrich Obarum."

"The Chosen of the Passionists?" Ara broke in.

Darlaene nodded. "For someone as new as Ronoch to become the Chosen of the Warborn party that quickly, apparently sparks a lot of commotion. Hence, Elrich wanted him investigated."

"What leads did he have?" Khendric asked.

"None really," she replied. "I didn't take his case because it looked like typical beast hunter work; rather, because he pays well."

"And you do like gold," Khendric added.

"Oh, let a girl be a girl," she said, smirking.

"So what have you found out about him?"

"Disappointingly little. As far as I know, he travelled from Brattora around one and a half years ago, to Ashbourn. He joined the Warborn Party and, without much merit, became their Chosen for the coronation."

Khendric hummed, sharing a look of mild disappointment with Ara.

"And who are you working for?" Darlaene asked.

"Some kid. His name is Adenar and he's an assistant for the Meritocrats."

"Sounds biased," she replied.

"And yours doesn't?" he snapped back. "And I don't think he is biased. In fact, he seems to be *very* earnest."

Darlaene stood up and walked to her chalkboard. "So, how did he end up in this mess?"

"Misfortune," Khendric answered. "He was unlucky to hear something he shouldn't one night at the Warborn Headquarters."

Darlaene frowned and turned to Ara. "So what happened out there? With those men?" Her eyes drilled into her.

"I don't know," Ara answered. "Suddenly I felt them close to us. Like they, out of nowhere, were consumed by dark thoughts."

"It's worth mentioning," Khendric said as Darlaene's brows creased. "Ara got the ability to sense if and where people are should they have sinister thoughts. We believe these thoughts to be: hatred, jealousy, thoughts of murder, and the likes. This stems from barely surviving a venom from some small tentacled beast with the use of my blood. After that, she got this gift *and* has an awesomely strong arm."

Brows raised, Darlaene looked impressed. "Well, you must have many uses."

"Thank you?" Ara replied.

Khendric filled Darlaene in on the events that transpired in Cornstead. "There might be a connection to what is happening here," he said. "And to tell you the truth, I begin to think the connection is in fact in Ara."

"The voice in my head appears to be relevant to what's happening. It said 'I will deal with her', and then those men appeared."

Darlaene went to her chalkboard and noted down key words. "That would mean the tentacled beast in Cornstead might somehow be linked to what is going on here," she said. "Which in turn might have something to do with the coronation."

"Well," Khendric said. "There is definitely *something* wrong with Ronoch Steelbane. I found a secret cellar with countless dismembered bodies being sunk into acid for dissolvement. Someone in that party has been doing a lot of killing lately."

"What?" Darlaene and Ara exclaimed. "That's horrible!"

"I agree," he said. "So I killed those men. When I think about it in retrospect, it might not have been clever, as they'll know someone's definitely on their tail. But I guess Topper took care of that already."

Darlaene noted furiously on the board.

"You know he's going to be furious when he comes back," Khendric continued. "I promised him I'd try not to let you kill him, and it's the first thing that happened."

"Well," Darlaene said, keeping her attention on the writing. "It was him or Ara to fall on the blade of the shadowwalker."

"Shadowwalker?" Khendric asked, frowning. "*That* was the assassin?"

"Yeah, and Ara stopped it from killing Eranna, which might not have been a good thing."

Ara blushed, feeling ashamed.

"Not that I blame you," Darlaene said, finishing the notation. "You acted out of instinct and saved a life."

It made Ara feel a tad better. "What's a shadowwalker?" she asked to shove the shame away.

"It's an assassin that anyone can summon," Khendric said. "But it requires the summoner to sacrifice an important limb. You need to perform an ancient ritual to summon it, and few books have this information. Shadowwalkers are incredibly hard to stop, as they're not slowed by mortal wounds, instead bleeding thick smoke upon being hurt. With enough damage, it dissipates."

"And not only that," Darlaene said. "They can disguise themselves as regular humans."

"Not to me," Ara said, becoming painfully aware of how hard her heart beat.

Khendric frowned.

"I saw its true form. That's why I was ready when it attacked. Why do you think I could see it?"

Khendric raised his eyebrows and looked to Darlaene, but she shook her head. "I have no idea either," she said. "I once heard a rumour saying they were somehow connected to the voreen culture, but I don't believe it."

Voreen culture? She didn't want anything to do with that. "It said something to me after I had grabbed its arm," Ara said. "That I was 'of him'?"

Both Khendric and Darlaene frowned, and she sat down.

"There is definitely something quite interesting about you." Darlaene studied her eyes.

"And I think it all stems from that foul tentacled beast in Cornstead," Khendric said. "Show her your arm."

Ara did and Darlaene didn't flinch at the ghastly sight. Instead, she seemed interested, gently turning it around.

"Well, look at that," she said. "And this is the enhanced arm?"

Ara nodded.

"I'd be lying if I didn't admit I was envious."

"I think I can barely feel your envy," Ara said. "But it doesn't feel as dark as other thoughts."

"Maybe because it's not the bad kind of envy?" Darlaene suggested.

Ara shrugged, not knowing what to say as anxiousness reigned in her mind. She hated the tinged, ugly arm. Yes, the arm was strong, but it came with an unnatural force looming over her at all times. When she said she wanted to become a beast hunter, she hadn't meant she wanted to be the target of an unknown mystery.

"How was the assassin stopped?" Khendric asked, breaking Ara out of her thoughts.

Darlaene stood, crossing her arms and paced back and forth. "It did behave rather abnormally. After Ara stopped it and it failed to stab her, it ran away."

"It ran *away*?" Khendric asked.

"It seemed scared of me," Ara said. "I caught up as it dealt with the guards, and when it saw me it turned frantic, desperately trying to hack and slash through them."

"Usually," Khendric said. "They'll attack their targets relentlessly until dead, and then just simmer away into smoke."

"It did," Ara said. "But it vanished while it fled."

"Then it was stalling," Darlaene interjected. "Trying to keep you away until it disappeared." She went back to her board and noted down the comment. "A lot seems to revolve around you, girl. Be glad we're here."

And Ara felt tremendously glad to be surrounded by immensely competent people. "So it's gone then?" she asked.

"I actually have no idea," Khendric admitted. "This is highly unusual."

"Anyhow," Darlaene said. "Something is definitely going on, and those corpses are disconcerting."

An idea sprouted in Ara's mind as she remembered something from earlier. "After the assassin vanished, I found myself in the slums. All the poor people fled at the sight of me, claiming the 'Dark Lady' returned. A blind man told me that a year ago, a woman, accompanied by guards, abducted people. He said that at least a hundred men had been taken. Maybe—"

"They were the dismembered corpses at Ronoch's house," Khendric finished.

"That's my guess."

"Where better to go if you need bodies?" Darlaene said, shivering. "The government doesn't document them, frankly because they don't matter. Those poor souls." She wrote more words on the board. "Do you know of any beast that would need that many bodies?"

"I can't think of any," Khendric said. "And I doubt it's a mere villagemother."

Ara grew more worried, but their nonchalant discussion about this calmed her nerves somewhat. Darlaene drew lines from Ronoch's name on the board to the text about the countless bodies, and from Eranna to the shadowwalker— and a line to Ara. Her stomach churned. *Perhaps it's nothing,* she tried to convince herself, but with no luck. Khendric rose and put his coat back on.

"I'll go see if I can find the young man," he said, and Ara hoped he'd find Adenar.

"You told him where we were going?" Darlaene asked.

"Only incredibly vaguely."

Darlaene's eyes lingered on the doorway as he vanished, a quick smile dawning on her lips. It was quickly tucked away when she met eyes with Ara. "I'm sorry for before."

"What?"

"For the way I acted. I just . . . hadn't seen Khendric in a while and, I *really* hate to admit this, but I got jealous. Could you feel it?" Darlaene asked. "Me—I mean, my . . . jealousy." She sounded embarrassed.

"Probably, but with so many thoughts from different people I couldn't distinguish it."

"I see. Still, sorry. I'll start working on our problems, and you can do whatever you wish." She gestured to the room and sat down in front of her board.

There wasn't much to do, and her biggest question was: who summoned the shadowwalker? *I won't be able to sleep tonight,* she realized. *And that might be my life for some time.*

Right now, it felt like she'd chewed off more than she could ever swallow. Perhaps this beast hunter business wasn't for her. A part of her wanted to flee. *Wait, what am I thinking? I thought I'd changed and become stronger. But I just want to turn my back and flee when it gets tough?* This wasn't how she acted in Cornstead. There, she charged head-on into danger. *I won't run,* she told herself. *I'll see this through.*

A surge of bolstering strength coursed through her body, pushing away the fear somewhat. It still lingered in her mind, but she wouldn't succumb to it.

* * *

The large metal door creaked open, followed by multiple muffled footsteps. Darlaene perked up at Khendric's voice, her eyes revealing excitement. Adenar's concerned voice rang through the wine cellar too. Ara quickly found the long glove and put it over her arm to conceal her veins.

Khendric opened the wooden door. "I found our stray rabdog. He was hanging out in front of the headquarters."

Adenar looked bewildered with his ruffled hair.

"You're trustworthy?" Darlaene asked, coming to tower over the young man, who looked uncertainly back at her.

"Yes-yes," Khendric said, pushing her aside with one arm and walking into the room. "I vouch for him, besides—he could probably beat you up, so don't be so tough."

Adenar shrunk even more under Darlaene's oppressive stare. "What? Why would you say that?"

"Because it gets her blood flowing," Khendric said with a grin.

"Please stop," Adenar pleaded, trying to pass Darlaene. "And I'm sure you'd beat me up. Easily—"

"It's fine," she said, chuckling.

Adenar's eyes flooded with relief, and he dared to fully enter, closing the door. "Where's Topper?" he asked and sat down on a chair.

"The assassin killed him," Khendric said.

"What?" Adenar freaked out, spouting apology after apology as tears formed in his eyes.

"Stop!" Khendric said harshly. "It's fine, I just forgot something, and I guess I have to tell you." He shared the secret of Topper's nature with Adenar and the young man calmed down. Khendric continued to explain the nature of the shadowwalker too.

Darlaene asked, "Do you know of anyone who would send a shadowwalker after Eranna? Someone who hates her enough to sacrifice a limb to kill her?"

Adenar slowly rubbed his hands together. "I mean, there might be so many, or almost none. It's almost impossible to know which of the politicians hate each other. They're so good at covering it up."

"We know Elrich hates her," Ara said. "He told me at the party."

"He did?" Adenar asked. "See? That is not known. Hence I'm afraid any lead I'd give you might be false too."

"That makes it harder," Darlaene agreed. "Tell me about the night that brought you into this mess?"

Adenar frowned. "Oh, that night." Adenar explained the encounter in great detail, shivering when talking about the horrific sounds.

Darlaene had found a smaller chalkboard to take notes on. "Tell it again," she ordered, keeping her eyes on the board.

When Adenar didn't start talking she waved her hand at him. "The whole thing?" Adenar asked.

"Yes."

Ara chuckled.

Adenar had to recall the event not only once more, but over and over again. Ara nodded off after a while. She felt sorry for him. He was getting tired too, but dared not object against Darlaene's resolution. She didn't sway or grow tired, which was mighty impressive.

"Why do I have to keep repeating this?" Adenar finally dared to ask after the seventh reprise.

"In my experience," Darlaene said. "After retelling the story countless times, some people remember details they previously left out, which might be important." Her voice was calm as she explained it to him. "I understand that you're tired though."

"Oh," Adenar said. "And . . . how many times did this work?"

"Well, only a handful," she admitted. "So it might be a shot in the dark. But try to think—is there *anything* else you haven't told me? Try and remember."

Adenar exhaled and stared hard into the floor for what seemed like an eternity.

Bored, Ara stood up and went over to a shelf of books. She took down a random book about the history of Paradrax, opened it, looked at a few pages, and put it back. Not something to explore today. She found another book, titled "The Abstract Cooking on the Daggered-isles." She sighed and put it back.

"Wait," Adenar said, determined.

Ara turned with book in hand.

He stared right at her. "There is something, and Ara just reminded me. I can't believe it worked!" He looked both bewildered and happy. "There was a woman." He sat back down, turning his attention to Darlaene. "An older woman at the receptionist's desk sifting through books. She was on edge the whole time before she left the room with a book."

"Good, good," Darlaene said, smiling too as she noted down his words. "I was about to lose faith."

"Describe her," Khendric said, lounging in his chair, his hat pulled over his eyes.

Adenar smiled. "There was one distinct thing about her: she wore an eye patch."

"Are you kidding me?" Darlaene asked.

Adenar's smile broke into uncertainty. "Ehm, no. I thought that would be useful information."

"And it is," she said. "I should have thought of this possibility—I'm almost embarrassed I didn't. Only one woman of nobility in Ashbourn wears an eye patch, and she recently disappeared: the widow of General Toran, Viessa Toran." She noted her name and circled it.

Ara felt butterflies burst to life in her stomach.

Khendric perked up. "She has to be our primary suspect for summoning the shadowwalker." He filled Darlaene in on the corpse of the general Adenar had brought them. He told her about the strange holes in his body, the lack of blood, and the secrecy of the burial.

Darlaene wrote everything on yet another chalkboard, revelling in all the new information. "I *am* glad I ran into you. Hopefully, this will all be easier from now."

"And it fits," Ara said. "I mean, if Eranna murdered her husband, Viessa would probably go to great lengths for revenge."

"And she couldn't go public about it," Adenar said. "Without proof, it would seem like a desperate attempt to discredit the Warborn Party."

"I think we should try to find her," Ara said. "If she's still alive."

"Agreed," said both Khendric and Darlaene.

Finally, they were getting somewhere. They couldn't go to more parties since Ara had been compromised, but now they had a new heading.

"How will we track her down?" Darlaene asked.

"Find out where she lived," Khendric suggested. "Get into her house, pop the paratis serum and see what we find?"

"Someone should also do some research on what kinds of beast needs a hundred bodies to sustain itself," Darlaene said. "We should try to conclude if there's a connection between the body count and whatever is going on with Ara; with the arm, the thoughts, and the voice."

Adenar's confused expression at that worried Ara, but luckily, he didn't ask about anything. She didn't want him to think of her as a freak.

Darlaene added, "We should search different libraries. There are some ancient scriptures in the ancient sections. There's got to be lore on something we don't know about. A children's tale or anything."

"That sounds like Topper-work." Khendric sighed.

"That reminds me," Darlaene continued. "We should lay low for some days. At least Ara and I. You're exposed, and I might be."

Ara sighed audibly. *Really?*

"I'm still anonymous," Khendric said. "So I'll—"

"You might not be," Darlaene interjected. "You entered the party hand in hand with Ara. We should conclude that Eranna knows as well. She might not see the connection, but I don't think we should risk it."

"Well," he said. "I doubt that. We were only together for a very short time and I wore a fake nose."

Darlaene merely sighed. "I can't stop you anyway."

"It's Topper I plan to look for," Khendric said. "If Eranna *is* looking for me, she's looking for a handsome dark-haired man with a ghastly nose. I'm going to dress up as a beggar, sitting at the Meritocrat gate to spot him."

"How will you know it's him?" Ara asked.

Khendric produced a most mischievous smile. "I told him to sing when he was at the gate."

"What?" Ara and Darlaene asked simultaneously.

"It was my turn to pick how to spot each other, and I said I would only help find him if he started singing at the front gate. Loudly. Topper hated it."

"I wish I could hear that," Darlaene said.

"None of the victims of his vocal cords will say so." With that, Khendric left the hideout.

"Hopefully, he will do *some* investigating as well," Darlaene said, making Ara chuckle.

Ara tried to process the thought of 'staying hidden' for a couple of days and looked for ways to relieve herself of boredom. The options were: read or work on the case. The latter seemed fun, but she felt so masterfully outmanoeuvred by Darlaene, who put even Khendric to shame. She fascinated her—so beautiful and certain, yet such a bookworm.

"I'm free to go, right?" Adenar asked.

Darlaene chuckled. "Only if you pay me a gold chip."

"Huh?" Adenar asked.

"Of course, you are free to leave," she said.

"I'll see you soon?" Ara asked.

"I hope so," Adenar answered. He bowed courteously to her and left the hideout.

CHAPTER 9

Of Kings and Beasts

Bored to death and not possessing the energy to eat the food Darlaene had made, Ara lounged on a chair. Khendric had been gone for three days and Darlaene wasn't talkative. Ara had read about countless more beasts, but even that grew tedious after a while.

Darlaene had drilled the names of all the different important people in the city into her memory. She even had drawings of them, some of which she'd drawn herself, impressively enough. Ara tried to draw her own sketch, but she threw it in the kindling fire in fear of Darlaene seeing it.

After running through sword techniques, she just wanted to go outside and do . . . well, stuff! Find the general's widow, or discover more about the voice in her head. Normally that thought terrified her, but it was better than this.

A hard knock came at the utmost door of the hideout. Darlaene sprung up, looking at a calendar. "Damn it. I'd forgotten about that. I have to go out for some time."

"Let me come," Ara begged. "I'm tired of being here."

"You can't, I'm afraid," Darlaene said, hurrying out of the room, into the wine cellar, and out the main metal door. How unfair! Suddenly she had *somewhere* important to be. Ara wondered how they'd react if she just got up, proclaimed she had somewhere important to be, and left. She barely noticed she was on her way out the door too in her thoughts. *I guess that settles it. I'm coming too.*

After slowly opening and making sure she was alone, Ara walked around the building. A carriage stood out front, facing away from her, and Darlaene's voice emanated from inside. Ara climbed onto the back and took a firm hold as it moved away from the headquarters and towards the centre of the city. Ara couldn't hear what Darlaene said or who she talked to, but it made her suspicious. Khendric trusted her, but Ara didn't know her at all. With so much trickery in the world—anyone could be an imposter.

The carriage continued towards the centre, through many crowded streets. Ara did her best to look inconspicuous, like she belonged on the back of the carriage. Several people noticed her, but probably had their own problems and didn't want to get meddled in other's business, so no one said anything.

The carriage continued towards the castle and the giant structure towered over Ara. *Darlaene is meeting with someone here?* she wondered. The driver steered through an open gate. Ara would surely be seen by guards at every corner. Fortunately, few people looked at the back of the carriage, which entered a large courtyard. It stopped before a smaller gate and the driver opened the door for Darlaene and whoever else sat inside. Ara's heart pounded so hard in her chest she had trouble hearing the footsteps climbing out of the vehicle.

"I'll get your chair," the driver said and his eyes widened at the discovery of a mysterious young girl at the back of his carriage.

"Hello there," she said, with no clue what to do.

After finally finding his words, the driver asked, "Who . . . who are you?"

Which in turn led the two people in front to investigate. "Lady Lordemure?" a familiar voice asked, sounding puzzled. It took Ara a moment to place the old man—Councillor Elrich Obarum, Chosen of the Passionist party. To him, Ara was still Lady Aviana Lordemure. But judging Darlaene's face, Ara was the biggest fool in the world. She sighed deeply.

"What are you doing here?" Elrich asked, as befuddled as was his right.

"She's actually with me," Darlaene said, laying a hand on his shoulder. "And she's in fact not Lady Lordemure. I'm afraid she played the same game as I at the party. This is Ara, another beast hunter I work with."

Elrich studied Ara. "Why haven't you told me about her sooner?"

"She recently came to the city. I did not know either."

"But I am not paying her. At least, I haven't agreed to. So if you think . . ." He trailed off, lost in thought. "Who are you working for and who are you investigating?"

Ara didn't know what to say. Frankly, she still held her breath.

"Buyers confidentiality," Darlaene said, luckily. "Ara discovered I work for you, and since our investigations align, we're working together. With the rise in crime, I told her to jump on the back of the carriage and see if we had a tail."

"And you didn't tell me?" Elrich asked.

"I didn't get time admits all your questions," Darlaene countered.

He considered her words, casually glancing at Ara. "Well, I guess what she's doing is no different than what you're doing. As long as you work together, I guess it's only beneficial." He extended a hand to Ara, and she shook, relieved. "Nice to meet you, Ara."

"Nice to meet you too," she answered, trying to keep her composure.

"I guess you'll meet the king too," he added, walking through the small gate and up some large stairs.

Ara fell into line with Darlaene up the giant steps. The stairs formed large half-circles, and at the top stood several guards, wielding large polearms. Their well-maintained armour looked dashing in the sun. Ara found it hard to keep her eyes off them, and she almost stumbled.

Two other men wearing silken vests and royal garments in various bright colours opened the doors for them. The insides of the castle took Ara's breath away. Large halls; giant staircases leading to different inside-terraces; wide corridors and paintings painted directly on the ceilings; it was all too much for her mind. Guards stood posted absolutely everywhere, all clad in polished plate, proudly guarding the castle. No dirt or dust tattered the floor, and multiple chandeliers hung from the ceiling above statues.

"I take it she's never seen this before," Elrich said with a small smile.

"Pardon me," Darlaene said. "But neither have I . . . and it *is* breath-taking."

The three walked up staircase upon staircase, through hallway after hallway until finally reaching a grand hall, with windows so large they threatened to break under their own weight. Countless benches riddled the hall, placed in rows. Far away, Ara spotted a beautiful silver throne on a plateau with its own stairs leading up to it. The king stood beside it, his blond hair making him easily recognizable, talking with a broad woman. A long blue carpet with a white trim led from the entrance and all the way to the throne. Guards stood posted on the sides. With this kind of protection, Ara would feel safe from anything.

They started down the long hall, and Elrich mumbled words to himself and gestured a greeting with his hands.

The king gestured for the broad woman to leave. "Councillor Elrich Obarum," he said, his strong voice reverberating through the hall. "Chosen of the Passionists."

Elrich and Darlaene went down to one knee, and Ara stood alone for a second before following suit. "King Koradin," Elrich said, staying on his knee. "The Ashen King of Ashbourn."

"Oh, stand up," Koradin chuckled. "I'm tired of formalities, and especially that title. For twelve years, everyone has kneeled and bowed and danced and sung . . . just get up and relax."

Ara's eyes widened at the casualty, and still barely dared to stand because of his strong and commanding voice. She rose with the others to see his long perfectly groomed blonde hair resting on the shoulders of his blue tabard with white lines. A sheathed sword with a beautiful, golden handle hung at his side. He towered over the three of them, his natural authority almost oppressive.

"Maybe you'll soon be the one everyone has to kneel to," the king smirked to Elrich.

"I don't think that's likely," he answered. "Chosen Ronoch has such momentum, I'm scared I'll be left in the dust."

The king's eyes surveyed his great hall. "That brings us to why we're here."

His gaze fell upon Darlaene and Ara, and her heart almost stopped. Unbelievable. She, a poor girl from the Rundowns of Kalastra, stood in front of the King of Ashbourn.

His determined, yet kind eyes loomed over her and stopped on Elrich. "I thought you were only working with one?" he asked the councillor, raising an eyebrow.

"So did I," he replied—as if Ara wasn't nervous enough already. "But they have their networks and have worked together for some time. Darlaene assures me they're working for a common goal, though it was a surprise to me too."

"Wait," the king said. "So, you've only hired one of them?"

"Me," Darlaene stepped forward. "My name is Dar-laene."

The King strolled down from his plateau and took her hand. "Pleasure to meet you, Darlaene" he said and turned to Ara, making her feel even smaller. "And you?"

"I . . ." she stuttered. "I'm Ara."

"Ah, and you're a beast hunter?"

"She is," Darlaene interjected.

"And who do you work for?" he asked.

"Buyers confidentiality?" Ara said uncertainly, looking at Darlaene.

"But I am the king," Koradin said with a smile.

Could she tell him? If she only had more experience with politics. Darlaene kept her stare at the king, offering no help.

"Just a young man," Ara said. "An assistant from the Meritocrat Party."

The King frowned, giving the smallest of chuckles. "An assistant?" he said, but turned to Elrich before Ara could answer. "I have summoned you because I know you sent a beast hunter to investigate Ronoch Steelbane."

"I figured as much, but *how* did you find out?" Elrich wondered. "Your letter said 'bring your beast hunter', but how did you know I investigated Ronoch?"

"I've been king for twelve years," Koradin replied. "It does come with some benefits, like loyal and clever friends. But you do not have a rat in your circles—do not worry."

"What I'm doing is not illegal," Elrich said.

"It is not. Espionage, or investigation, is a necessity in the world we live in. I want to know what you know, that is all."

"What?" a befuddled Elrich mumbled.

"For too long I have investigated these rumours of war that the Warborn have been spouting within the city and found nothing. I know Ronoch comes from Brattora, but why he left or why he would warn us, I do not know. I've stated, in numerous speeches, that I cannot find any proof

Brattora will go to war with us, as they are already busy in another war. However, our citizens swallow his words like a hungry wretcher. I'm convinced no war is coming, but they believe him, and I am genuinely scared he'll lead us into destruction." The king's eyes fell upon Ara and Darlaene. "Now I see he's also attracted the attention of two beast hunters. I'm failing in disproving his rumours, hence I ask you. Have you found anything that can discredit the man?"

"Hold on," Elrich said before either Darlaene or Ara could speak. "Though Ronoch is probably in the lead to win, you're surely second to win the throne for a third time, meaning that if you discredit him, you secure your own throne, whilst I gain nothing."

"Yes," the king said bluntly. "That's true. I'll be honest with you about how I see this. I think we can count both you and Chosen Tennar Nataro, of the Royalists, out of the race."

Elrich's face didn't flinch at the king's words.

"And I assume," Koradin continued. "Both you and I don't believe the Warborn's words of war, and we believe Ronoch will indeed lead the kingdom into a war that might be pointless except for conquering more for ourselves. Am I wrong?"

Elrich's face held stern. "You are not."

"I believe the only way we can stop this would-be war is if I can somehow best him in this coronation, though I understand that's not the outcome you wish for. I do not ask for you to aid me, only that I am given possible means to save our soldiers and citizens, if I am right."

"And you're not doing this *just* to become king once more?" Elrich asked.

"It will probably be impossible to fully convince you," Koradin said, "but being king grows tiresome, and none of my daughters wishes to rise for the position, hence I still remain the Chosen for the next term as well. Hopefully, someone new can step up within the Meritocrat Party soon."

Ara envisioned Adenar in Koradin's place. After all, he was the only Meritocrat she knew, but he lacked the imposing presence surrounding Koradin.

Elrich emanated dark thoughts, but not too strong. It had to be because the king intruded into his work and the fact that he had trouble countering his arguments. His facial expression stayed surprisingly calm. *I could never be a politician,* she thought.

"Anyway," Koradin said when Elrich didn't provide an answer. "These beast hunters are free to do as they like and don't need your permission to answer. So I ask again, do you have any information that would aid Ashbourn?"

"They *are* free," Elrich said, "but I could refuse to pay them."

King Koradin blinked twice, which Ara interpreted as slight annoyance. "I'm trying to go about this graciously. The truth is, I could simply offer to pay many times more than you. While it would go against my morals to do so, I don't hold them as high as I hold what I believe to be best for the capital."

Elrich clenched his teeth, but otherwise remained still.

"You know what I'm about to ask for a third time," King Koradin said, turning to them both.

"I have investigated Ronoch the longest," Darlaene said. "Unfortunately, I haven't been able to find any dirt."

Ara frowned, wanting to tell the king about the corpses in Ronoch's hidden basement and how he lied about General Toran's death. But she held her tongue, trusting Darlaene had her reasons for not divulging.

Koradin sighed, looking irritated and thoughtful. Ara realized she couldn't feel any dark thoughts coming from him.

"And you?" Koradin said. "Ara?"

"Uhm," she stuttered, immediately feeling like a fool. "That is all we know, for the time being." She hoped to sound professional, but was so nervous the words came out almost as a whisper.

"And these are your true words?" pressed the king.

Darlaene nodded, prompting Ara to mimic her response.

"If so, maybe there is nothing more to him, and I am losing justly. And the assassin, the . . . shadowwalker?"

Both Darlaene and Ara's eyebrows rose in surprise.

Koradin chuckled softly. "I do know a thing or two about beasts. Do you know who would send one after Eranna Carner?"

Darlaene didn't answer, so Ara kept her tongue as well.

"I do know you were there," he continued. "Hair as red as that is not easily missed, not even by kings."

Darlaene couldn't keep her mouth from curling into a smile.

"Though," Koradin continued, "your reluctance to say anything on the matter does make me question the 'scarce' information about Ronoch."

"We're trying to figure out who summoned the shadowwalker," Ara finally said

"And?" Koradin asked.

"We're not sure about anything," Ara said.

"Do you have any suspects? I need to know who can summon such monstrosities, as it is a serious crime. Not to mention incredibly dangerous."

"We think it might be the general's widow," Ara said. He seemed so earnest Ara felt she had to help him.

"Lady Viessa?" Koradin asked. "Why? What could be her motive."

"Well," Ara started. "Maybe the general didn't die the way the Warborn claims."

Koradin slowly nodded. "There is . . . something off about it. And I have people looking into that too. I wish I could help on this matter, but as far as I know we can't locate her at the moment. She's been silent since General Toran died. If you do find her, please guide her to me, even if she summoned the shadowwalker. General Toran was a dear friend, and I know Viessa well. I want to protect and hear her side of the story, before carrying out any justice."

"We will," said Darlaene, giving a little bow.

Koradin nodded. "Also, there's a shortage of food in the city, and it is getting serious. Normally, I wouldn't tell you, but there's something off about the circumstances of the surrounding villages supplying us. I've sent emissaries to investigate, and they reported back that nearly everyone in the villages was dead. Women and children too. Murdered quite brutally. I don't suppose you know anything about it, but if you do, let me know."

Ara thought of the tentacled beast from Cornstead. Left to itself, Cornstead would probably have suffered the same fate. If more of those horrible little beasts existed, they could be the cause of the mayhem. Ara didn't voice her thoughts, however, both because she didn't have any proof, and because Darlaene had withheld information from the king too. Ara guessed she would explain why after this meeting.

"We'll look into it," Darlaene said. "But I don't know anything, I'm afraid."

The king sighed, looking troubled. "This might be a far stretch. But, I'm getting reports of a rise in deathwalkers lately, while coincidentally three people from surrounding villages and two citizens of Ashbourn have gone missing." A grim expression crossed his face. "I'm fearing a voreen might be lurking in the forests."

Darlaene and Ara's eyes shot open. Ara cleared her throat and Darlaene composed herself. Ara found the king's beastly knowledge impressive, despite it regarding such a terrible creature.

Koradin tilted his head as if bemused by their reactions. "As a king, it's important to know what kinds of creatures are potential threats. And a voreen is a grave one, one I hope I never have to fight or fend off. Though you should know, there exists an official mandate where if more than ten people are murdered by the same beast, the king has to personally attend to the issue. If this happens when you are still in Ashbourn, I'll be forced to send you on this case, breaking your current contracts. Let's pray it doesn't come to that."

"I understand," Darlaene said.

You understand? Ara thought. *That's utterly terrifying.*

"If there is something else," he said, "contact me. I will give your descriptions and names to the guards. Once inside you may schedule a meeting with a servant."

"We will," she agreed.

A woman dressed in lavish, purple clothes entered from a door and strolled over to them with elegance. Ara recognized her to be the queen, so when Darlaene kneeled, she did too. All that studying in her very boring spare time had been good for something, at least.

"You may stand," she said with a calm and soothing voice. "Having everyone bow to you does grow tiresome."

Ara rose nervously in the presence of kings and queens. Such powerful people were frightening to say the least.

"Hopefully," the queen continued, addressing Koradin. "You will lose this coronation and I can be free of all this useless kneeling and bowing."

"Ara and Darlaene," Koradin said, gesturing towards the queen. "This is Queen Lenda of Ashbourn."

"You are the beast hunters?" she asked, and they nodded. "I'm afraid I need to steal my husband away from you. Other business calls."

The king sighed, excusing himself and his queen before retracting from the hall. Elrich gestured for them to follow him. "It's nice to see where your loyalty lies," he said in a hushed whisper.

"This was not a matter of loyalty," she answered without whispering. "It's simply a matter of policy."

They left the giant castle—which took a fair amount of time—and got in a carriage back to the hideout. Ara didn't sit inside, but resumed her earlier position at the back, keeping her story intact. Once inside the hideout, Darlaene sat Ara down.

"That was foolish," she said. "I can't have you sneaking onto carriages like that."

"I'm sorry, but it caused no harm."

"Let's hope not. You did blow your cover to Elrich and King Koradin—"

"Why didn't we tell him anything?" Ara asked. "The king, I mean. He was nice. Not like I'd picture a king, actually."

"We're here to kill beasts," Darlaene said. "Not get mixed up in politics. He seemed like an earnest man, I agree, but he was clearly using us to try to win over his opponent."

"But—"

Darlaene silenced her with a wave of her hand. "Listen, I don't know where the line goes with how much we should interfere, to be honest. If we find hard proof or something so outrageous we're certain we cannot let the city fall to the Warborn, we'll tell him. We'll hear Khendric's thoughts on this matter too, before doing anything. And no more acts like that, got it?"

"Yes," Ara yielded and promptly sat down. This was the nicest Ara had ever been yelled at. Her father would slap and scream at her. The nerves she felt when Darlaene had sat her down faded. Perhaps physical punishment wasn't the most effective tool? She learned so much about herself and other people, understanding why the way she'd been brought up was not okay.

"I'm terrified by the thought of fighting a voreen," Darlaene said. "If Koradin asks us to take care of one, I'll flee. But they're so rare I doubt it's the case."

Ara already feared the voreen, and if Darlaene would flee, that spoke volumes. Ara tried to push the phantom worry away. *It probably won't come to that.* She sighed, deflated, and got back to reading.

CHAPTER 10

The Widow

Three more days had passed after Khendric broke into poor General Toran's estates, but he'd been unable to progress on the hunt for the general's widow, Viessa. He'd searched through the entire estate, and did find a disposed of dress in a drain with someone's scent on, but that was it. Fed up with not getting anywhere, he'd handed the reins to Ara and Darlaene and for two days, he had been pretending to be a beggar, sitting slumped over at the main Meritocrat gate into the city, waiting for Topper to return. He guessed enough time had passed for Ara and Darlaene to not 'lay low' anymore. They currently investigated the estate trying to find any clues that could help them.

Having had to ask Darlaene for help, she made snarky remarks as usual. If she managed to solve it, Khendric would never hear the end of it. The thought of her beautiful, smug face smirking at him was nauseating. The thought of Darlaene doing potentially dangerous work too, nagged him, but he had to let go of his need for control. He hated how the only thing to save her was her wits. Ara had her arm and Topper could reincarnate, but Darlaene didn't have anything like that. He exhaled, remembering why they split, years ago.

His worry had strangled her, and it broke Khendric's heart to leave her.

On every possible occasion, the two had snuck away to spend some time alone, talking beneath the stars, reminiscing about the wonderful hunts they had done. Poor Topper had probably died around twenty times. Darlaene was like the wind, an unstoppable, gracious force he felt on his skin and he revelled in its soothing comfort. Khendric did his best not to be overprotective—not that she ever let him, but he had to control his emotions on the subject. She always did what she wanted, and Khendric both admired and hated her for it. *Stop being so obsessive, Khendric.* But the obsessiveness probably came from his childhood and—Khendric pushed those thoughts away. They'd surfaced more frequently lately.

He sat back, sighed, and surveyed the people on the street instead, waiting for Topper. The stakeout had become tedious. Naturally, he'd toyed with the guards and other people leaving and entering the city, from throwing pebbles to trying to get guards to stab him. Nobody had ever stabbed him before, no matter how much he tested them, until one day ago.

Two of the guards actually pulled their swords and stabbed him, and they hadn't needed much encouragement either. They both had that look in their eyes—a grey shadow over the pupils, like they weren't fully present. Khendric terrified them when he continued playing drunk and wandered off, but he had to return in new clothes.

It was easy to get new beggar clothes. Either climb and steal from people who hung them out to dry or trade with other beggars. But now, even annoying the guards couldn't lift his spirits. He understood how Ara felt during the three first days of being locked away—utter boredom.

He chipped a pebble at a wall and leaned against the stones forming the enormous wall around the city. The stream of people leaving Ashbourn was larger than the one entering. Some left with all their possessions on carts as the food shortage got worse, affecting more and more. Darlaene had Elrich's backing, luckily.

A persistent man outside the gate had been preaching for the Warborn Party every day, and the crowd grew in size. *Only three more days until the coronation*, Khendric reminded himself, which bothered him, because it felt like a deadline. A most horrible singing broke his trail of thought.

"I once fell in love with a beautiful woman in the mists," a croaky voice sounded from somewhere in the mass of people outside the gates. Khendric's smile grew, as he knew instantly Topper had arrived. "I fell in love with her, but she turned out to be a mire woman."

Khendric stood up to get a better view and saw the voice's origin. Topper's new, tall vessel was an elderly crooked-nosed man with a constant look of annoyance on his face. He looked to be in his late fifties, but with a brawny build. Perhaps he'd been a soldier?

He'd torture Topper some more, and let his horrendous singing continue.

"Then I met a beautiful young woman again," Topper continued. People turned their frowning heads at him. "She took me to bed, and a child we had. Then another and more and more. She turned out to be a villagemother. Then I met another one and we fell deeply in love. She fell sick and I stayed by her side, forever and ever and ever. She never got better, she needed me more. Then I found out she was a luster." Topper stopped after finishing the first verse of the children's song, to teach them about some of the beasts in the world. Topper scanned the area, annoyance clear on his older face.

"Come on!" he bellowed, scaring some people. "Please don't make me do more!" Khendric enjoyed the moment one last time, and tossed a small rock at Topper's head.

* * *

Khendric and Topper strolled through the gate and into the busy streets of Ashbourn.

"I can't believe it," Topper complained. "I meet her and not even an hour later she uses me like a sack of meat and I die!"

Khendric rolled his eyes at the all-too-expected nagging about Darlaene. At least, he didn't blame Khendric—yet. "She did save Ara's life though," Khendric suggested, to calm him down.

He turned sharply with an annoyed stare. "*I* saved Ara. My body took the dagger."

"But without Darlaene's push—"

"Are you serious?" Topper asked, aghast.

Khendric gave him a sincere look. "I'm always serious."

"Listen. I'm angry, furious even. I just need you to empathize with me."

"Oh," Khendric said mockingly. "Poor two-hundred-year-old Topper. Did the mean woman get you killed?"

"I hate you sometimes." Topper scowled. "Where is Darlaene now?"

"Working with Ara. We think the general's widow, Viessa, sent the shadowwalker after Eranna. We're trying to track her down."

A stream of children's laughter hit them as they rounded a corner, and the many backs of parents halted them. Khendric and Topper both smiled when they saw the cause for the chatter and cheers. In the middle of the children, on a tall cane reaching high above the crowd rested a sparkling browar. The many long tails of the large multicolour bird reached down to the ground, which the children wrapped around themselves, relishing in the many magical and shifting colours. The browar relaxed on the cane, supported by its owner's hand who smiled cheerily at the happy children, gently showered by the bird's sparkling dust.

Khendric and Topper slowly moved through the crowd. Khendric said, "How nice of the browar, and the guy." Usually, a hat would lay on the ground with the expectancy of coin for the display of the exotic beast, but not this time.

Khendric led him into a carriage and they headed for Darlaene's hideout, giving him plenty of time to fill Topper in on the recent clues. He told him about Ara's strange thoughts the night they were attacked by the criminals.

They went down into the hideout and Khendric gave him his stuff back. The sword, hat, and too short coat.

"How's the new body?" he asked.

"Pretty good," Topper replied. "For an older gentleman, he's in decent shape."

"Too bad the shape of his nose was only half-decent, at best."

"Function over looks," Topper retorted, walking over to the chalkboard.

"I guess. We can't all have both, like me," Khendric said smugly. Topper turned to him. "So, what do I do then?"

"Well, it might not be too exciting, but I was thinking you could search the library for anything useful. Either about shadowwalkers, small tentacled beasts or whatever else you think could help."

"Gladly," Topper replied. He appeared to be a bookworm in any body. "As long as I can stay away from that woman, I'm satisfied."

"Yes, she's quite amazing, isn't she?" Khendric jabbed.

Topper gave him a flat stare.

Khendric sighed. "I'm sorry you died again, truly, and so quickly."

"I don't blame you. You weren't there."

Khendric nodded, before they heard a commotion sound from the hallway. Adenar stumbled through the door with an older woman leaning heavily on his shoulder. They looked stressed, both panting heavily. Adenar sat her down on a chair and turned to Khendric and Topper.

"Are you hurt?" Khendric asked them.

"Uhm, no," Adenar said. "This is my mother, Olenna."

She had to be in her late forties, and fairly beautiful. Her long, brown hair hung down past her shoulders. Her dress had probably been a clear white once, but now it was tattered and dirty.

"What happened?" Topper asked.

Adenar's eyes went back and forth between the two. "Is . . . is this Topper?"

"Yes," Khendric said.

"That's going to take some time to get used to," Adenar admitted. "Anyway, we were assaulted. Men came to our home trying to hack through the door. We managed to escape through the back door, shaking them off in narrow streets and got into a carriage. I didn't know where else to go, so I took us here."

It hadn't been what Khendric had expected at all, but he was glad Adenar brought her here. "The men," Khendric began, "did they look like your stereotypical ragged thieves?"

"We didn't get a good look—"

"They did," his mother said. "I got a better look than Adenar."

Khendric wondered if there was a correlation between those thieves and the ones that attacked Ara, Darlaene, and himself the other night. *Something is definitely going on here,* he thought. *And someone is trying to get rid of us.* Those men had to be controlled by someone or something, but Khendric knew of no beast that could do such a thing. He felt as lost as he had in Cornstead, with too many loose ends. How was Ara connected to all of this? Did the tentacled beast in Cornstead have anything to do with this?

"Thank you," Adenar's mother said, reaching out her hand.

Pulled out of his thinking, he shook her hand.

"My name is Olenna Varnor," she said. "Adenar has excessively explained to me that you're *not* to blame for the dangers he has apparently been in lately. Though I do wish you would just have turned him down in the first place."

"Well, he went to great lengths to get us on the case and got himself in great danger fully without my help."

Olenna looked to her son. "He is stubborn."

Adenar looked back and forth between them, still panting. For being a pencil pusher, the youngster was a man of action. All the things Adenar had done were impressive for only signing papers every day.

"So what now?" Olenna asked.

"The less you know, the better," Khendric said. "If those people come here and you know more than you need to, they can torture you for information."

"Well, that's morbid," she said and sat down, looking dissatisfied.

"Yeah, sorry. Just try to get comfortable and we'll get back to saving this city from whatever's going on. Hopefully, you'll have a house to go back to."

Khendric gestured for Topper to follow him outside and Adenar and his mother began conversing privately

"I'll head for the library," Topper said.

"Good idea. Try to find anything on shadowwalkers—or if anyone has rented any books about them lately."

Topper nodded and turned to leave. Khendric planned to team up with Darlaene and Ara in their search for Viessa. He ached to get back to her.

* * *

Ara grew bored once more. They'd been searching the general's house for hours upon hours without finding any clues.

They even tried following Khendric's trail from earlier, but came up short there as well.

Now they simply searched the house over and over. Darlaene never tired however, attacking each and every room with fierce determination again and again. Ara tried to motivate herself to do the same, but after a couple of minutes, her mind wandered to other things. Not knowing what they were looking for was the hard part. What could they possibly find? A letter Viessa had left, telling them her location? A map?

Frustrated, she sat down in the massive office chair, located in the general's office. Mountains of paper rose from multiple desks. Weaponry hung proudly mounted on the walls. Tons of books about war laid on the floor as Darlaene and her had gone through each one. The massive desk in front of her had several drawers, which she'd already searched through many times, but hearing Darlaene work from another room, Ara felt she could do it again.

The same pencils, ink, crumpled papers, and documents hid inside. In frustration, she pulled everything out of the drawers and tossed the office supplies on the floor. No new important documents surfaced, and she had read through all of these already.

Once more, she fell back into the large chair. From this sitting position, she saw something strange in the bottom drawer. Not an object, but rather . . . the floor of the drawer looked weird. She squinted, seeing intricate patterns. She picked it back up.

Her eyes widened. "Darlaene!" she yelled.

Darlaene stormed through the door, and Ara handed her the bottom of the drawer. Her frown deepened and she glanced at Ara. "You found a map."

"I think so."

A detailed map had been scratched into the bottom of the drawer, with crosses at various locations.

"This could be interesting," Darlaene said, putting it on the table. "This looks like the Warborn District."

"What do you think those are?" Ara asked, pointing to the crosses.

"I don't know, but I want to find out. This one is closest to the trail Khendric found, maybe we could start there." Ara nodded and they took off, bringing the wooden map.

Leaving the house, they met Khendric in the courtyard.

"I found a map!" Ara said excitedly.

"No way," he answered with a wry smile on his face as Darlaene put it in his hands.

"She did—I mean, we did."

"That's a little annoying, but this seems to be—"

"The Warborn District," Darlaene interrupted him.

"Yes, and this cross is—"

"Closest to the trail you found."

He sighed. "You're taking away all the fun."

They wandered through the Warborn District to locate the cross marked on the map. A troubling number of people in the streets asked for food, almost enough for a riot. They flocked around the beast hunters until Khendric and Darlaene handed them the little food they carried, and flashed their weapons. After that, they were left alone.

The guards treated the beggars rougher than they did, and there was no shortage of patrols. Khendric said that the increase in guards had to do with the escalation in crime. Whatever caused the food shortage started influencing the city greatly.

Ara had seen some carts on an earlier day, surrounded by guards, handing out food. Darlaene had told her those guards were the king's army. Their armour bore the mark of a pharlanax. The ones in the streets, however, were the Warborn army.

The group found where the cross was marked on the map, which placed them in front of a dilapidated, abandoned pottery factory. Loads of ruined ceramics lay strewn around the old building. With no door, Ara walked through the doorway, while Khendric and Darlaene went around back. Ara only found more pots inside, and sighed.

Shortly after, Khendric and Darlaene entered through a window nearby. An ever so faint blush clad her face when she met Ara's eyes.

"Nothing in the back," Khendric said, stealing Ara's attention.

"Why would this be marked with a cross?" Ara asked, her voice echoing down two hallways.

Darlaene examined the ruins, looking thoughtful. "This place is rarely or never visited," she said. "Which would make a perfect—"

"Safe house!" Khendric burst out. "I said it first."

Darlaene rolled her eyes and nodded. "That's my best guess. And I bet that if it's not on this first floor, then it's underground."

"It is imperative that we win . . ." the voice in Ara's head said. She repeated the words aloud.

"'It's imperative that we win'?" Khendric asked. "Win the coronation, maybe?"

"My first thought too," Darlaene agreed. "At least if the voice has something to do with anything here in Ashbourn. At this point, I'm fairly certain that's the case. The night with those criminals, and Ara's pre-emptive thoughts, is almost proof enough."

"And it's somehow connected to Cornstead then," Khendric said. "Because that's where you got these . . . powers."

"Maybe," Ara said, trying to push worry away. "Maybe Ronoch is involved too?" She couldn't put her finger on why she thought so. It was simply a gut feeling.

"I'm thinking the same," Khendric agreed. "There's something going on with him, and with all those corpses."

He shivered. "But, there's not really anything connecting the two."

"So until we find something," Darlaene said. "We must try to keep an open mind to other possibilities too."

Ara and Khendric nodded in agreement.

"Good thing you brought this to our attention," Khendric said. "Let us know if anything else pops in."

"I will," Ara said, trying to keep her cool about the voice.

They reinitiated their search for a safe room and went systematically through the old structure. They discovered an old shack behind the building, made up of rotting wooden walls and a creaking door. There was nothing inside—except for a trapdoor.

"Well-well-well," Khendric said. "This looks promising."

Darlaene went down to one knee and rustled the big chain and lock denying them entry.

"I don't suppose you found a key?" she asked.

"No, but perhaps Ara can be of help."

Ara frowned questioningly, and he inclined his head towards her arm.

"Ah," she said. Whether it would work or not, she didn't know, but it was worth a try. She kneeled and grabbed the chain.

"Try to yank it," Khendric said.

Heaving the links, it didn't break, but she managed to stretch some of the metal, so she kept going and the chain gave in, snatching apart. Both Khendric and Darlaene looked mighty impressed, their eyes wide. Ara smiled broadly, a comfortable feeling spreading in her body. Khendric patted her on the back and Darlaene lifted the door open.

Complete darkness stared at them and nothing to light the way with. Khendric disappeared carefully down the steps, and he returned with a lantern in his hand, motioning for them to follow. A dank smell met her nostrils inside the short narrow tunnel before they reached another door. A metal chain and lock laid on the ground.

"Someone has been here," Khendric said. "But the place seems empty now." He opened the door and lit the room. Canned foods on shelves and barrels of water were stacked in a corner. Khendric found a set of clothes piled on the floor next to a wardrobe. "She changed clothes here—if it's indeed Viessa we're chasing."

"And ate," Ara added, holding up an opened can.

"Looks like she was in a hurry," Darlaene said, searching the table and bed. "Not bothering to lock this door."

"Maybe," Khendric agreed. "I can't see any signs of struggle."

"Any idea of where to go next then?" Ara asked.

"Well," Khendric huffed. "We got lots of places, so I guess we'll start here." He pointed to the cross nearest their location and they left the hideout shortly after.

* * *

They spent the rest of the day systematically visiting the marked safe rooms. They were inside taverns, beneath fake bushes, behind hidden doors in walls, in attics, and even an entry through a mock privy. Ara's arm came in handy again and again to force their way inside, and time and time again the rooms were empty. Unlike the first safe house, nobody had visited these. Ara feared the trail had gone cold. If Viessa hadn't gone to a safe house after the first one, how could they ever find her?

Night fell upon them as they approached the last safe house, furthest away from the first one. Close to the tall stone wall surrounding the Warborn District, it abutted the river bank separating the district from the Royalist's. Approaching on foot, they neared the wide river.

The only lights in the area came from the windows of nearby taverns. The beast hunters approached the riverside, and Ara couldn't really spot anything peculiar. They got as close to the vine-ridden wall as they could, but no safe room showed itself.

"This is where the cross is," Darlaene said. "Guess we'll start searching."

They always had to spend some time looking for the previous doors, but Ara had an idea of where to start this time. She grabbed the vines on the wall and forcefully shoved them aside and just as she expected—a door hid behind.

"Well," Khendric said. "Why didn't I think of that."

"I feel foolish." Darlaene rubbed her forehead. "Of course it's there."

This door didn't have a chain, and Ara opened it. A warm breeze hit her face, which was new. Khendric noticed it too and looked questioningly at her, before walking inside.

They pressed through a narrow tunnel, leading to a closed, but not locked door. Ara opened it and light streaked through. Khendric pulled her back and entered first. Letting out a small gasp, he ran further into the room. Ara followed, trying to get a look at what he had seen.

"Darlaene!" he yelled. "Come quick!"

Inside, on a chair, sat a barely conscious, ragged woman. She didn't respond to Khendric's touch or slaps. Darlaene moved past Ara as she neared.

Khendric checked for a pulse. "It's faint."

The pale woman missed her leg from the knee down, only a crude bandage tied around the stump. She also wore an eye patch.

"It's her," Ara said.

Khendric brought up a canteen with water, splashing it in her face.

She mildly reacted, blinking her eyes and wheezing out a word. "Water."

Khendric carefully poured some into her mouth and she started coughing. When she stopped, he poured some more and she managed to keep it down. "The book," she said, waving her hands around, eyes looking everywhere. Blood pooled on the floor beneath her stump.

A table stood next to Viessa with some canned food on it, and even more on a shelf further away. Ara found trails of blood too, back and forth between the chair and the shelf. *The poor woman,* she thought. *That must have been painful.*

She turned back to see Viessa more alert, focusing on Khendric and Darlaene's faces, but Khendric had to support her head.

"Kill . . . me, then," Viessa said looking at Darlaene, voice a mere wheeze. "Like you did my . . . husband." Her head fell back and she fell unconscious.

"We have to get her back to the hideout," Darlaene said. "She's in a bad state and needs water, food and a disinfectant for that leg."

Ara examined the room further and frowned upon seeing charred wood on the floor, surrounded by three chalk circles with various signs or glyphs inside. Ara got to one knee and felt a ghastly smell. She got a better look at the charred wood and saw what it really was—Viessa's severed leg all black and burned. Ara turned away in disgust.

"I think this is where she performed the ritual," Ara said, holding her hand over her mouth. "To summon the shadowwalker."

"I think you're right," Khendric said, hoisting Viessa over his shoulder.

They hurried out of the safe house and onto the street. Luckily, no people roamed outside to see them, and several carriages lined up close to the main road not far away, which connected the Warborn District to the Meritocrat District.

They got the attention of a carriage, and Khendric and Darlaene ignored the questioning driver as they laid Viessa inside. He was a man in his mid-thirties, with ruffled hair and a meagre build.

"To the Passionist Headquarters," Darlaene ordered.

"Uhm, what is—"

"Just take us there. Now!" Khendric barked and the driver accelerated with haste. The hooves of the two horses thundered on the cobblestone, and Ara held Viessa firmly with her strong arm.

"That will be six silver chips," the driver shouted to them.

"Six?" Khendric asked.

"Because of the cost of food these days. My family has to eat. You won't find anyone doing it for less."

"How is she doing?" Khendric asked, looking back at Viessa.

"Not better," Darlaene said as they headed back to her hideout.

CHAPTER 11

The Black Book

The beast hunters had carried Viessa back to Darlaene's hideout and treated her wounds. She already looked better, eating and drinking to further improve her state. After hours of sleeping, she came to her senses, realizing they didn't intend to torture or kill her.

Ara had gone to sleep on the floor for what remained of the night. The crowded hideout only had one bed. Still, she felt rejuvenated. Topper was back from the library, and Ara had met his new body. For being so old, he seemed strong and healthy. He had been thrilled to see her again. Getting used to him changing bodies went surprisingly well, and she talked to him as easily as before.

Khendric finally carried Viessa from the small bedroom and into the crowded common room, where everyone else sat, including Adenar and his mother.

"Glad to see you are doing better," Ara said, breaking the silence.

"Thank you," Viessa said. "I'm sorry you had to see me like that. I hadn't eaten for a long time and couldn't take the pain of getting back up to get more." She slowly shook her head. "I should've carried the food and water over before"—

Viessa swallowed and sighed heavily—"before performing that idiotic ritual."

"Right," Topper said, eating what was left of a piece of bread. "We're hoping you can shed some light on a few things for us."

"I figured as much. You're beast hunters, right?"

"Yes," Topper said. "Well, at least Khendric, Darlaene, Ara, and I."

"And the rest of you?" Viessa asked.

"We're collateral, I guess," Olenna said, giving a slight chuckle.

"I'm the one who hired them," Adenar said, getting Viessa's attention.

"You're the son, right?" she asked.

He frowned in confusion, but nodded. Viessa's eyes darted to Olenna, and a questioning smile grew on her face, but Olenna's hard expression remained immovable.

"Hired them to do what exactly?" Viessa asked, eyes lingering on Adenar.

"We can tell you about that later," Khendric said, getting up in front of the chalkboard. "But in short, we're investigating Eranna Carner and Ronoch Steelbane, whom we suspect killed your husband."

"I thought I was alone," Viessa said, eyes falling to the floor. "I was sure they would kill me too, once they got around to remembering me."

"So they did kill Toran?" Topper asked.

"They did. She murdered him."

"Are you certain it was her?" Khendric asked.

"I *feel* it was her. I wasn't there when—"

"I met you there," Adenar interrupted. "That night . . . in the reception. You grabbed a book and ran off."

Viessa looked at him. "I had almost forgotten. That was you?"

Adenar nodded.

"Which book was it?" Khendric asked.

"This is going to be easier if I start from the very beginning." Viessa inhaled. "To say it simply, Pether Toran and I weren't the best couple. Our marriage was not a matter of love, but rather a political contract we were both forced into. We fought a lot . . . but we had some great moments too. We did fall in love with each other in our own way." Tears welled in her eyes. "And I truly did love him." She blinked them away. "Anyway, Pether was married to his work more than me, hence he didn't tell me anything. But leading up to the coronation, something bothered him. He was constantly annoyed and prone to frustrated outbursts. He didn't let me in on much, just that Eranna was turning the council over to a new direction. 'An unnatural direction', he said. I prodded for more, but his shields returned as soon as he noticed they were down. It nagged him more and more, eating him up. He couldn't sleep or eat and decided to take matters into his own hands after Eranna had convinced the council to follow her plan. Pether said that if she succeeded, Ashbourn would cease to exist. He gathered his most loyal men and marched against her." She turned to Adenar. "That brings us to the night we met. Pether told me what he was going to do. If it got really bad, I was to leave the city. A carriage was ready with people he trusted. It would take me to Kalastra, and he promised I would be safe. I cried and begged him to come with me—to leave it all behind. I *knew* that would never happen. Pether would give his life for Ashbourn, holding loyalty above everything else. Loyalty to the crowned king, and the people. Going against a council decision went against every fibre in his body, but still, he pressed on. And . . . then he gave his life for that cause." Viessa had managed to keep her composure well, but this tore her apart. "I don't know how he died exactly, but he never returned. When they declared he died in an ambush, I knew he was gone. I couldn't come forth. They'd stop me. Eranna is fiercely clever and has probably been searching for me since the moment my husband died."

"So," Adenar said gently, "what were you doing there that night?"

"Pether didn't know I had a plan of my own. A long time ago, I learned about shadowwalkers. When I saw how Eranna ruined him and began to understand how severe the situation was, I wanted her gone. I thought of a last resort, something that was in *my* control. There was a book in the council's private library about shadowwalkers, not available to the general public. I strategically snuck the book out bit by bit. I hadn't gotten further than the receptionist's desk before Pether assaulted Eranna. Maybe if I had, I could have saved him. Anyway, I fled to one of our safe houses and stayed there for some time, before fleeing to the one you found me in. I gathered enough courage and hatred for Eranna to perform the ritual. I sawed my leg off. It was excruciating, but the creature appeared. I uttered her name before fainting. Then I thought it was done, I thought she was dead for certain. After bandaging my leg, I managed to get out on the street the next day and learned there had been an assassin . . . but no murder. I gave up. In all my pain and suffering, that vile woman got to live."

Ara almost vomited, her stomach churning like soup in a cauldron. She stopped the shadowwalker from ending Eranna's life that night. She grabbed its arm. Khendric clearly saw how she felt. He shook his head slowly, meaning for her not to say anything. An overwhelming shame came over her. This could all have been over if Ara hadn't saved Eranna, and luckily Viessa didn't notice their silent exchanges, staring at the floor.

"So, that's what happened," Viessa said.

"I'm very sorry for your loss," Olenna said. "I met your husband a couple of times, a long time ago, of course. He was a man of honour. Truly."

"Adenar will tell you how he got us on this case," Khendric said. "It involves General Toran, but it will have to wait. Are you certain you don't know what is going on at all with Eranna? Or maybe Ronoch?"

"I don't," she said, tone regretful. "But I do know what you need . There's a book—a cursed book. Pether mentioned it many times, how Eranna clung to it, presenting it as 'the path to Warborn victory.' He said it was a book of dark and foul magic. He wanted to snatch it from her and burn it, putting an end to Eranna's plans. I think you have to find that book. She holds it dear. I haven't seen it myself, but I know it has dark pages, with white text. The cover is also completely black, but that is all he said. Eranna is probably protecting or hiding it somewhere in the headquarters."

"A book?" Topper frowned. "Well, I guess it's something, at least."

"You *have* to get it," Viessa said, voice hard. "I'm sure there will be answers inside, and if not . . . destroy it. Eranna cradles it like a child—that's how important it is."

"She wasn't carrying it at the last party," Darlaene said.

"Of course not. That would have been risky. People would ask questions. Please, I beg of you: find the book."

"This is the only lead we have," Khendric said. "The coronation is two days away, and from what Ara heard, I think we have to act before that."

Ara nodded, trying to force away thoughts about the shadowwalker.

"Adenar," Khendric continued, "go into the other room with your mother and Viessa, and tell her what you know about Toran."

Adenar sighed heavily. Ara understood why he didn't want to tell her about digging up the general's corpse and dragging it around Ashbourn. But it was better than what Ara had done. Adenar and his mother helped Viessa into the bedroom and they closed the door, leaving the beast hunters alone.

"What do you think?" Khendric said. "This is turning into something big. If everything she says is true, and with what we have discovered, this will undoubtedly be dangerous, but we also might save the city if we succeed."

"I've already died once for this cause," Topper said. "I can probably die some more."

"This could all be over already. If I had just let the shadowwalker do its job—"

"There's no way you could have known, Ara," Khendric said. "You did the rational thing; save someone's life. I think it's best you don't mention that particular event to Viessa."

"He's right," Topper said. "You did the right thing. It was actually Darlaene that did the wrong thing and got me killed . . . again."

Darlaene rolled her eyes. "Really?"

"That was like ten minutes," Topper said. "I met you, and after ten minutes I was stabbed by some dark dagger, which by the way—"

"You saved my life though," Ara said.

He completely lost his momentum. "Well, I suppose that's true."

"So," Khendric said. "We need to decide if this is something we want to do, and if so, how to approach it."

"We have sacrificed a lot for this case," Ara said.

"I'm not surprised you want to continue," Khendric smirked. "It seems the more danger you're in, the more eager you become to push through." He looked to Darlaene and Topper. "You two have been in the business for a long time. What do you think?"

"We have no idea what the ramifications are if we leave this to run its course," Darlaene said. "If it is true what Viessa said—that the whole city is doomed if Eranna gets her way, I guess we have to continue."

"There is definitely something grand happening," Topper said. "And it's not like us to back away from a challenge."

"I didn't think you would back out," Khendric said. "Though I would prefer to lock Darlaene away."

"I know you do, dear. But you're going to need me. The coronation is two days away, and we should try to get that book before then."

"That doesn't give us much time," Khendric said. "What are we going to do?"

"You can't just sneak in like you usually do," Darlaene pointed out. "They know someone's on to them, especially after you slaughtered those men in the cellar. I'm pretty sure their security is tighter than ever, but don't worry." Darlaene rose and shooed Khendric away from the chalkboard. "I think maybe I have a way in. You're lucky I actually do my research."

Khendric sat down on his chair. "The boring part I elegantly leave to you, as always."

Darlaene waved his comment away. "The last day before the coronation, the Warborn Party, just like any other party, hosts one last great feast before a new king is chosen. It's a great tradition, known as 'the Coronation Dinner.' Everybody who works at the headquarters attends this dinner, therefore a lot of work is needed beforehand. I think this feast is our entry into the building. From there, we can search for this book."

"It could work," Topper said, nodding.

Sneaking again? Ara wondered, hoping she could do better this time around.

Khendric gazed at Darlaene with a bright fire in his eyes, and Ara saw how much he loved her. "That is probably our best chance." He got up and grabbed the chalk out of her hand, reclaiming the board.

Ara sat in silence, watching the professionals work. It took her mind off the shame.

"So, how do we do this?" Khendric asked. "I have a complete set of Warborn armour. With my great charisma, I can easily sneak in and get close to Eranna or Ronoch. Neither knows what I look like, and I can handle myself." He wrote his name on the board as an imposter-guardsman. "Now, I'm thinking Eranna wants more cleaning personnel both before and after the feast."

"Yes," Darlaene agreed.

"Cleaners again?" Topper said, sighing.

"Of course," Khendric answered. "It's just too good an opportunity to pass up."

"Cleaning personnel?" Ara asked.

Topper leaned over to her. "We've done some infiltration before and I guess you've seen the uniform cleaners use?"

"Yes," Ara answered. "But it changes from place to place."

"Except for one thing," Topper said.

"The mask!"

"Exactly," he said. "They use strong chemicals from silkeaters to clean, but they're toxic, hence the mask. I'm just sighing because I'm tired of being a cleaner."

Ara had no idea what silkeaters were. In Kalastra, she had seen official cleaning personnel, and they always wore masks, but she had never known why.

"You won't be this time," Khendric said. On the board, he wrote Ara and Adenar as cleaning personnel. Both excitement and worry grew in her mind. "Adenar too?" she asked.

"Yes," Khendric answered. "We need as many heads as we can muster, and cannot use Viessa or Olenna, as they're public figures. The reason you'll be cleaners is that you've both been exposed."

"I can get the outfits," Darlaene said, noting her tasks on her side of the chalkboard. "Elrich must have tons of them, I'm sure it won't be a problem."

Khendric glared at her for taking space on his board. "That leaves you and Topper then."

"We need something that's easy to fix," Topper said. "Something where the attire won't be a problem."

An idea sprung to life in Ara's head. "What about a cook?"

There was silence as they all thought the suggestion over.

"That's not a bad idea," Darlaene agreed.

Khendric wrote Topper up as a cook.

"But I don't know how to make classy food," Topper said.

"You always make food," Khendric said.

"That's road food. And you eat anything."

"Nobody is going to pay attention anyway."

"Why can't it be Darlaene?" he protested.

"Because she's too pretty to be a cook, while you are, well . . . not."

"That's the stupidest thing I've heard," Topper muttered.

Darlaene wrote herself up on the board as an 'arranger.'

They all frowned. "Arranger?" Khendric asked.

"For you uncultured ones," she joked. "Large parties like these have people who actually set them up, making sure everything's in order and well prepared."

"And how do you plan on becoming an 'arranger'?" Khendric asked.

"There are no official clothes. They wear what they want. I'll find something flamboyant and fabulous. Then I'll come sweeping in, talking down anyone who dares question my authority."

"That doesn't sound safe," Khendric said.

"Oh please," Darlaene shrugged. "I'll charge through the door, claiming to be the famous Madame Oyster from the far regions of Karatan, called upon by some noble. Then, I immediately yell at Topper for some phantom mistake, further proving my non-existent authority. It'll be easy."

Khendric didn't look convinced, worry plain on his face. "Maybe. Perhaps you can be a lookout, from outside?"

Darlaene snorted and underlined her role on the board.

"We each have our roles to play then," Khendric said. "Once inside, we don't know where to look. We'll ask Viessa if she knows any good places to begin. Other than that, just search where you can and get out if you think you're compromised. Listen in on conversations and pay attention to your surroundings. We'll get back here during the following night to discuss where to go next, depending on what we found. Sounds good?"

* * *

Viessa hadn't known any places the book could be. Her deceased husband had once said Eranna carried it on a chain around her torso. She was quite certain it wasn't in the Warborn library where she found the book on the shadowwalker.

Khendric and Darlaene had adjourned to the one bedroom in the hideout after the meeting ended. They bore mischievous grins before shutting the door, Khendric telling everyone *not* to open it for any reason, unless they wanted their eyes removed. Ara had giggled at that and sat down with Adenar.

She informed him of his role and he took to it more easily than she thought he would. Topper, Viessa, and Olenna had all fallen asleep, leaving just the two of them awake in the candlelit room.

"Your mother is really nice," Ara whispered.

Adenar smiled broadly. "Yes, she is really something. Awfully strict, but a great mother. She worked her heart out in politics when I was younger. She was thrilled when I went into the university to study 'politics, leadership and warfare.' But eventually she got tired, and luckily, thanks to my job, I can support us. We're not living a life of luxury, but we get by."

"Your job as everyone's assistant?" Ara said, giggling.

He chuckled. "Yes, that one. It's almost been a relief to be chased by murderous thieves that are just after my life, instead of all the snobby people in the headquarters that want my time." They shared another muffled laugh. "But I keep my spirits up. King Koradin began the same way and now he's . . . well, king."

"He started the same way?"

"Yes. Only, he was somehow hired into the council straight out of the university. He was quite the man, I've heard. Charming, dazzling and a fierce debater." Reverence twinkled in his eyes.

"Well," she said. "You got hired too."

"Yeah, though I have no idea how, and it doesn't seem anyone at the headquarters does either. I've asked all of my superiors and none of them can answer how I got the job. I'm always scared I will lose it, so I strive to do my best."

"I'm sure you're great," Ara said, feeling a couple of butterflies flutter to life in her stomach.

Adenar had his own fire in his eyes. He wasn't imposing in any way, but rather sincere. Ara thought it next to impossible for Adenar to be anything but true to himself. She found something attractive about that, and never wanted the conversation to end.

"I appreciate that," Adenar said, looking into her eyes. "I'm not always great at my job, but I appreciate the compliment." The conversation quieted—Ara had to say something quickly.

"Elrich Obarum called King Koradin 'the Ashen King.' Why?"

Adenar looked mildly surprised. She had no idea how that question popped into her mind.

"There is a story about Koradin," Adenar said. "It goes along the lines of: a village outside of Ashbourn burned to the ground and everyone died but a boy. And that boy was Koradin."

"That's it?" Ara asked.

"I guess you can add some heroism, but that's the core of the story. I don't know whether it is true or not." There was a short break before Adenar said, "Ara?"

"Yes?"

"Do you think we can stop whatever this thing is?"

Hearing Khendric and Topper's snoring while laying next to Adenar, she felt safe and dared to say, "Yes, but not the two of us alone. I think we have parts to play, but with Khendric, Topper, and Darlaene on the case, we have a fair chance."

"Good," Adenar answered. "Are you worried? About to-morrow?"

"Do you mean the 'pretending to be a cleaner' part?"

He nodded.

"Not really. I've already pretended to be a high lady, and that was without a mask. I don't think this will be too bad."

"You're very brave," he said and Ara blushed. "You risk your life to chase a shadowy assassin, you infiltrate a massive political party, and fight criminals in an alley."

His words warmed her heart. She'd never thought about it that way. She wanted to be modest, but pride swelled in her chest. "Well, you're not so bad either. I mean, you started all this and you had to do quite the amount of convincing."

He cast back a smile, and she enjoyed his company. He said it was time to sleep and Ara went to bed with her stomach full of butterflies, gnurgles, and other slithering beasts.

CHAPTER 12

One Clumsy Cook

Ara and Adenar easily slipped into the Warborn Headquarters, no questions asked. First, they snuck onto the official transport shipping cleaners to various locations and went off at the massive Warborn structure. With so much activity in the courtyard, nobody paid attention to two extra cleaners, and they snuck past everyone with their large trolley with cleaning equipment. Ara didn't know what half of it was for.

At first, they roamed free inside the building, but ultimately an important woman directed them to a large room for cleaning while waving her arms around.

"In here you go," she said, opening large doors. "Now clean. Come on. You have a lot to do today." She closed the doors behind them, her footsteps disappearing down the hall.

"This is the room," Adenar said muffled through the mask. He pointed at a window. "That is where I hid."

The room was large, with a small stage barely elevated above the rest of the floor. Except for a small throne on the stage and an elaborate chandelier, the room was empty of furniture. Adenar went over to the window and opened it.

"From here I listened to the most horrible sounds I've ever heard," he said, pointing to the cobblestoned ground beneath the window. "Steel on steel and steel on flesh. And I *heard* the terrible wounds on General Toran be inflicted."

Ara didn't quite know what to say. "Well, they cleaned the room really well at least."

Adenar frowned.

"Should we search it?" she suggested. "Maybe we'll find something useful."

"Sure," Adenar agreed. "It looks clean enough. Maybe we don't need to work so much first."

"Wait, you're going to clean?"

"Yes," he answered. "Aren't we?"

"No, we're here to infiltrate." She grinned.

"But what if they come in and we haven't cleaned anything and they see?"

"I don't know," she said. "We'll get yelled at I guess, but they won't kill us . . . right?"

"Well no. I don't think they will."

They searched the room for any trace, but it had been thoroughly cleaned. No patches of blood, no hair on the floor, nor anything else out of the ordinary.

"I need to feed on him," the voice uttered in her mind, but she didn't tell Adenar. What could they do? They were already inside the headquarters, so she kept it to herself.

* * *

Topper wore the outfit of a professional chef and had entered incredibly early in the morning with the rest of the kitchen staff. Not long after getting into the immense kitchens on the first floor, he had been put to hard work for hours. In fact, it had been so challenging he'd considered killing himself just to get out.

The Master Chefs had been on him constantly for not cutting perfect potato wedges or preparing the onions correctly. Too many herbs, too few herbs. The meat wasn't sliced in the right way, and he had burned the vegetables. Then he overcooked the meat and had to be throw it out. The Master Chefs sent him to peel potatoes before sunrise, their anger overflowing. Never had he been in such a stressful environment. He'd gladly be a beast hunter any day over this insane profession.

"You need to peel them faster," one of the Master Chefs bellowed. "We need two thousand potatoes for dinner service!"

The man was short and plump with a round face and next to no hair on his head. Topper almost threw the potato peeler into his neck, but restrained himself. Instead, he used the anger to quicken his pace. "Why do I always get these parts to play," he muttered under his breath.

Maybe Darlaene wasn't so wrong, he thought. *Maybe arrangers really are needed.*

As if she read his mind, Darlaene opened the door into the kitchens, oozing confidence. She wore light blue linen clothes, a dark vest and a large hat with a peacock feather attached.

Topper sighed, knowing what was coming. Darlaene put her hands to her waist. The cooks started working even faster, clearly intimidated. She spotted him and began her determined walk toward him.

"You!" she snarled. "What are you doing?"

"I'm j-just," he stuttered, trying not to get annoyed.

"You need to peel faster! And why aren't you preparing any food?" Darlaene snapped her fingers, shouting for a Master Chef. One of them scurried over, wiping a sweaty forehead.

"Yes?"

"What is this man doing?"

"Uhm—"

"Well, speak up!"

"He was slow at preparing the food. And didn't know any of the dishes. So I put him on peeling duty."

Darlaene narrowed her eyes at Topper. "Good idea. But perhaps you should give him another task. One that gets him out of the kitchen would be best, I think."

Topper raised his eyebrows. She was clever, trying to help him cover more ground.

"He can bring the food up to the feasting hall," the plump chef said, not questioning her authority at all. "We have errand boys, but I can throw him in with the bunch."

"Perfect," Darlaene said and left them both, picking on someone else. The Master Chef leaned closer to Topper.

"You're never working for me again," he said, his belly almost poking Topper's face. "I never want to see you again. You're an embarrassment to the culinary arts."

"Yeah-yeah," Topper calmly said, trying to stop himself from hurting him.

"Over there," the man motioned with his hand towards some trays. "Whenever a tray is fully loaded, bring it up to the feasting hall. Think you can do that?"

Topper looked him straight in the eyes, frowning and clenching his teeth. "Yes," he pushed through tight lips. Topper put the half-peeled potato into the batch with the fully peeled ones before heading to his new assignment.

* * *

Just as Darlaene hoped, the other arrangers approached her. They'd seen—or probably heard—her display with Topper. She felt sorry for him, but it was necessary. Hopefully, running to the feasting hall would offer an opportunity to sneak away.

Four other lavish ladies strolled elegantly towards her with grim expressions. They wore hats, dresses, and lots of jewellery, with more make-up than Darlaene had used her entire life.

"Who are you?" the apparent leader asked. She was a slim, gorgeous woman. She hid her hair beneath the hat, except for two curls placed strategically down her long face.

"I'm—" Darlaene began, but the young woman raised her hand and looked away.

"I don't have time for this. I need to check on the arrangements in the hall." Then she pointedly turned and walked away.

Darlaene recognized the display—an act to place herself above her in the hierarchy. Quickly, she disappeared out the same door Topper exited with the errand boys. The other two remained with piercing eyes. "As I was saying," Darlaene said with a perfect smirk. "I am Serah Morningdew, the arranger from the Berfast Isles. I have come at the whims of Councillor Taris Hunitar. I'm here to add sprinkles of the beautiful Berfast culture, as requested by said councillor."

The arrangers narrowed their eyes, obviously not liking the competition Darlaene provided.

"We have a lot to do, ladies." Darlaene clapped her hands sharply. Shock was written all over their faces, exactly as she expected. Following the example of the previous arranger, she too walked away, leaving them in the dust. No words of complaint arose from them, and they stalked behind her, giving in to authority.

* * *

Khendric stood amongst a group of soldiers waiting for today's duties in the courtyard. The working soldiers were ending their shifts, and Khendric was only here to find out who was to guard the upper levels of the headquarters. A sergeant exited the barracks, handing out different assignments, and Khendric eavesdropped his name as he strode over.

"Remember," he said while finishing up. "Today, safety needs to be on top! Nothing can go wrong. That would be an embarrassment. And stay out of Eranna's way, she's in a ... mood." A common understanding spread among the soldiers with a chuckle.

They dispersed down various paths and into hallways, and Khendric followed a group of soldiers going to the upper levels. He had noted the name of one of the younger soldiers who looked new.

The small garrison went up some stairs, relieving soldiers from their duty along the way. Khendric took a guarding post close to the stairs and watched them leave. When they were gone, he pulled out a small knife and stuck it in his finger. On the wall, he wrote in blood "The assassin is coming." When done, he ascended the stairs to the upper level.

He didn't know where the band of soldiers had gone, though armoured footsteps clattered ahead. It would be best to get into a position and stand guard quickly. If found walking around randomly and alone, it wouldn't be long before someone asked tough questions.

Luckily, he found the young soldier from earlier. "Soldier Rhaegen," he said in his best Captain's voice.

The young man immediately saluted.

"I am here to relieve you of your duty right away." The soldier frowned. "You are needed elsewhere. Orders from Commander Hartmen."

"Commander Hartmen?" he answered, eyes growing big.

"Yes, now go to the barracks."

The soldier scrambled off. Now Khendric just had to wait.

* * *

Ara and Adenar had been sent to many different locations by many different people. She was experiencing how it was for Adenar to be everyone's assistant. It sucked. Fortunately, they'd been moved up a few levels, so perhaps they could discover something here. But for now, they'd been set to cleaning a whole hallway and it was really hard work. Ara's back ached, and her eyes were watering from the strong chemicals.

Soldiers ran up and down a nearby spiralling staircase, creating a fuss. A man in glimmering armour, perhaps a sergeant, gestured at Adenar and Ara.

"You two!" he yelled. "Follow me!"

The stern tone felt like a stone dropping into Ara's stomach. *Does he know?* Adenar dragged the trolley towards him and Ara followed.

"Leave that," the sergeant commanded. "Just bring simple cleaning equipment. Come on, hurry!"

They rushed up the stairs to the next level, finding a group of soldiers forming a perimeter. Ara and Adenar were let through along with the sergeant.

"See this?" he said, motioning for some writing on the wall. It read "The assassin is coming" in blood. "Wash this away."

Ara frowned at the writing. *Will it come back?* she wondered.

"What are you waiting for, do it now!"

Adenar quickly doused the writing with water and they began scrubbing it away. The soldiers around them kept their perimeter tight.

"Should we tell her?" one of the guards whispered. He was of the same rank as the sergeant, proven by the lines on their red cloaks.

"No," the sergeant answered. "She told me *he* had taken care of the assassin." They both disappeared through the wall of soldiers. Ara and Adenar continued removing the words in blood and Ara secretly hoped the shadowwalker would return to finish off Eranna.

* * *

Following the commotion after his writing had been found, Khendric slipped away and found the great hall where the feast was being prepared. The room was in a general state of organized chaos. Tons of people were involved, placing cutlery, pouring drinks, and setting up chairs, while cleaners washed the floor furiously.

Khendric snuck past the great hall, passing through some narrow corridors. To his relief he met no guards. In case someone wandered by, Khendric would post himself somewhere and hope he looked natural.

A barely audible wheeze reached his ears. It grew louder the further he went. He frowned when his arm began to itch where the tentacled beast had stung him. *Other people itch like this all the time? Think I'd end my life a long time ago if I had to deal with stuff like this on the daily.*

The hallway expanded into a grander, decorative space with numerous doors on each side. A huge, red carpet laid on the white marble floor. Various paintings and weapons were displayed on the walls. The light wheezing kept increasing the further he went.

Faint voices were audible through two large doors at the end of the hallway, one female and one unnaturally deep, male voice. Khendric slowly snuck up to the door to eavesdrop.

"There is no point to this," the male voice beckoned. "I don't have time for your ritual."

"It's tradition, Lord," the female answered. "You have to be there."

"Such a puny thing; a ritual for devouring food. I don't understand you." A few heavy footsteps rung through the door. "I'm not sure Ronoch can withstand much more. He is weak."

"We just need him tonight and tomorrow."

"He cannot die before tomorrow," the male voice continued. "But then he will meet his demise."

"That will suffice, Lord," she answered back. "As long as we win—"

"It is imperative that we win. I must grow stronger than I am. If we lose, then it has all been for nothing."

"The people of Ashbourn believe us," she said. "They have swallowed the rumours of war like children eating candy. It's all coming together." A silence followed. Was this Eranna? They talked about Ronoch as if he was a piece of the puzzle, rather than the playmaker. *Have we been wrong?* It was tempting to break the door down, but not knowing what was on the other side was dangerous.

"There is something in the air," the dark voice said after a short while, and Khendric considered returning to the great hall, afraid he'd been discovered. "*She* is here—somewhere close. I can feel her."

"What?" the woman asked sharply. "The girl?"

"Yes, at least I think so. I can find her once more like I did before."

"We don't have the manpower for such a bloodbath again. I'm sorry, Lord."

"Then find her," the dark voice rumbled.

Understanding the conversation was over, Khendric silently made his way back through the hallway. He heard the door opening behind him, but just snuck around the corner.

With haste he moved back to the great hall, stationing himself in a doorway without being noticed. Everyone was so busy putting up ribbons, placing dinner plates, and sweeping the floor. A woman hurriedly walked past Khendric and into the hall—Eranna. *Now I just need to figure out this Ronoch-business.*

* * *

Darlaene opened one of the many doors leading into the great feasting hall. It was enormous, housing thirteen long tables and a large stage. Countless people were busy placing all kinds of food on the tables.

From behind her entered more people with food to place, Topper amongst them, carrying overloaded plates. How he didn't trip remained a mystery.

Following Topper with her gaze, Darlaene's eyes landed on Eranna. She wore dark robes and gloves, examining the hall with her piercing eyes. Darlaene tried to look inconspicuous, pretending to inspect the nearby tables. She had no idea how well Eranna knew her arrangers, and she wasn't going to risk getting into a debate about it. She helped the errand boys spread the food selection on the incredibly long table to blend in.

Eranna scouted through the room for something, her eyes crawling past everyone.

A terrible debacle rang through the hall, the sound of plates upon plates crashing to the ground, spilling food all over the floor. Glasses broke on the marble, their contents flying into the air, and in the middle of it all stood one very wide-eyed Topper.

Oh no, Darlaene thought. He'd single-handedly been the cause of all the commotion.

Deadly silence filled the hall; all eyes on him. He stood frozen in place, waiting for someone to start yelling—he wouldn't wait long.

Eranna marched over, eyes of fury. "What have you done? You must be the clumsiest man to ever have been employed here!" Poor Topper had a *really* bad day. "Consider your employment here over as of right now. Get out!" Eranna's eyes searched the room anew, this time locking eyes with Darlaene. "You! Get over here. Everyone else, get back to work, now!"

Darlaene hurried over and bowed before Eranna.

"Get this mess cleaned up right away," she said.

"Yes, my Lady," Darlaene said, turning to the mess. She snapped her fingers at some of the errand boys to help her, but they just frowned.

"What are you doing?" Eranna asked her, voice hard. "I meant to go and find the nearest cleaning personnel. These people have other jobs to do and have no time to clean up this mess. The incompetence . . ." Eranna muttered, flurrying past Darlaene to open the nearest door to the hallways. "I don't know who hired you, but I'm going to find out."

Darlaene's heart pounded, sweat forming on her forehead. She stood proudly still and snapped her fingers for the boys to return to their jobs. Eranna burst open the doors, yelling for some poor cleaner to deal with Topper's mess.

* * *

Torn out of her deep conversation with Adenar, Ara almost jumped out of her skin as the closest doors to the feasting halls burst open.

"You two," a hard voice uttered—Eranna Carner. "Come in here!"

For a moment, Ara forgot she wore a mask and almost bolted. However, Adenar tugged at her to follow with haste into the hall. Eranna spared no time and ordered them over to a great big mess on the floor. There were broken plates *everywhere,* together with spilt food and drinks.

"Clean this up, now!" Eranna snapped. Her eyes drilled into Ara, and the fear of getting caught became all too real.

She wanted to start cleaning, but her feet froze in place.

"What are you waiting for?" Eranna asked, voice like ice.

Ara stumbled into action, clumsily falling forward and breaking another plate with her knee.

"What kind of incompetence am I surrounded by today?" Eranna roared through the hall.

Ara got up again quickly. "I'm sorry," she muttered with a meagre voice, but Eranna trampled towards her.

"I will make sure you are never hired here again." Before Ara could think, Eranna pulled the mask off of her. "I will report you to—"

Ara had no idea what to do. She ended up simply standing at attention. Eranna examined her, eyes widening. She stepped away from Ara. "Guards!" she yelled. "Arrest this girl! Now!"

Ara looked wildly around. From all sides, guards approached from the entry points of the hall.

"Arrest her now!" Eranna commanded again.

Ara spotted one guard at the far end of the hall remaining at his post. He gestured something to her, for her to stay calm. *Khendric.* The other guards seized her hands behind her back and kicked her to one knee.

"Take her to the dungeons," Eranna commanded. The guards led her away. On the way out, Ara spotted Darlaene too. They had seen what happened, luckily. The guards blindfolded and brought her down countless steps, ultimately shoving her into a cold and dank cell, seating her roughly on a chair. She was all alone in the clutches of bad people. Her body shivered as blood rushed through her veins, and a fear of being killed in a cell all alone turned very real. *How will they find out where I am?* she thought, worried. Her breathing quickened. The door of the room closed, placing her in complete darkness.

CHAPTER 13

Seeing Double

Khendric remained at his post in the doorway to the great hall, even though every instinct urged him to defend Ara. Leaving her in Eranna's clutches were dangerous, but he was pretty sure she wouldn't execute Ara right away.

Pretty sure.

She would want to interrogate her, and Khendric hoped Darlaene or Topper would rescue her quickly.

After Ara was arrested, Eranna pointedly walked towards Khendric. She snapped her fingers at him and continued past. "Follow."

Khendric hurried after her. Not to his surprise, they ended up outside the same room where he'd eavesdropped earlier.

"Stay here," Eranna said. "If anyone follows us, sound the alarm. They'll be her accomplices." She went inside the room and Khendric put his ear to the door. He could make out the muffled voices.

"I found her," Eranna said. "She was disguised as a cleaning lady. Given she was a spy, I suspect there are more inside the building. There's a red-haired arranger who I believe is the woman from the party. I will apprehend one of the cooks who looked out of place too. I'm not sure, but he might be the last beast hunter. The leader of the group." She was actually talking about Khendric, but it was natural to assume Topper's new body was the missing piece.

"Pst!" another voice sounded through the hall. Darlaene—she had followed him. Khendric crossed his arms, giving her the agreed-upon sign they had been compromised. In an eyeblink, she disappeared to his great relief.

"I will heighten the security, getting all guards on this."

"Did you place her down below?" the trembling, dark voice asked.

"I did, Lord," Eranna confirmed. "I think we should kill her—"

"You will not. I want to be near her to see what she is."

"But Lord—"

"Silence. Her death will come."

"Yes," she said.

"I will find Ronoch and meet with the girl," the dark voice said.

Eranna exited the room, walking towards the hall with Khendric towing after. When they got back to the hall, she told him to stay posted. Inside the hall, everything returned to the normal stressed atmosphere. Khendric waited for Eranna to turn the corner before quickly injecting himself with the remaining paratis serum. He sniffed up her scent and followed.

* * *

Darlaene found Topper outside of the hall and snatched him up. Together, they ventured into the dungeons in the lower levels before a horn sounded the alarm.

"I'm so sorry," Topper said. "It was impossible to balance all those plates and—"

"Let's just focus on finding Ara."

"So we're forgetting about the book?"

"I'm not sure. After we find her, maybe we can try. It depends on how freely we can move around."

They continued down stairs until they reached the bottom and went through a metal door. They were presented with cells upon cells, all empty.

"Why do the Warborn have their own dungeon like this?" Darlaene wondered.

"It's peculiar. You need some place to imprison unruly soldiers for some time, but this seems excessive."

The scream of torture that followed filled Darlaene with dread.

"Ara?" she asked.

"I don't know."

They stormed through the dungeon, finding more and more empty cells, coming to a halt where the screaming was the worst. It was a male voice, which was a relief.

"No!" it screamed. "No more, it's mine! Stop!"

Darlaene couldn't see what was happening as they had to hide due to two guards standing posted outside of the cell.

"Please, no more! Dark, dark, dark and red."

"What do we do?" Darlaene asked.

"It's not Ara," Topper said. "Let's see what happens. Do you have a weapon?"

Darlaene lifted her dress and revealed a concealed dagger.

"Good," Topper said. "We might have to kill them. I think we have grounds to do so."

"It's torture," Darlaene said.

After a short time, the screaming stopped. The metal door to the cell unlocked and opened. Out came a man they both recognized immediately.

"Ronoch?" They whispered in unison. The guards snapped to attention.

"See to it that he does not die," Ronoch said before moving on, disappearing down the other side of the hallway. One of the guards produced a bag of blood and they both went inside.

"We have to check this out," Darlaene said, and Topper nodded.

They slowly approached the open cell, reaching either side of the door. Darlaene snuck her head around the corner.

A pale man laid on the floor with a syringe in his arm. Blood flowed from the bag into the man's vein. She couldn't get a good look at him, as the guards obscured her view. The cell was filled with all kinds of fresh food and drink stacked up against the walls. Topper signed that they should take the guards out. Darlaene nodded, feeling her heartbeat quicken.

"Just incapacitate them," he mouthed and counted down on his fingers.

The first guard turned towards them surprised, meeting Topper's booted foot. He crashed to the ground, but his comrade was quick on his feet and jumped up, back against the wall with an unsheathed sword.

"Intruders!" he roared.

Topper went at him to shut him up, but the soldier turned his sword in time to ward him off. It gave Darlaene a window to lunge forward. She took no chances and plunged her dagger into the man's throat. Blood spurted from the wound as he gurgled horribly. Darlaene drove her dagger through his heart, ending his suffering. Topper lifted the head of the other soldier to find him knocked out.

"Lucky guy," Darlaene said.

"Yeah, not as lucky as that guy." Topper pointed to the dead guard.

"He shouldn't have screamed."

Examining the tortured man, they were stunned. On the floor before them laid an unconscious, pale Ronoch.

"Some kind of shapeshifter then?" Darlaene suggested.

"Fuelled by blood," Topper said. "Or that's my best guess."

"We have to bring him with us," she said. "He can tell us so much."

"I agree." Topper lifted the blood bag and smacked him hard on the cheek a few times. His eyes opened slowly.

"No," he muttered. "No more . . . I just want to die."

"We're here to get you out," Topper said, hoisting him up, and handing him to Darlaene.

"We have to get going," Darlaene prodded.

"We need to change attire," Topper said, undressing the unconscious guard as quickly as he could.

Ronoch started pathetically slapping Darlaene. "Tendrils, I hate them . . . everywhere, they go."

"We'll get you out," Topper said, and Darlaene sat Ronoch down against the cell door, awkwardly changing into the male guard's too-large uniform. After what felt like too long, they could pass for Warborn guards.

Reluctantly, the real Ronoch was led out of the cell. "They force the food down my throat," he said, eyes wild at being brought into the hallway. "Until I can take no more. All he wants is my blood."

She snapped her fingers in front of Ronoch's eyes. "Who is *he?*"

"The dark monster," he answered. "Big and black. He is darkness!" he screamed.

"We have to get going," Topper said. He put a bag found in the cell over Ronoch's head.

* * *

Someone entered Ara's cell. A strong presence unlike anything she'd ever felt had pressed on her mind from outside the door, but now it entered. Vague light became visible through the fabric of her hood, probably from a lantern. It was pulled off her head, and before her stood Ronoch Steelbane. He gazed down at her with a look of deep interest, his eyes meticulously studying her. He towered over her, the light of the lantern somewhat cloaking his features.

He wore a red vest, with a black linen shirt beneath. On a chain around his torso hung the black book.

"Finally, I have found you," he said.

Ara flinched beneath his dark voice and intense eyes.

He looked at her with wonder and desperation, his eyes piercing her. "I have felt you. Not like I feel my own people of old, but I *have* felt your presence in my city. Have you felt me too? You must have. I have *wanted* you to feel me, to sense how truly powerful I am. I have yearned for someone to feel my presence." Ronoch ran his finger calmly over Ara's cheek, then into her mouth. She jerked away and he retracted his finger.

"How did I create you?" he asked and leaned closer, smelling her face, his lips an inch away. Ara writhed in her chair. "You must answer me, child."

"I don't know what you're talking about," Ara whispered.

"What are you," Ronoch asked rhetorically, sniffing her skin. He turned to her arm and ripped off the clothing covering her veins. His eyes lit up like a starved carnivore finding prey. "There it is . . . my imprint on you."

Ara considered breaking the chains that arrested her to grab him, but she had no idea what he was. Ronoch was definitely not human.

"How did I create you?" he asked again, calmly.

Ara didn't know nor wanted to answer. The pressure he left on her mind was intense and oppressive.

"I felt you enter the city," Ronoch went on. "So it must have been my minions that gave you my gift. You survived them, didn't you?"

He gently punctured a vein on her arm with his nail. Ara didn't react, doing her best not to seem intimidated.

She couldn't keep a straight face when he licked her arm, tasting her blood. She fought not to move, but it was disgusting, feeling his spit on her skin. "I can taste my venom running through your veins, little one." He stood back up, looking down upon her. "Could I control you as I will control them? You could achieve great things. But you are also dangerous." He grabbed her arm. "For you to have even a fraction of my power is a threat."

Ara flinched under his tight grip.

"I believe you must meet your death." Ronoch faced away from her. "Though you are of great interest to me, you are also a liability."

"What are you?" Ara asked, voice shaking. Dark smoke churned around his hand. It looked like a trick to the eye in the dim light. Darkness coalesced around—

The door to the room burst open, and Eranna stormed in. "They got him!" she exclaimed, Ronoch snapping his head towards her. "They got Ronoch."

Before Ara could blink, Ronoch left the room. Ara remained with Eranna and the four guards posted outside. Every muscle in Ara's body wanted to break her bonds and grab the woman, but she couldn't deal with all the guards herself. Eranna looked at her with pure hatred, before marching out of the room.

"Kill her," she casually told the guards.

Ara's heart pounded in her chest as the two guards turned toward her. Their eyes were dark, almost invisible under the helmets in the dim light. One unsheathed a dagger and walked toward Ara.

In a mighty yank, she snapped her chains with her arm and grabbed the man's hand, tightening so hard she heard the crunch of bones. He bellowed in pain and dropped the dagger. Ara picked it up with haste and pointed it at them. The three remaining soldiers drew their swords, but didn't attack, keeping their distance while getting their wounded man back on his feet.

"Kill her!" he roared, clutching his broken wrist. The soldiers didn't advance. "You have swords and she a butter knife! Go!"

The sound of metal entering flesh came next and a sword protruded through the wounded soldier's chest. He fell to the ground when the sword retracted. Behind him stood Khendric, who quickly advanced on the others, swinging his blade at them. They barely had time to turn before he assaulted them with a flurry of quick stabs. In the chaos, Ara broke the last chain and dashed to one of the soldiers, plunging her dagger through his chainmail with all her force. He flew into the others—one skewering himself on Khendric's blade, but the last one managed to keep his balance. He got his guard back up to block Khendric's quick blow.

Ara picked up a sword and swung it down upon the soldier's shield. He didn't expect the enormous force behind her attack and let out a scream as his shoulder jerked downward. Khendric seized the opportunity, ramming his blade into the man's heart. He slumped to the ground.

"You ok?" Khendric asked.

"Yes," she answered, panting. "How did you find me?"

"The paratis serum let me follow Eranna undetected, and she led me here."

"Thank the stonepudders. Ronoch is not what he seems. I don't know what he is, but he is not human."

"We'll get to the bottom of this later. We have to go."

"No!" Ara protested. "He has the book. He's wearing it around his torso on a chain."

"We've been exposed. We have to get out."

"Khendric," she said, voice steady. "There is something wrong here, something grave. Ronoch is . . . I don't know, but we have to stop him. We have to get that book."

Khendric considered her words. "Listen, we'll try, but as quickly as we see it becomes too hard, we flee, agreed?"

"Agreed," she answered without hesitation.

* * *

Darlaene and Topper escorted their gagged prisoner up the stairs leading to the first level of the headquarters. According to Darlaene's estimations, this entrance should be nearest to one of the exits to the courtyard. She'd also thought about using the back door that Adenar had talked about, but she was uncertain as to where it was and didn't want to risk everything by searching blindly.

She was hoping there was a lot of commotion upstairs, making it possible for them to escape unnoticed, but it was a slim hope. Two guards walking a hooded prisoner away from the building was suspicious, but he was too valuable not to give it a shot.

Slowly, she pushed the door open. Guards searched all the people who had been there to make the feast ready. Patrols ran through other corridors, only seen in glimpses as they passed by pillars. Captains screamed commands from all directions, and the commotion made by countless soldiers hurriedly running back and forth with steel boots reverberated through the air. There was a lot of stuff going on, which greatly increased their chances. Sounds of padded footsteps also became audible from the dungeon beneath them.

"We have to go now," Topper said.

She nodded, and took a moment to adapt her best pompous look, throwing her shoulders back and chest puffed out. They stepped into the hallway. It wasn't a long walk to the gates, but the hallway teemed with soldiers and commoners all trying to either do their job or get away unscathed.

"Move aside," Topper commanded two florists and pushed them to the wall.

Nobody stopped them, but they hadn't passed any guards either. The gate entrance was ahead, but Ronoch squeaked a lot through his gag and moved erratically. Topper kept pushing them past people, some of who offered discomforting looks.

They neared the gate, but they had to pass through the huge courtyard too. The knot in Darlaene's stomach tightened. Her worst nightmare came to pass when a high ranking officer walked past, noticed them, and stopped.

"What are you doing?" he asked, voice quick and hard.

Topper didn't break stride. "We are taking this prisoner to—"

"Prisoner?" the officer said and frowned. He grabbed the hood on Ronoch's head and pulled it off. "Here!" he bellowed, "Ronoch—"

Darlaene and Topper each planted a foot in the man's armoured chest, sending him tumbling down the stairs behind him. They took off running in the same direction.

"Damn it!" Topper said as the guards began shouting. An arrow ricocheted off of one of the marbled steps, almost taking Darlaene in the foot.

"Only fire with a clean shot!" someone yelled. "You could hit him!"

Darlaene and Topper made their way quickly towards the outer gate. The going was easier out in the empty courtyard, but Ronoch slowed them down. It sounded like the guards had trouble organizing with all the people inside the headquarters. *We might actually make it,* Darlaene thought, but they would need to flee further before the Warborn soldiers dropped pursuit.

"Fire!" a hard voice protruded through the general buzz. "Don't let them get away."

Darlaene briefly turned her head to discover a wave of soldiers pursuing them and gaining. Multiple arrows flew, just barely missing. A thud followed, and Ronoch became a lot harder to move forward. An arrow stood from Topper's back and he crashed to the ground, lifeless. Alone, she hadn't the strength to push the unyielding Ronoch forward.

The soldiers caught up, the gate closing ahead, effectively trapping her inside. In a flash, she turned, raising her dagger to Ronoch's throat. "Don't come any closer!" she roared. "Or he's dead."

The soldiers did not approach her further, instead encircling her. Darlaene scanned the area for opportunities, but she was running out of options.

* * *

Ara and Khendric entered on the first level, in a hallway close to the feasting hall. She was determined to find the book, but the building crawled with guards.

"He must not die yet," the voice in her head said, but she pushed it away. Ara had been worried by the things the faux-Ronoch had said. Stopping him was of utmost importance. They *needed* that book.

"If I say that we're making a break for it," Khendric said. "We are, alright? I can't have you disobeying me."

Ara gave him a stern look, but nodded.

"Good. It's better to come back and fight another day." He scouted the hall. "Too many people running about. We need another way. Follow me." He opened a door leading into a hallway covered with a large red carpet.

"We have him," the voice said, making Ara flinch slightly.

"The voice in my head is very talkative at the moment. I think it's Ronoch."

"What do you mean?"

"I mean the words that I occasionally hear, are some of Ronoch's spoken words, or so I believe. I think we are connected. He spoke as if he had created me and wondered what I was."

Khendric frowned. "Then I wonder what he is? And how that all ties together with the tentacled beast from Cornstead?"

"He said something about minions," she remembered. "I think we really need that book."

"She's alive," the voice said.

"I think he knows I'm free."

"How?"

"He said we were connected somehow, but he seemed as perplexed as I am about it. We need to hurry."

His ominous presence dominated her mind, making it hard to focus. They hurriedly walked through the hallway and up one floor. Luckily, the place was void of guards. They came to a large windowed door leading to a gigantic outside terrace with lots of soldiers. They must be close to the feasting hall still—she could smell the food.

Where is Adenar? Was he still inside the feasting hall? In case he was, she should probably go and get him.

"They are too many," Khendric said, interrupting her trail of thought. Ara looked through the windows; the soldiers all faced away from them. The terrace faced out towards the courtyard and the city. Ara easily spotted Ronoch, both with her eyes and the pressure on her mind. He stood in the centre of the mass with Eranna by his side.

"He's there," she said, pointing.

"I can see that," he answered. "But how are we going to get the book?"

"You're wearing the correct armour. Just walk up behind them and blend in. Then snatch it off his person and take off running. None of these guards can keep up with you."

He let out a sharp breath and examined the scene again. "That will never work."

"Intruders!" yelled a soldier who had spotted them through the window. In an instant, Ronoch turned his head sharply and stared into her eyes.

Ara froze.

Ronoch said something inaudible and Eranna turned as well. *Her* voice was clear as day.

"Guards!" she yelled. "Get her!"

The small army of soldiers moved. Khendric locked the door with haste, unsheathed his blade, and pulled Ara with him back the way they had come. They didn't get far before the sound of padded footsteps met them. Guards were rushing up the stairs.

"Get back!" he yelled to Ara and they pulled back towards the terrace. "We'll go through the feasting hall!" They reached the terrace door and pressed on to the feasting hall. They blasted through the doors, scaring the regular people still inside. They did not get far before they stood face to face with soldiers once more.

"Go back again!" Khendric ordered her and they ran back as quickly as their legs would carry them.

"What do we do?" Ara said, looking desperately at Khendric. He was staring out the window facing the terrace. Outside, a perimeter of guards had formed around the door. Ronoch stood in the centre, a challenging look on his face, blade in hand. Khendric scouted all possible routes, but soldiers were approaching rapidly.

"I guess we're going outside," he said and opened the door, stepping into what felt like certain death. The guards stood their ground, menacingly surrounding them, and Ara had never felt this small.

"It is a shame I cannot let you live," Ronoch said to her, looking regal in his robe. The soldiers pointed axes, spears, hammers, and swords at them, but no bows. "You are a danger," Ronoch continued. "However, I am most interested to see what you can do, before you meet your demise."

"How very poetic of you," Khendric said. Ronoch's oppressive gaze fell upon him, but Khendric seemed rather unaffected.

"Puny human," Ronoch answered back. "You are of no interest to me."

"What are you?" Khendric shouted back.

For what seemed like an eternity, Ronoch did not answer. Eranna's eyes darted back and forth between Ronoch and Khendric, her jaw clenched.

"I am what will bring this city greatness," Ronoch said. "With the eternal night comes Ashbourn's destruction and renewal. Sadly, you will not see it."

"I bet neither will you," Khendric snapped back.

A bemused look dawned on Ronoch's face and a sly smile spread across his lips. "You are brave . . . or stupid."

"Let's fight," Khendric demanded. "You and me. No need for any of your soldiers to die."

"I have not fought in many lifetimes," Ronoch replied. "I must admit, it is tempting." Ronoch caressed his sword. "But it would be foolish of me. If you are as skilled a warrior as you present yourself to be, I would honour your calling with a blood oath. But I cannot yet—first, I must win the coronation. If the right hand of fate had not put you here in front of me prematurely, I would have accepted."

"Coward," Khendric said.

Ronoch uttered a short mocking laugh. "You are a mouse taunting a giant, a brave mouse, but a mouse nonetheless. Kill them."

The guards advanced towards Khendric and Ara, but like a spring, he burst into motion, lunging at the nearest guard holding an enormous two-handed battle-axe. He skewered the man with his blade, catching the axe before it hit the floor. The other men fell a step back in response, dragging their wounded soldier away. Khendric lobbed the large axe toward Ara, and she grabbed the large weapon. To her, it weighed almost nothing. Khendric got back to back with her and held his sword warningly against approaching soldiers.

"Time to see what that arm can do," he said.

She'd never realized how dangerous such a weapon would be in her hands. She grabbed it by the hilt the same way she would hold a sword. It looked ridiculous, but the soldiers looked confused. Ronoch studied her too, a deep intense stare and a smile curling upon his lips.

The guards stepped too close; Ara readied a swing. With ease, she moved the large battle-axe like a knife. Three guards were within her reach. The first one was cut in half as her axe passed through him, pushing the second man into the last one. Blood and guts flew in all directions as the axe embedded itself into a skull. She pulled it free with a sickening crunch, trying to stomach how much of a macabre destructive force she could be.

Behind her, Khendric spun into action, but she concentrated on her part of the fight. She swung the axe in the opposite direction stepping forward, reaching a new set of guards. The first soldier to meet the incredible force of her weapon raised his shield in vain. The shield hit him like a battering ram, tumbling the adjacent soldiers with him. The axe dented and bent, and she hoped it had one more swing in it, as Ara had to continue the brutality.

If one soldier got past her mighty defence, she'd be dead. But they actually feared her, none daring to advance on her. She could see it in their eyes. *Good*, she thought. If they understood that only her arm was enhanced, they could quickly counter her.

She dashed at a soldier with a battle-hammer, but he stepped back. Yet Ara was too quick, flinging her rapidly deteriorating axe in all directions. Soldiers were sent flying around her as it slammed into foe upon foe, breaking bones and shattering flesh. Her axe was a mere metal pole by now, but remained quite destructive. The great battle-hammer laid before her. In the wake of her onslaught, she picked it up. Their eyes were terrified, but they held their ground.

"Ara!" Khendric yelled. "Some help?"

Khendric fended off three guards, with more converging on him.

With an upwards swing, she sent an approaching soldier flying into the air. The sound alone boomed in her ears. Her mighty weapon came down on another foe, crushing him like a crab under a rock. The soldiers around Khendric retreated.

"Thanks," he said through breaths. He bled from his thigh and shoulder, but the wounds were already closing.

"Come on!" Eranna roared, voice desperate. "What are you waiting for, kill them!"

None of the guards approached.

Khendric got back to back with her again. "You're doing better than I expected," he said.

Ara could practically hear his smile. "I've impressed even myself."

"I'm not sure we're going to get out of this, but at least we're giving them a good fight."

She believed they could escape, but the sheer magnitude of soldiers surrounding them was daunting.

"How are you doing?" he asked.

"Good enough," Ara said. Though she was breathing heavily, the feeling of power was incredible.

"Good," Khendric said.

Troops charged, and Ara threw the hammer around, crushing bodies and breaking metal, sending soldier upon soldier flying into the air. Some fell over the fence of the terrace, others through windows or into walls. Swinging upwards, she crushed a man's jaw. Her hammer came around for a swing into another's side; his body broke. Using the head of the hammer, she pushed it into a charging soldier's chest, crushing his sternum. Strike upon strike connected with metal or flesh, and gut-wrenching sounds filled the air. "Switch with me!" Khendric roared as he had trouble keeping them off.

They flipped sides in a blink. With all her force, Ara devastated the men who were too close with a swing of untold might. Their bodies crashed into other soldiers. The floor turned red and slippery, moans of pain ringing through the air. Ara had to not think of the terrible things she was doing, instead trying to think she was defending her and Khendric's lives. Together, they continued to fend off the attackers as long as their breaths held, not giving them any chance to advance.

"Step back!" Ronoch bellowed.

The soldiers stopped. Both Ara and Khendric turned to gaze at him. He looked confident still.

"You are great warriors," Ronoch said. "You fight with passion for life. Had I been stronger, I would grant you the chance to become my new rosh'gar. But at this time, you must still die." He unbuttoned his robe and removed the chain with the book around his torso.

"What are you doing?" Eranna asked as she was handed the book. "You cannot do this, what if—"

"Silence," Ronoch commanded, eyes locked on Ara.

To Ara's shock, Eranna grabbed Ronoch's arm. "I'm begging you, Lord," she said, but Ronoch shrugged her hand off.

"I have not fought in a long time," he said, striding towards them.

Khendric stepped defensively in front of Ara and raised his sword. "It's you and me."

"Then you will surely die," Ronoch answered calmly. "But I respect your courage, little healer. Your regenerative powers won't be enough."

Ara came up to Khendric's side and readied her hammer.

"He's right," she said. "I appreciate the gesture, Khendric. But surely our chances are better together."

Ara actually felt confident they could take him on. Perhaps Ronoch was as strong too, but she'd just have to wait and see.

Ronoch sniffed the air like a hound. "What's that?" he asked Khendric, who still had his sword pointed against him. Ronoch gestured to where the wound from the tentacled beast had been on Khendric's forearm. "I see. You have felt my touch too."

Without warning, Ronoch advanced lightning-quick at Khendric and easily pushed his sword aside with his own. Ara leapt towards him, but Ronoch extended a foot and kicked her in the thigh, stopping her momentum completely. Khendric let out a roar as Ronoch grabbed his arm and tightened. The skin on his arm tore open and blood sprayed on Ronoch's face. He stepped back, licking his bloody lips. Khendric clutched his forearm as it healed. In a sickening display, Ronoch tasted his blood.

"Ah, Khendric," he said, a devious smile spreading across his lips. "What a childhood you had. Do you miss your parents?"

Khendric's eyes turned sharply on Ronoch, his jaw tightening.

"Have you seen them lately?" Ronoch continued to press. "Any hallucinations perhaps?"

Khendric's face turned molten.

"Had you only been able to protect them . . ."

That was the last drop for Khendric, and he lashed forward, hate and anger fuelling him. He slashed his sword viciously at Ronoch, but the man parried or dodged every single blow with ease. Ara charged with her battle-hammer, but he sidestepped her swing, placing himself so Ara clumsily obstructed Khendric from advancing. Khendric pushed her aside, keeping his fury and swings overly aggressive. Ronoch dodged his attack, and jabbed his sword through Khendric's arm and kneed him in the face. Khendric fell backwards, but

Ronoch stopped his attack due to Ara's large hammer almost crushing the back of his head. Khendric got back up, arm and face already healed. He panted heavily, but looked calmer.

"Feeling better?" Ara asked.

"Yeah. It just took 'almost dying' for me to realize how foolishly I'm fighting." Ronoch stared at them, not even slightly out of breath.

"Don't you wish you could have protected them?" he goaded.

"Don't let him get to you," Ara said.

"Do not speak of them! You damn monster!"

"They certainly wished you could," he continued. "But you were too weak."

Khendric threw caution to the wind, renewing his relentless swings. Ara did her best to assist him, but Khendric fought solo.

* * *

If there was one person everyone seemed to have forgotten about, it was Adenar. He had stayed in the feasting hall through everything, even after Ara's arrest. He stood with all the regular people on a large terrace, looking at Ara and Khendric fight Ronoch. Naturally, everybody wanted a look at the ongoing duel, and they found it exciting, but Adenar found it terrifying. He caught glimpses of the fight through the thick of soldiers, and they were both currently alive. Sweat poured down his forehead, thankfully the mask hid it.

He was tempted to join the fight, but he had no experience—and no weapon. Even though he felt like a coward, it was probably best he stayed back.

From what he could see, Ara and Khendric fought Ronoch with all their might, but the man danced around them. Ara had been spectacular and really, *really* frightening, single-handedly knocking people several feet away, killing countless foes.

But what can I do? he thought to himself, trying to look for any way to assist. When he tore his eyes away from the fight, he spotted someone standing outside the group of soldiers. Eranna clutched . . . a book. That had to be *the* book. She shivered even more than Adenar, eyes locked on the fight.

Adenar subconsciously tightened his hands around his broom. Would he go as far as violence? Eranna hadn't really done anything personally to him, except *maybe* setting a lot of criminals on him and his mother, but he had no proof of that. *Hold on. I am really debating whether it is morally correct or not to inflict physical pain on Eranna?*

With a knot tightening in his stomach, he walked slowly towards her, with no protests coming from behind.

Eranna kept on staring at the duel, and with the cheers of the soldiers, she did not notice his approach from the side. The broom was in range, and he clutched it tightly, stilling his stomach as best he could.

The hard piece of wood crashed into her face, cracking on impact, throwing her to the ground.

The book launched into the air and Adenar rushed to pick it up as it landed. Without giving his surrounding another glance, he ran as quickly as his feet could carry him. He went towards one of the empty exits on the other side of the terrace. He couldn't believe it had worked, it had actually worked!

"The book!" Eranna shouted. "The cleaner stole the book!"

Adenar kept his quick pace down into a hallway. There were a few people here, but no guards. Nobody intervened as he passed them. Countless shouts grew audible behind him from guards however. Running in the voluminous cleaner's outfit wasn't easy, but it beat running in plated armour.

He came out on an empty terrace with multiple braziers burning. He removed the vest with haste and tossed it in the fire. Multiple footsteps and shouts approached. Removing the pants took too long, but getting out of the outfit meant he could blend with the crowd.

The pants came off, but there was no chance for him to cross the rest of the terrace before being noticed. He gazed over the ledge of the terrace—only one floor above ground level, and there was a tent to land on. People wandered back and forth, but no guards.

The pursuing soldiers were too close for any more consideration. He jumped feet first and landed on the tent, collapsing it. Despite almost twisting his ankle, it made for a decent landing pad. He shot to his feet to find three people staring at him; two older women and a plump man.

"Good day," he said. "I tire of the party." Without waiting for their response, he walked hurriedly away. They said nothing. It wasn't easy to stay calm, but he did his best. Guards ran across the terrace above him, but none shouted for him to stop.

* * *

Ara and Khendric had been left virtually alone, just a few soldiers left. She was still baffled that Ronoch took off with the rest of the small army, as a cleaner had run away with the book. It had to have been Adenar. Except for the few soldiers still standing, the terrace had turned into a place of death. Blood seeped from slits in the armour of so many dead, and the gravity of her power revealed itself. She was dangerous and capable of a lot, and she hoped this wouldn't haunt her. She held her hammer up warningly against the remaining soldiers.

"That book must *really* be important," Khendric said. "I hope he gets away."

Ara's throat closed at the thought of Adenar being caught, killed or worse . . . tortured. *Please get away,* she begged. He was among the kindest persons she'd ever met.

"We have to follow them," she whispered to Khendric.

"We're leaving." He walked right towards the few soldiers. Ara followed close behind, ready to fight, despite breathing heavily. Khendric didn't raise his sword, and still, the soldiers parted like fish fleeing from an octinara. They bore resentment, but still scattered.

Amazing, Ara thought.

Khendric started jogging. The soldiers gave no chase. They ran down a large flight of stairs on the opposite side of the terrace Adenar had fled through. Ara feared more soldiers—or even Ronoch—but none stood in their way. They entered a courtyard, where two dozen regular people tried leaving through the gate. A couple of guards inspected them, but that was it. Shouts came from behind them, screaming to find the cleaner. *Why are there not more guards here?* Ara thought. *This is the main entrance.*

Khendric pushed through the people and Ara followed in his wake, dropping the hammer in the crowd. They approached the guards, which told Khendric to stop. In an eyeblink, Khendric struck the man in the throat and pushed him towards the other armoured man. They crashed to the ground.

The commoners, with Khendric and Ara, flowed through the gate. Ara spotted a young man with a book in hand and blond hair that looked familiar—Adenar! In the small mass of people, he also blended in as one of the bystanders, and she grabbed him by the arm

"You're alive?" he asked. "I'm alive!"

"We have to go," Khendric said. "Now. Have you seen Darlaene or Topper?"

"No," Adenar said.

Khendric adopted a grim expression and gave the large structure behind them one last glance. "They probably made it out," he said. "Let's move." Something dark hid behind his eyes. She felt it, like a dam built in a hurry, ready to cave in to immense pressure.

They blended with the people a short distance before shooting out into a smaller alleyway heading back towards the hideout.

"How did you know to take us out the front entrance?" Ara asked Khendric.

"I took a chance."

"A chance?"

A short silence followed. "There are so many other places and ways to exit the headquarters. I hoped they'd think that's where we would go, instead of leaving out the main entrance. Also, I heard a lot more commotion from behind us than in front of us. We got lucky."

The mood turned sombre. Both Ara and Adenar had trouble keeping Khendric's pace, but he didn't seem to notice.

They had escaped. She was alive, despite the circumstances. It all felt surreal. She hoped Darlaene and Topper were safe too. No one spoke during their long trek back. They were all tired.

CHAPTER 14

The Coronation of Damnation

Except for Viessa and Olenna, Ara found the hideout empty, grinding her teeth as she wondered where Darlaene and Topper could be. Khendric tightened his hands, vibrating with anger. Night had come and gone, and dawn approached. Ara's muscles ached, and her eyes almost fell shut. Adenar yawned constantly, and Olenna slept soundly, still recovering, but Adenar's mother was awake and embraced her son.

"They're probably alright," Ara said, walking closer to Khendric.

He rubbed his hands against his forehead. "You're probably right. She's gotten out of worse situations. It's the waiting that kills me."

Adenar put the book on the table. "We actually made it, though."

It didn't feel like a victory, not without all members there. She wasn't afraid for Topper, he'd always be back, but for Darlaene. Sure, she was magnificent, but as far as Ara knew, she lacked abilities like Khendric, Topper, or even herself. "You're right," Ara said. "Even Ronoch turned from the fight to get this book. It should shed some light in the darkness."

"We actually need to get reading too," Khendric reminded them. "The coronation is tomorrow, or today, I guess."

"I'll let you work, and I'll look after Viessa," Olenna said, leaving them alone.

The title of the book was 'The Dark Traitor.' Ara opened it and began to read out loud . . .

>**The Dark Traitor** *was written by the only literate voreen and edited to make it readable by her only friend, Avina.*
>
>**Editor's note:** *I(Avina) managed to befriend a female voreen named Vho'rha over four months. I taught her the basics of reading and writing. She wrote this book, which is of vital importance to mankind if the horrors I have lived ever resurface again. For writing this book and befriending me, Vho'rha was banished from her people and had to defend us in countless duels so we could live. Vho'rha gave her life in the ultimate sacrifice for this book. Through some voreen magic, she made it near indestructible, providing it with a way to survive in perpetuity. My hopes and dreams are that one copy will someday be found in every library. This is Vho'rha's gift to us.*
>
>*I, Vho'rha, write this book because I must. I've seen the destructive ways of my kind, and I only realized it too late. Though I despise humans, I see my race will not survive for long. Voreens are too violent. I have murdered thirty-four of my own—for rituals, vengeance, and any other possible reason. Humans are kinder, I have seen that. Perhaps they deserve this book, perhaps not, but I have decided to write it.*

> *My people worship our ancient god. We fight and die for him. He gave us life and endless lust for blood. This book tells how to defeat him. Within these pages lies the secrets you need. How my god works and why he must be destroyed.*
>
> *He is a god of followers. This is important. His power grows as the number of people worshipping him increases. This god's name is Chronor, The Breaker of Wills.*

Ara looked up at Khendric and Adenar with big, round eyes. Khendric returned the look.

"Are . . . are we fighting an ancient voreen god?" she asked. Absolute silence.

"I must say," Khendric began, "if so, that is *not* what I expected."

"What did the book mean by 'god of followers'?" Adenar asked, swallowing dryly.

"Uhm," Ara said. "The more people who worship him, the more powerful he becomes?"

"And we're talking about Ronoch here, right?" Adenar asked.

"I think so," Ara answered. "Khendric, you suggested he is a shapeshifter, somehow, right? The book probably says how he does it."

"Think!" Adenar said sharply. "We're talking about Ronoch, the guy that might very well be chosen to be the next King of Ashbourn. The people are loyal in this city. They will get behind whoever is chosen. How much power do you think that will give him?"

Khendric and Ara shared a look, before the older beast hunter grabbed the book. "Somewhere it must say how to kill him," he said, sifting through the pages. "Look here." He put the book down on the table so all three could read.

Summoning and Killing Chronor

I will write down the ingredients to summon Chronor, but not how to perform the ritual, for obvious reasons. I do this to help reveal signs someone is calling forth this terrible god. To summon Chronor into this realm, you need:

- *The blood of a hundred souls*
- *The heart of a bear*
- *The heart of a wretcher*
- *Twenty wretcher's talons*
- *Two Varghaul eyes*
- *The ribcage of a boulderbeast*
- *The tentacles of an octinara*
- *A thousand rura scales*
- *A trollman skull*
- *Ten shadestones*
- *The wings of a Gorewing*
- *Eight tentacles of a corpsewalker*

All eyes met once more, pieces of the puzzle falling into place.

"The blood of a hundred souls," Khendric said. "That must have been the people I found in Ronoch's basement being dissolved!"

"Eranna has been clever too," Ara continued. "Who would miss a bunch of homeless people? She is 'the Dark Lady.' Those poor men were murdered and drained of blood to bring forth this Chronor creature."

Khendric looked down on the ingredient list once more. "A trollman skull. Damn. I should have picked up on that before. When we first entered Ashbourn I went to my favourite sparring club, 'The Troublesome Sailor'. A skull used to hang on the wall, but now it's gone. The owner told me someone came and forced him to give it up."

"And when we were at the beast hunter store," Ara began, "they were out of wretcher's talons, probably because they're needed to summon him. How long does it take to get new ones?"

"A long time," Khendric told her. "Chronor must have been summoned a long time ago. Getting a new supply of twenty wretcher's talons back into the city would take a year at least. They're big, bad, and mean to kill, meaning their claws have a high market value."

"So that checks out too," Ara confirmed. "I really think this is what we're up against."

"So," Adenar said. "How do we beat this . . . Chronor?"

Their heads turned back to the book.

> *Chronor is a god with one goal: To become the world's sole dominator. He is a tyrant that wishes to enslave all others. To achieve this he has many tactics, cruel ones that will twist the minds of men to his will as his powers grow. He operates in seven phases, each more powerful than its predecessor. As he gains devoted followers, he will progress through these levels.*
>
> *Phase one:*
>
> *When Chronor is first summoned he is in his first phase. He has thick grey skin, like all voreen, but stands a head taller than most of us. The key difference separating him from us is his ability to summon his deadly voreen blade: Shraz'tah. (Editor's note: I(Avina) think the best translation for this is: The Souleater.)*
>
> *Phase two:*
>
> *Somewhere around a hundred followers, he reaches his next stage. From his shoulders, a dark, looming smoke will emanate, and his eyes glow with a red fire. Tentacles grow forth on his left forearm, clutching around his hand. These give him a mighty grip, but ultimately serve a more sinister purpose. The big change in this*

phase is that he gains the ability of 'blood transfor-
mation.' Chronor can inject his tentacles into someone's
flesh and drink their blood. Doing so will earn him their
appearance for a time, before reverting back to his darker
self.

"So," Ara said, "when we met Ronoch, that wasn't the real Ronoch? It was Chronor that had drawn his blood?"

"It must have been," Khendric agreed.

"When I was in the cell," she said. "Being interrogated by . . . him, we were interrupted by Eranna storming in saying 'they got Ronoch.' I didn't think much about it at the time, but Darlaene and Topper must have kidnapped the real Ronoch, because Chronor was gone the very next moment." Khendric's expression darkened.

Adenar said, "Because if they kidnapped the real Ronoch, he wouldn't have had any blood to use to transform again. It would destroy their whole scheme, as all of the Chosen have to meet in person later today at Castle Square for the announcement."

"That makes sense," Ara agreed. "If they got out with him, we've already won."

"Then why aren't they back?" Khendric asked sternly.

Ara thought for a moment. "Perhaps for safety. In case someone followed us back here or the Warborn know of this hideout. The fact we're not seeing them here could be a good sign."

"But it could also be a bad one," Khendric retorted.

"Yes, it could," she yielded

"Guys," Adenar said. "These tentacles that the book mentioned. It said Chronor uses them to 'inject' into people. That must have been what happened to General Toran. Remember those weird wounds that looked like holes?"

"I guess we know for sure then," Ara said. "General Toran was against the summoning of Chronor and finally decided to go against his beloved Warborn Party."

"I wonder when he was summoned," Khendric said. "It must have been way before we ever entered Ashbourn."

"It's hard to say when, I guess," Ara said. "We should read on."

> Chronor is immensely strong and skilled with his deadly blade. I recommend not using the weak swords humans fight with. He will chop them in half with one swing. But he can still die from regular mortal wounds.
>
> *Phase three:*
>
> The third phase occurs around three thousand followers. When reaching this phase, Chronor's appearance continues to change. Horns grow out of his forehead and smaller spikes grow from his chin. Darkness looms around him. Typically, the vermin population will grow in the area. Look for an increase in packs of rats, rabdogs, heartflies, narworms and so on. This can be an indicator Chronor has been summoned.
>
> There is another peculiar thing happening with some men when Chronor reaches this stage. My people, the voreen, have a natural evil within ourselves. My contempt for humans is strong, but I cannot fathom where it originates from. I think it is because of this, that we do not feel the effect Chronor have on our minds. Chronor's mere presence, over a longer duration, can influence those around him who are prone to evil. Thieves, murderers, and oppressed people grow restless and agitated, more often getting into dangerous situations. Chronor can still be destroyed with your regular weak weapons, though a voreen blade would fare much better against him.
>
> *Phase four:*
>
> Reached around a hundred thousand followers, this is a dangerous step for Chronor to advance to. Before Thrak'sha beat Chronor in a duel, he ascended to this

*phase by conquering land and cities. Through his con-
quering, many joined his side. Some of the voreen began
to see the utter destruction he cast upon the world. Human cities like Shieldnar, Silvermountain, and Darkeid
were burned to the ground. Everyone was either killed or
swore allegiance to him. Men, women, or children, it did
not matter—to Chronor they were just more followers. I
have killed over a thousand souls in his name with my
voreen blade. Even the deathwalkers I created followed
Chronor. Not out of loyalty, but by the force of his powerful presence. I could hear their screams day and night,
cursing his name, pleading to be freed from the damna-
tion they had been forced into.*

*I am getting side-tracked here, but it is still im-
portant. This is how he operates to gain followers, so if
you just now discovered that he has been summoned, pre-
pare for full out warfare. He can still die from mortal
wounds even at this stage.*

*His tentacled arm has grown to its fullest. This
brings me to a tedious ability of his. He can bathe the
tentacles in blood and cut them off. They grow into small
foul monsters. With these, Chronor can cripple villages
and cities alike. These disgusting creatures have glands
that emit spores, causing males to flare into unfounded
killing sprees, and render females completely dormant,
not even getting up to eat or drink. Besides that, they are
given a venom that derives directly from Chronor's blood.
Their stinger injects the venom into someone's blood-
stream. Nobody lives through this; it is said to be a terrible way to die. Chronor haunts the victim's mind, tor-
menting them with vision and pain.*

Ara stared at her arm and at Khendric. "In Cornstead,
that's what we met! I was infected with Chronor's blood,
which was supposed to kill me, but your blood saved me!"

"That's probably why all the surrounding villages have stopped shipping food to the city," Khendric said. "Because Chronor's minions are making everyone kill each other."

"But why?" Adenar asked. "Why would he try to create a famine?"

"Maybe to create contempt towards Koradin?" Khendric suggested. "Though that seems like a thin theory, even to me."

"Khendric," Ara said. "My powers, they stem from Chronor, right?"

He nodded.

"So we can assume that he is as strong as me, but not just in his arm. And I can feel people's dark thoughts around me, so we should assume he can do the same too, agreed?"

Adenar looked puzzled, but said nothing.

She continued, "Do you think that's why I could hear the whispers from the deathwalker out in the forest that night?"

He frowned.

"Because deathwalkers are created from voreen blades, and I have gained a fraction of the powers of their ancient god?"

"Possibly," he said. "At least we know your connection to him now, through the tentacled monster. We need to pin down what phase he is in and get to taking him down fast, so let's read on."

> *Phase five:*
>
> *Somewhere around three hundred thousand follow-ers, he reaches phase five. It is a dangerous one, not because his powers grow immensely, but because this is the last phase of simple mortality. Upon reaching phase six, my god becomes a lot more difficult to kill. If you find Chronor in this phase, you must kill him quickly. Though it takes Chronor time to ascend to his next phase, he will reach it.*

To protect himself, Chronor can finally craft his powerful armour. To do this he needs shadestones and a lot of blood. He takes it from unfortunate victims—or even his own followers, if needed. Upon drenching the shadestones in the blood he can meld them to his skin where they will form a crude-looking armour that can withstand any blow. However, this armour is not without the usual weak points of any armour. It is full of random spikes resembling a crab shell, and is completely black and impenetrable.

His followers have up until this point had their free will, but that changes for the weakest minded at this stage. Those who have felt and been affected by his influence in phase four, feel his presence even stronger. Upon consuming blood, Chronor can boost his infliction on them, gaining complete control over their functions. These poor souls will usually be outcasts like criminals—homeless and such, and have been prone to his strong emanating power for a prolonged time. Those who have remained unaffected will undoubtedly begin to feel him pressing on their mind. He seeks control over everybody in the end. A free-willed follower is a liability.

"He must at least be in phase five then," Ara said, interrupting them from reading further. "That must have been what happened that night of the shadowwalker. I remember how I felt all these different presences around me all of the sudden. That must have been Chronor seizing control of criminals in the area so they could kill me. Do you remember how they didn't even seem to care about the guards? That must be because they were of no concern at all to him. Only I mattered . . . for some reason."

"I believe you're right," Khendric said. "Damn . . . that means he has at least three hundred thousand followers already."

"Do you know if shadowwalkers are somehow connected to him as well?" Ara asked.

"I have no idea," Khendric answered.

"When I stopped the shadowwalker from killing Eranna, it said I 'was of him' and fled. It must have meant Chronor. They are probably connected to him somehow too. It seemed terrified of me."

"It looks like Chronor has his fingers in many things," Khendric said. "Weird we haven't heard of him before."

Adenar looked down at the book again, finding a specific sentence. "Here," he said. "The book references cities of old; Shieldnar, Silvermountain and Darkeid. I've only heard of Shieldnar, but it was an ancient city that existed around nine hundred years ago. I'm guessing nobody has tried to summon Chronor since then. Do you know when the voreen culture crumbled?"

He asked Khendric, whose thoughts had been on something else. Ara could see it in his eyes; anger, thoughts about the past. She was terrified he was going to go dark again, triggering hallucinations, becoming that angry, cold man.

Khendric said, "Some sources suggest it vanished around eight to nine hundred years ago, but it's unreliable."

"Well, according to this book," Adenar continued, "that could be true. Avina and this voreen woman probably wrote this book the last time Chronor was summoned. If the voreen culture perished soon after, we can assume Chronor was not summoned again . . . until now. And that might be his most dangerous weapon: being forgotten in time. Nobody in the city knows what's going on. Not the citizens, nor the king. They don't know they're about to crown an ancient voreen god, bringing the end."

"We have to keep reading," Khendric said. "We have to know if he is in phase five or six and how to kill him in both."

Daylight shone through the windows. The coronation neared quickly. Luckily, adrenaline helped Ara stay awake.

Still in phase five, Chronor can be killed with regular weapons. Strike him down now if you can! If you are a great warrior, challenge him to a duel. Chronor holds high respect for duels, because of the blood oath.

Phase six:

At around eight hundred thousand followers, he reaches phase six. Chronor must not be allowed to reach it, as his powers become incredibly strong. In phase six, Chronor will have all his followers drink his blood. Doing this will give him full control of them and their thoughts. In other words, he gains a mindless army to attack at his whims, no questions asked. Often, he will use his fanatics to force his blood on those who refuse to drink it.

His appearance changes: an ever-burning cloak woven of smoke and fire appears like mist over his shoulders. His veins turn a molten red colour and his eyes alight with flame.

The most important part of phase six is his mortality. Chronor can no longer be killed with regular weapons. As far as I know, he stems from a time before us voreen. A time of gods and mighty creatures. I overheard a conversation where he called it 'a time of divinities.' I don't know much of what divinities he is talking about, but any weapons forged from anything divine can kill him, I believe. Our voreen blades are forged from voreen blood and shadestones, which are also used to summon Chronor. Our blades can kill him. This is the only weapon I know that can be used.

Editor's note: *I(Avina) believe other items can be used to kill him too. I've heard of a rare metal called doorn which I believe can end him. I've met the people of the Iceblood clan and they said doombringers are divinities, or part of a divinity. If that is true, that probably*

means a doombringer can kill Chronor, but unfortu-
nately they are rather hard to control. However, when a
doombringer dies, it leaves behind metallurgic dust that
decays rapidly. If this dust is quickly coated with slime
from centitars, it won't deteriorate. It can then be used to
forge weaponry I believe can be used effectively against
him. There might be other such divinities too out there
that could work."

Khendric shoved the book away from them and directed himself to Adenar. "How many people live in this city?"

"A little more than a million."

"We can assume he does not yet have around eight hundred thousand followers then. Right?"

"That would be hard to believe, yes."

"Then we can assume he has not yet reached his sixth phase," Khendric said. "Right?"

Both Ara and Adenar nodded.

"And if he wins, will the people of Ashbourn turn to follow him even if they did not vote for him?"

Adenar's face paled. He adopted a grim expression. "Yes."

"You seem certain," Khendric observed. "How so?"

"The people of Ashbourn loyally follow whoever is chosen. In our past, we have let it divide us and civil wars have threatened to tear the city apart. Since then, we learned from our mistake, and all citizens vehemently support whomever we crown. That's why I said I would follow Ronoch if he won a long time ago—but obviously not now I know what I know."

"Damn it," Khendric said. He walked to the window, the sun bathing him in its rays. "We don't have time to spread this to the population of the city now. We know for a fact that if he wins, he will reach his sixth phase and become almost impossible to kill. That means we must act now. How long until the official coronation?"

"At midday," he said. "That doesn't give us much time."

"What do we do?" Ara asked frantically.

"Something drastic," Khendric said without turning. "I'll kill this damn monster before he's crowned." He grabbed the door handle and stormed out, not listening to Ara's or Adenar's objections.

"We need some sort of plan!" Ara screamed.

"What is he thinking?" Adenar exclaimed. "He can't just walk up and shoot him. Ronoch is surrounded by guards and Khendric would be executed on sight."

"He isn't thinking clearly. I could see hatred behind those eyes of his. The past haunts him, I think, and now he's acting too hastily. Though I don't know what else we can do. There isn't time to plan anything."

Adenar let out a strained breath and sat back down. "Let us hope Darlaene and Topper got the real Ronoch, or killed him—so Chronor cannot transform."

Ara nodded, looking into his eyes. Adenar was truly concerned. He really cared about his city and had been right all along. She only wished they had come to Ashbourn earlier and met him. That's what they would have needed—more time.

***

Koradin rose from his chair to address the immense crowd gathering at Castle Square, which could contain over thirty thousand people.

To his surprise, Ronoch had not arrived, which was peculiar. All four Chosen were supposed to sit on their designated chair and give one last speech before the announcement of the new king. Elrich had just finished his, leaving only Koradin and Ronoch left to speak. Without showing up, Ronoch couldn't win. The votes had been tallied and this was first and foremost just tradition, but it was also enforced by law for the Chosen to appear.

Koradin went to the panel for his speech. There were criers placed evenly that would echo his words down through the endless masses.

I must be the first king to do this for the third time, Koradin thought. The first time, he'd been nervous beyond belief, but today it felt like any other day. He gripped the wooden sides of the panel in front of him.

His people were displeased, that was easy to see. They were starved and angry. He was disappointed in himself that he hadn't been able to disprove the rumours of Brattora readying for war, and it had certainly brought the downfall of his campaign. If it *was* just rumours, it had been a genius move. More and more he felt played by Eranna, kept too busy to meet with citizens, give speeches, and hold rallies, which must have lost him his support.

Usually, whenever he faced a crowd, hope sparked in their eyes, but times had changed. By phantom threats, they had turned against him. He still feared for them—his people. Not for a second did he trust Ronoch. If Ronoch were to win, Koradin would be on his toes for anything out of the ordinary. And so was his army. Hopefully, he was wrong, and Ronoch was just another politician, but his gut feeling said something else. If that 'something else' was correct, he would fight for Ashbourn. *Hopefully, it will not come to that.*

"My people!" he beckoned, the criers echoing his words. "I stand before you yet again with hopes that you have chosen me to be your king! Under my rule, Ashbourn has prospered!" His voice held the same strength as before. He still felt as young and strong as in his youth, even though he was in his forty-eighth year, though he *did* have an unfair advantage. "I will not keep on talking about how our economy has put coins in all pockets. I will address what you're all concerned with." There were no smiles. Instead, the people were filled with contempt. "We have arranged for new trade routes with distant villages and cities. Caravans are on their way with supplies. Investigations have been conducted in our villages to find out why they abruptly stopped supplementing the city. I am not sure what has happened there yet, but something did indeed happen. Reports from my most trusted people tell me all the people in these villages have died. Either by themselves, or some vile beast."

He really wanted to say that it all must have been planned. There was no way one beast could hit all the villages that systematically. Koradin was sure it was an attack by someone—and not the Brattorans. His best trackers and foresters had been on the case, and if the mayhem was caused by people, he would know. There was something else happening, but he could not blatantly say so to the crowd without proof. "But food is on its way. In the meantime, we are rationing the emergency storage, but are running out quicker than anticipated—"

"What about the war?" someone shouted. *That is new,* Koradin thought. Nobody had interrupted him during a speech before. That person was either brave or desperate.

"—However, the food shortage is my number one priority," Koradin said without skipping a beat.

To his surprise, more people took up the man's call and shouted questions about the war. Before long, the mass roared uncontrollably, demanding answers. It was a spring ready to escape its hold. Koradin gently lifted his hand and waited for the screaming to die down, and eventually, the crowd stilled.

"I can assure you," he said. "If an attack against our city is to happen, I am ready for it! I have doubled the regular patrols for months and have twice the number of trackers at our border. If Brattora marched with forces into our kingdom we would know well in advance. We are ready for an attack and have been for a long time. I can't do anything more than I have done, except actually launch an attack!" Koradin's voice was hard. He tired of this foolish talk. There were no signs of war—at least none that could be taken seriously, except for the rambles of the Warborn. He would not believe for a second that General Toran had suddenly gone to the Paradraxian border, gotten ambushed, and killed.

It had been unprofessional to let his annoyance bleed into his voice, but what more could they expect of him? "What have you all been thinking? That I've been sitting on my throne without doing anything? Of course *any* rumour of war will be thoroughly investigated, and that has been done. But despite there not being any signs of Brattoran aggression, I have ordered the city to be on alert. I would never sit idly by and do nothing with a potential threat. My emissary talked to the royalty of Brattora. She came back with exactly what I thought she would. Brattora was alarmed at these accusations and frightened we were going to pull our already existing trading agreements with them. War does not seem likely, but even so, the city and our armies are prepared! Rest assured, I will defend this city with every muscle I have, even if I lose today."

Silence followed from the audience and many hung their heads low in . . . shame? *Did they really think I was doing nothing?* Koradin felt a stab of disappointment until suddenly the crowd cheered. He frowned in confusion and wondered if his words had inspired something in their hearts—until he noticed they weren't looking at him. Turning his head, he saw Ronoch take the stage and sit down on his chair. It had been too good to be true, and with a sigh, he thought it natural to end his speech there. He let go of the panel in front of him, realizing he'd been clutching it harder than he meant to. His speech hadn't been an inspiring one, rather one that scolded thousands of children, and he sat back down with a sour feeling in his guts.

Ronoch got up from his chair and walked to the panel. He raised his arm and the people filled anew with vigour, chanting wildly at the sight of him. It was harder to swallow than Koradin would have thought, and the sensation that he would have to step down settled. He did not like the taste.

* * *

Upon seeing Ronoch step up on the stage behind Koradin, Khendric's hatred flared. He'd been watching the king's speech from a rooftop nearby, but he climbed down into the crowd, making his way towards the stage.

Flashes of his past lurked in the corners of his eyes, and the smell of phantom blood danced in his nostrils. Now and then, people in the audience resembled one of those bandits from long ago, but when Khendric fixed his gaze, they were just another commoner.

Whispers from his mother reached his ears, uttering heart-breaking words. *"You did nothing,"* it said. *One step at a time*, Khendric told himself. *Just get to that stage.* Ronoch—or Chronor, held his speech, and the mass was ecstatic. Khendric made way as quickly as he could without raising too much suspicion.

"You just watched," his father's voice rang in his head. *"You watched them kill me."*

"It's not real," Khendric whispered and kept moving. *What about Darlaene?* he thought. If Ronoch was here, then what had Darlaene been doing during their infiltration? Where was she now? *Is she dead?*

The uncertainty led to fear, then to panic. It manifested in his chest, solidifying with every step. *"You've lost her,"* a voice from the past whispered. He was about to faint. *"You couldn't protect me . . . or your mother . . . and now not even your beloved huntress—"*

"Get away!" Khendric shouted, startling the few people in the crowd around him. Overall, his words were drowned in the chanting.

His eyes fixed on Ronoch far ahead as he pushed through faster than before, subconsciously gripping his pistol. The peripherals of his eyes darkened. Sweat ran down his fore-head. *Breathe, just breathe.* A strong chant reverberated through the square so loudly it hurt his ears, and Ronoch disengaged from the panel. Anger didn't mix well with panic. Khendric pushed himself forth violently.

"Move!" he bellowed. Someone else took the stage. It was a tall, scrawny man with a scroll in his hand. He began reading it, criers throughout the crowd echoing his words.

"The votes have been tallied!"

Khendric moved frantically, the time for subtlety over. "Get out of my way!" He neared the stage.

"The sixty-ninth king of Ashbourn!" the man on the stage shouted.

Khendric slowed his pace as the place in front of him was riddled with guards. *I just need one well-placed shot,* he thought. *Before he's crowned.*

"Chosen by the people themselves!" the scrawny man bellowed with a powerful voice. "From all corners of the Sangerian Grassland."

Face to face with the guards, they looked at him with cau-tion; worry clear on their faces.

Time slowed as adrenaline pumped through Khendric's veins. The two closest soldiers tightened their grips on their spears. One turned towards the stage to call out the impend-ing danger—Khendric himself.

"All hail the new king," the man continued.

Khendric lost his focus on the guard for a second. *I have to stop him.* He pulled out his gun to point it at Ronoch, but it stopped halfway, the soldier holding his arm down.

"King Ronoch Steelbane!" The crowd went wild with cheers and applause.

"No!" Khendric shouted. He stared deep into the sol-dier's eyes. They were at a standstill. The soldier's eyes darted back and forth, begging Khendric to remain still.

"I'm sorry," Khendric said and they both spun into action, but Khendric was faster, elbowing him with such force he crashed into another guard. Khendric aimed his gun, but couldn't get a good shot at Ronoch. He needed to advance up the nearby stairs, but guards converged from all directions.

Flashes of his family disturbed him. Darlaene dropped into his mind again and all of Khendric's hatred culminated at once. *I have to kill that damn god,* he thought.

The soldiers came at him with weapons high, but Khendric dodged and spun out of reach. He didn't want to kill any of them, instead shoving them off balance.

Nearby citizens tried fleeing the zone, but the ecstatic crowd trapped them. The cheers served as a shield; officers couldn't get any commands through, but more people picked up on the growing danger, and Khendric needed to act fast. He toppled soldier upon soldier from the stairs leading to the stage, and midway up he saw Ronoch walking towards the panel, clear in his sight, completely unaware of the pistol aimed at him.

The soldiers on stage noticed him storming towards Ronoch and lunged to protect him, but they were too slow. Khendric fired.

The bullet soared through the air with the force of a hundred arrows. A soldier dove in front of Ronoch, but the projectile went under his arm, continuing on its deadly path, burying deep into Ronoch's chest. The force carried him backwards, arms flailing in the air, and Khendric prayed he was still in his mortal phase.

A knee landed on Khendric's back, forcing him to the ground. On impact, he cracked the floorboards of the staircase and some of his ribs, knocking the air from his lungs. Someone grabbed his arm and forced it behind his back, popping his shoulder out of its socket. Khendric turned his head as chains locked around his wrists. The man holding him down was . . . Koradin? His vision swam from the impact, but it looked like the king himself. Koradin punched him in the head and a knife entered his back. Khendric roared in pain as the steel intruded its way into his flesh. Koradin struck him once more, and all went black.

BEASTIARY

Octinara

Known location: Ocean

Type: Beast

Weakness: General weaponry. Harpoons are effective.

Rarity: Common

Vicious creatures of the sea, Octinaras are often described as 'the sailor's nightmare.' Their round body is about the size of a rowboat, with gelatinous and slimy skin. This ball contains all their organs—a terrifying mouth and eyes as well. The mouth contains countless serrated teeth, making sure that anything caught won't get away. They have four spiderling-like legs that can be used for walking on the seafloor. They only rarely walk on land, as the pressure their bodyweight put on their skin would cause it to tear. The legs are used to capsize boats.The octinara utilizes sixteen strong and nimble tentacles with spikes of various sizes.

Octinaras are aggressive by nature, often killing their own to sate their hunger. How they procreate is unknown, as their bloodthirst seems insatiable. Stab it, hit it, and do whatever you can to penetrate its slippery skin. Harpoons are efficient and an absolute necessity. These creatures are the reason all large ships have harpoons installed.

Alec

Shadowwalker

Known location: Summoned

Type: Assassin

Weakness: General weaponry.

Rarity: Rare

Shadowwalkers are sinister entities, brought to life with one purpose; assassination. Few people know about these creatures, which is good. Else, there would be more murders in the night.

By a sinister ritual and by sacrificing a precious body part, shadowwalkers are summoned. How precious the limb has to be is quite individual. Rumours foretell of a musician who only sacrificed a finger, whilst a black-smith sacrificed his arm. Whether the sacrifice is enough is a gamble.

The limb is lowered into a fire, while citing words from old scripture. Few books left contain information of this summoning ritual, and it's debated whether spells are written in the ancient language of the voreen or not. The shadowwalker appears to the summoner, demanding a name. They're intelligent and may cloak themselves as regular humans—making them perfect assassins.

The shadowwalkers are woven in smoke, with the form of a human. Their face is barely visible through the churning smoke and dancing around their being. They have a physical form and can be damaged. The easiest way to deal with a shadowwalker is to kill its summoner

—their anchor into this world. Or else you must simply damage it with weapons until it fades. It isn't staggered by attacks, but goes to great lengths to avoid being struck. So in short, either kill the summoner or damage the shadowwalker until it fades.

- Alec

Villagemother

Known location: cemeteries

Type: Infiltrator

Weakness: General weaponry

Rarity: Rare

Villagemothers are foul creatures able to wipe out villages if not handled properly. Before climbing into the corpse of a beautiful, young, dead maiden, they are hideous creatures. Small, brown, with random patches of hair, rubbery skin, large toothless mouths, drooping ears, and a truly foul odour.

Villagemothers loom near graveyards at places of disasters, searching for a dead young woman to serve as a host. Upon discovering one, they somehow 'enter' the corpse, taking over its bodily functions, and travels far away to find a village.

In a village, the villagemother, now a beautiful maiden, makes some poor fellow fall in love with her. After fooling him into their clutches, they procreate. The villagemother's pregnancy is accelerated and gives birth to more children at once. The offspring look normal at first, but as they grow older, eyes move too far apart or too close, ears grow to unnatural sizes, their jaw grows too large, and other disturbing traits. The villagemother won't wait long before making sure she is pregnant again, birthing yet another series of children.

The children grow faster than regular children, and are prone to violence. They commit more and more heinous acts. From killing critters to beating up other kids, and ultimately to gang violence, usually resulting in murders. When the villagemother's offspring think they can overpower the village, they violently cul the regular people. If successful, the villagemother keeps on producing children with the poor father, kept alive solely to create more of monstrosities. With no people to kill, the children— adults at this stage, turn on each other, relentlessly murdering each other, while more children are born.

To deal with this monster, simply fight past the villagemother's creations and kill the villagemother herself. Then the rest will sort itself out. Or, you may kill your way out in a blaze of glory.

- Alec

Scribbler

Known location: caves along the vast mountains of Carnagan

Type: Magical

Weakness: Weapons with the correct signs

Rarity: Common within caves

Scribblers are small, pale creatures, reaching up to the hip of a grown man, with long snouts and ears and two arms and legs. They spend most of their lives in caves, and are extremely sensitive to sunlight.

Instead of a hand on one arm, they have a large stub made of chalk. They use this chalk to draw signs that can be infused with magic to perform different tasks. If infused, the chalk lights up with a crisp yellow light, easily visible inside the darkness. If spotted, be wary. The magic can heat your sword handle if you lack the counteracting signs. Stone can fall from overhead, water can freeze or items combust. Exactly what these signs can do, or their limitations, is unknown.

The scribblers don't have an endless source of magic to fuel their signs. Though morbid, they eat the hearts of other scribblers which fuels their magic.

A scribbler lays around thirty eggs to eat its own offspring. The scribbler l continues this, until growing too old and one of its children kills it instead. Bloodshed follows, as all the surviving children murder each other to become the next grown-up scribbler, continuing the circle.

When fighting a scribbler, avoid its traps and magic, and make sure you have properly warded yourself before-hand. The other option is to sneak and destroy its eggs to starve it.

- Alec

Puppetmaster

Known location: Cities and large villages

Type: Imposter

Weakness: Being compromised and general weaponry

Rarity: Rare

Puppetmasters conceal themselves under large cloaks. Their voice sounds like an old lady's to fool children or parents into buy their handcrafted dolls. Beneath the cloak, the puppetmasters have light brown leathery skin, two large, yellow eyes, and a bent beak used for eating the flesh of children. Beneath their beak is another ghastly human-like mouth, which they use to mimic human voices.

The puppetmasters roam cities or villages, concealed under their cloaks while pushing a cart full of dolls. It sells these dolls to children. The child carries the doll home and at night the dolls come to life. It grows to about the size as a child, prancing and dancing around, before transporting the child to the puppetmaster, who will eat it. How the doll transports the child varies, and there are some interesting variations. Some dolls eat the child and the puppetmaster tears its stomach open. Another one becomes a coat and dresses itself onto the poor child, thereafter walking the child to the puppetmaster.

The puppetmasters are truly horrible when it comes to preparing their prey. Some cook them in cauldrons, others roast them over a bonfire, or simply eat them alive.

To kill a puppetmaster drag its hood off, revealing the bald, leathery face underneath, and stab it. They are fairly strong, but if you are quick enough, they don't pose much of a threat.

- Alec

Scrumts

Known location: The dry plains of Varanos

Type: Undead

Weakness: Wretcher talons, silver.

Rarity: Common

Scrumts roam the large deserts and drylands of Varanos in packs, where they viciously attack anyone they encounter, may it be nomads, villagers, or patrols.

Scrumts are people who died and rose due to a small insect. It's called naonadai in the Varanos tongue, which roughly translates to 'cursed death'. In hordes, they feed upon the dead and when doing so, inject the corpse with a liquid. Somehow, this liquid reanimates the body, but the mind is reduced to a very primitive state.

The skin of the undead blackens, becoming rugged and hard. They suffer hair loss and growth of nails. Some seem to remember how to grasp a weapon and even swing, but most end up with a blank mind, only set on one thing: bloodshed.

Scrumts are violent and seek to kill anything with a pulse. They'll hunt prey until killing or being killed, be it children, animals, or soldiers. That's why the king-dom of Varanos has lots of patrols.

To kill a scrumt, use either the talons of a wretcher or a weapon made of silver. Cut them and gut them with either of these and they will die . . . again. You can also *dismember it enough to reduce the threat it poses, but when a horde comes at you, it's best to dispose of them as efficiently as possible.*

   - Alec

Borlin

Known location: forests

Type: wooden insectoid

Weakness: Fire

Rarity: Common

Borlins are not dangerous unless they are searching for mates. They live in forests and are often referred to as creek diggers. They have a barrel-like body with six legs and a head resembling a canine. From a distance, they appear to have fur, but it's actually made of thick leaves attached to a wooden body. Their front legs are shaped like shovels, which they use to dig for fresh roots and insects. The vigorous digging for food in long interconnected patterns and lines usually creates small creeks in forests come rainfall.

Borlins are often playful or at least interested in humans, and may approach to see what's going on. They are skittish, so it's advised not to pet them, as their talons are sharp.

For a short period in the summer months, borlins seek to find mates and appear to have one or three genders, as three of them are needed to procreate. During this time, they shed their leaf-like fur, and grow short spikes used to combat other borlins, or humans they view as competitors. Stay away from leafless borlins.

- Alec

Corpsewalker

Known location: The moist forests of Mandranar

Type: Aquatic

Weakness: Fire

Rarity: Common

Corpsewalkers live near waters and rivers, spending most of their time submerged, but occasionally encroaching on dry land. The corpsewalkers look like giant sea stars, with the mobility of an octopus. Their five thick, strong tentacles are connected by a head with four eyes. These eyes are located evenly in a circle, providing vision in all directions. The mouth, or beak, is placed on the underside of the body. It's short, but can extend with extreme force to twice its length. This is used to crack ribcages.

Corpsewalkers are believed to be intelligent, and often attack humans if the opportunity presents itself. They lunge from the bank of a river, wrapping their arms around the human, wrestling the arms, feet and head down. When positioned, its deadly beak shoots through the victim's sternum. Then it cracks the ribcage open with its tentacles and pushes itself into the body. The corpsewalker eats what it needs to fit inside and pushes its arms into the legs, arms and head. It controls the human as best it can, walking around erratically, hence the name. The corpsewalker will often seek villages nearby, scaring the villagers with its manic look. The way it controls the corpse is truly horrifying.

To kill it—once it is inside of a corpse—stab it repeatedly in the abdomen. If the corpsewalker is not inside of a corpse, try to avoid them. But if you are caught in a battle with one, try to keep it at a distance. It will overpower you if it gets too close, and it is not a pleasant way to die.

- Alec

The Lumberer

Known location: the Great Forests of Kavadash

Type: spectral

Weakness: unknown

Rarity: horror

While there are many specimens of one beast, for example there are countless gorewings, a horror is a beast of which only one exists.

Reports claim the lumberer appears as a deranged man, his head completely hairless, while his arms are riddled with fur. A single-edged axe rests on his shoulder.

In Kavadash, it's common knowledge to not look into the Great Forests at night. If you do, you might spot a man standing at the edge of the forest, staring back at you—the lumberer. He'll stand completely still, axe resting on his shoulder. If you look back at him, you'll be marked, and anyone marked by the lumberer will be dead before dawn. There are no reports of survivors, and, many foreigners are murdered in the kingdoms of Kavadash, unaware of the lumberer and the danger he poses to the unaware.

As far as I've heard, he's never been seen inside the forests.

Beast hunters have tried to stop the lumberer from killing his victim, but as far as I've heard, he cannot be stopped, not even when beheaded. It seems that someone marked will definitely die—unless someone can figure out where and how the lumberer came to be. There might be a hidden weakness we don't know about.

- *Alec*

Kindler

Known location: Bound to no location

Type: Elemental

Weakness: Water, rain, cold weather

Rarity: Common

Kindlers are the sole reason corpses aren't burned, but instead buried or placed in caskets. They spring to life from burning bodies. It's unknown why some burning corpses spawn kindlers and some not, but there's a lot of superstition regarding them. They're simpler to understand when visualizing the 'birth':

A dead man is burned, like in the old days. His corpse twitches slightly before it grows more violent. The corpse's stomach tears open and out gushes an inferno of thick smoke and fire, coalescing in the air. A red, spectral head emerges from the stomach, along with a slender serpent-like body. The kindler's skin is on of mystery. They're partially scaled, and wherever scales are lacking, they have crimson translucent skin through their being. From these 'holes', occasional bursts of fire erupt. An ever-burning mane runs down the whole length of the body, with a reptilian head on top. Kindlers swerve above the ground, making them versatile, their slithering movements propelling them forward.

Birthed from fire, they set fire to anything in their vicinity. Their constant dancing flames can burn down villages and whole cities if they're not extinguished. A kindler's nature is violent, wishing to set fire to as much as possible.

There are theories about who spawns kindlers. Some think it's a form of latent disease. Others think it is a punishment for evil people, though that doesn't make sense. Why would a punishment harm other people after said evil person is dead? In short, nobody knows.

To kill a kindler, douse it with water. Upon dying, it becomes pure white ash. Many kindlers often die to rain. But can do real damage before their demise.

The lesson is simple. Don't burn the dead, or you might risk killing everyone else.

- Alec

The Voreen

Known location: Mountainous forests

Type: Humanoid

Weakness: General weaponry

Rarity: Extremely rare

Little is known about the voreen, as their culture perished at an unknown time and for unknown reasons. Some sources claim the culture fractured around eight to nine hundred years ago, but it's only speculation. All that is certain is that they were an ancient and savage culture. If there's a voreen in your vicinity it's best to flee the area and not look back.

With a humanoid shape, their skin and teeth are completely grey. Their eyes are deep orange with no visible pupils. Their heads are hairless, instead covered by short spikes, pointing to the sky. It's speculated they might be used in combat.

A voreen seeks solitude, even from their kind. However, do not think they're peaceful. Many scriptures claim voreen culture was brutal and violent, but again. From experience, these creatures thrive on merciless killing. And that brings up another important aspect of the voreen: their blades.

Every known voreen carry a massive dark blade on their back. It's as long as a man, yet the voreen wield it easily and expertly. A mysterious power rests in these blades, a certain kind of dark magic. Dull on one side and incredibly sharp on the other, they shear through most materials easily. Smoky tendrils emanate from the blade's surface, enveloping the weapon in dark, dancing smoke. Do not get killed by one of these terrible blades, as you'll turn into a deathwalker.

If you must fight a voreen, it's best to do so when the sun is at its zenith—then the voreen are at their weakest.

During the day, the voreen lack most of their magical abilities and merely resemble an extremely skilled fighter. This aspect can't be overstated enough: they are extremely skilled. In my personal experience, it's ill-advised to duel a voreen no matter how good you think you are—the voreen is better. And not only that, their blades will quickly slice through normal weapons. They have the dexterity of a trollman at night and can close distances quickly. The best strategy is using ranged weapons, though they are next to impossible to hit, due to their enhanced reflexes. Gather a crowd of skilled archers, concentrate your fire, and pray someone hits a critical shot.

Here's the dangerous part. After a voreen is engaged in combat, daylight slowly disappears replaced by night, as if it's somehow blocking out sunlight. Kill the voreen within an hour at least, or retreat, as it will never tire. When darkness takes over, the voreen wields uncanny abilities. I can only speculate on them, as very few make it out alive beyond this point. One self-claimed survivor said the voreen could disappear and reappear somewhere else, but this is not confirmed by secondary sources.

It's believed the voreen had no written language, hence very few books from their time are available.

- Alec

Deathwalker

Known location: Forests.

Type: Spectral humanoid

Weakness: Silver and certain times of day

Rarity: Rare

Deathwalkers are extremely dangerous to those who don't know their rules. With a skeletal appearance, they float above the ground, missing their lower body. They wear tattered remains of the clothes from their deaths. Their eyes are intriguing, emanating a red glow from their sockets, giving the beast a maniacal look—besides already being a flying skeleton.

A deathwalker haunts the woods, slowly hovering through the air without purpose. It's speculated they're both in the real world and partially in some other realm, but again, this is only speculation. They don't hear or see others, and objects pass right through them.

Never look a deathwalker in the eyes, because if they look back, it will charge you, springing into action, flailing its arms around, rushing its victim. Upon reaching its prey, it will rip and tear at the person's flesh, tearing them open. Note the victim cannot physically touch the deathwalker, even when the creature is certainly touching him or her. After killing the unfortunate person, they go back floating through the forest.

Deathwalkers used to be regular people before they fell victim to a voreen blade. We know little about the voreen race, but if anyone is killed by one of their gigantic black blades, they'll become a deathwalker.

A deathwalker is killed by silver objects and for some unknown reason, they're also vulnerable at sunset and sunrise. Exactly why this is, remains unknown. Many think it has something to do with the ancient voreens worshipping some aspects of the day, but their culture is extinct, and they weren't a species known for their writing. A strong sense of mysticism and magic surround the voreen, and those who tried exploring it mostly died. If interested, read more about the voreen later in the book.

- Alec

AUTHOR'S NOTE

If you're reading this, it means you read through all of book 1 and also all of book 2, and to me, that's amazing! Thank you eternally for your interest. I love this second book in the series, as we get to see Ara's growth sprout into greatness. She's got such an amazing drive to solve mysteries, and her connection to the things going on in Ashbourn just roots her deeper. My favourite moment is when Darlaene first appears and Topper gets killed immediately. Writing that part made me laugh.

Book 1 was a smaller mystery, and even though this book builds on what happened in book 1, the scale increases. That's what makes this book stand out more than the first one, I think. It's not just a small village anymore, but an enormous city. They finally know what they're up against, and it sure is something bigger than the Cornstead case. I always knew it was going to be a sort of god, but I had such trouble figuring out how he should work. One day while walking my dogs I realized that I already had an ancient, dead, mystical culture. It became easy then, and thus Chronor was fleshed out.

Writing this book was fantastic because I got to knit the bigger picture together, but it was also far more demanding. The infiltration scenes had to be planned out way before I started writing them, as well as what to reveal and when. But when it all came together, I think it formed a great cliff-hanger at the end. I hope you feel the same way too.

STAY IN TOUCH

Thank you so much for reading *The Beast Hunters Dark Sovereign*, the second book in the *The Beast Hunter of Ashbourn* series. If you enjoyed the second book, and haven't read the short story about Khendric and Topper's final case before they met Ara, you can get it for free following the website link below, as well as read news about my author life, offers, and releases:

https://www.authorcalende.com/newsletter-signup

Facebook: www.facebook.com/christer-Lende-108798154062930

Twitter: twitter.com/ChribsterL

Author website: www.authorcalende.com/

Instagram: www.instagram.com/christerlende

ABOUT THE AUTHOR

Christer Lende began writing in a library, which sounds fitting, only he was supposed to be there working on his engineering degree. He is a professional screenwriter, working with the Norwegian movie producer behind 'One Love,' 'Who Killed Birgitte?' and 'All About my Father', Bjørn Eivind Aarskog. Together, they are developing the manuscript for a Norwegian thriller. Bjørn hired Christer after reading *The Beast Hunters*, trusting he could bring his vision to life.

Christer lives in what Norwegians call a city, but people from actual cities would call a town. Of proud Viking blood, he honours his ancestors by heroically sitting in front of a computer writing Fantasy and Science Fiction books. He believes in writing a little every day, through weekends, Christmas, New Year's Eve, even his own birthday. When he's not writing, he takes care of his two dogs and tries to broker peace with his girlfriend. He's often found at the gym, trying to compensate for his height issues, or lazily playing video games.

Christer did get that Master's degree in Electrical Engineering, despite procrastinating by writing fiction in the library, and works for a large IT firm, but writing and storytelling are his passions.

For more information, you can visit:
https://www.authorcalende.com/about.

Milton Keynes UK
Ingram Content Group UK Ltd.
UKHW030059190324
439691UK00003B/74